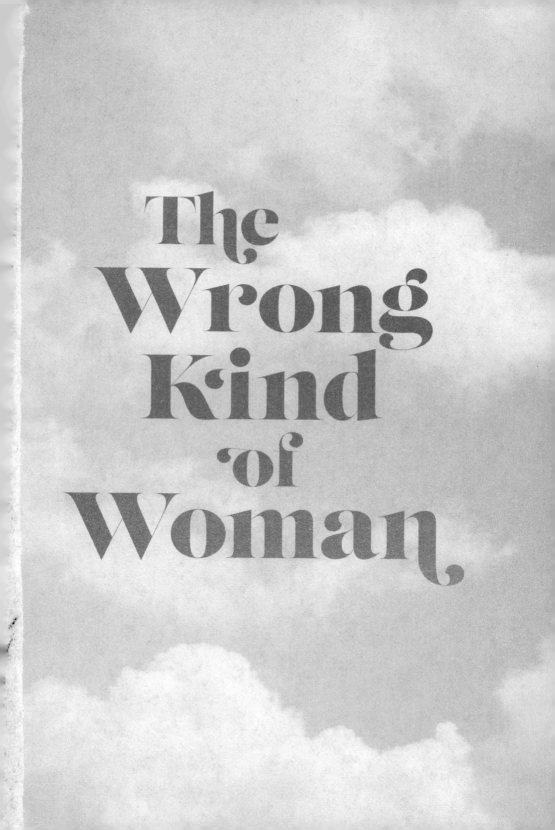

The Wrong Kind of Woman

The Wrong Kind of Woman

SARAH McCRAW CROW

mira

mira™

ISBN-13: 978-0-7783-1007-5

The Wrong Kind of Woman

This edition published by arrangement with Harlequin Books S.A.

For questions and comments about the quality of this book, please contact us at
CustomerService@Harlequin.com.

Mira
22 Adelaide St. West, 40th Floor
Toronto, Ontario M5H 4E3, Canada
BookClubbish.com

Printed in U.S.A.

The Wrong Kind of Woman

Clarendon! Clarendon!
The mountains call her name
Unto death a Clarendon MAN I'll remain!

—Clarendon College Alma Mater, 1895

Chapter One

November 1970
Westfield, New Hampshire

OLIVER DIED THE SUNDAY after Thanksgiving, the air heavy with snow that hadn't fallen yet. His last words to Virginia were "Tacks, Ginny? Do we have any tacks?"

That morning at breakfast, their daughter, Rebecca, had complained about her eggs—runny and gross, she said. Also, the whole neighborhood already had their Christmas lights up, and why didn't they ever have outside lights? Virginia tuned her out; at thirteen, Rebecca had reached the age of comparison, noticing where her classmates' families went on vacation, what kinds of cars they drove. But Oliver agreed about the lights, and after eating his own breakfast and Rebecca's rejected eggs, he drove off to the hardware store to buy heavy-duty Christmas lights.

Back at home, Oliver called Virginia out onto the front porch, where he and Rebecca had looped strings of colored lights around the handrails on either side of the steps. Virginia waved at their neighbor Gerda across the street— on her own front porch, Gerda knelt next to a pile of balsam branches, arranging them into two planters—as Rebecca and Oliver described their lighting scheme. Rebecca's cheeks had gone ruddy in the New Hampshire cold, as Oliver's had; Rebecca had his red-gold hair too.

"Up one side and down the other," Rebecca said. "Like they do at Molly's house—"

"Tacks, Ginny? Do we have any tacks?" Oliver interrupted. In no time, he'd lost patience with this project, judging by the familiar set of his jaw, the frown lines corrugating his forehead.

A few minutes later, box of nails and hammer in hand, Virginia saw Oliver's booted feet splayed out on the walk, those old work boots he'd bought on their honeymoon in Germany a lifetime ago. "Do you have to lie down like that to—" she began, while Rebecca squeezed out from between the porch and the overgrown rhododendron.

"Dad?" Rebecca's voice pitched upward. "Daddy!"

Virginia slowly took in that Oliver was lying half on the lawn, half on the brick walk, one hand clutching the end of a light string. Had he fallen? It made no sense, him just lying there on the ground like that, and she hurtled down the porch steps. Oliver's eyes had rolled back so only the whites showed. But he'd just asked for tacks, and she hadn't had time to ask if nails would work instead. She crouched, put her mouth to his and tried to breathe for him. Something was happening, yes, maybe now he would turn out to be just resting, and in a minute he'd sit up and laugh with disbelief.

Next to her, Rebecca shook Oliver's shoulder, pounded on it. "Dad! You fainted! Wake up—"

"Go call the operator," Virginia said. "Tell them we need an ambulance, tell them it's an emergency, a heart attack, Becca! Run!" Rebecca ran.

Virginia put her ear to Oliver's chest, listening. A flurry of movement: Gerda was suddenly at her side, kneeling, and Eileen from next door, then Rebecca, gasping or maybe sobbing. Virginia felt herself being pulled out of the way as the ambulance backed into the driveway and the two paramedics bent close. They too breathed for Oliver, pressed on his chest while counting, then lifted him gently onto the backboard and up into the ambulance.

She didn't notice that she was holding Rebecca's hand on her one side and Eileen's hand on the other, and that Gerda had slung a protective arm around Rebecca. She barely noticed when Eileen bundled her and Rebecca into the car without a coat or purse. She didn't notice the snow that had started to fall, first snow of the season. Later, that absence of snow came back to her, when the image of Oliver lying on the bare ground, uncushioned even by snow, wouldn't leave her.

Aneurysm. A ruptured aneurysm, a balloon that had burst, sending a wave of blood into Oliver's brain. *A subarachnoid hemorrhage.* She said all those new words about a thousand times, along with more familiar words: *bleed* and *blood* and *brain. Rips* and *tears. One in a million.* Sitting at the kitchen table, Rebecca next to her and the coiled phone cord stretched taut around both of them, Virginia called one disbelieving person after another, repeated all those words to her mother,

her sister Marnie, Oliver's brother, Oliver's department chair, the people in her address book, the people in his.

At President Weissman's house five days later, Virginia kept hold of Rebecca. Rebecca had stayed close, sleeping in the middle of Virginia and Oliver's bed as if she were little and sleepwalking again, her shruggy new adolescent self forgotten. They'd turned into a sudden team of two, each one circling, like moons, around the other.

Oliver's department chair had talked Virginia into a reception at President Weissman's house, a campus funeral. In the house's central hall, Virginia's mother clutched at her arm, murmuring about the lovely Christmas decorations, those balsam garlands and that enormous twinkling tree, and how they never got the fragrant balsam trees in Norfolk, did they, only the Fraser firs—

"Let's go look at the Christmas tree, Grandmomma." Rebecca took her grandmother's hand as they moved away. What a grown-up thing to do, Virginia thought, glad for the release from Momma and her chatter.

"Wine?" Virginia's sister Marnie said, folding her hand around a glass. Virginia nodded and took a sip. Marnie stayed next to her as one person and another came close to say something complimentary about Oliver, what a wonderful teacher he'd been and a great young historian, an influential member of the Clarendon community. And his clarinet, what would they do without Oliver's tremendous clarinet playing? The church service had been lovely, hadn't it? He sure would have loved that jazz trio.

She heard herself answering normally, as if this one small thing had gone wrong, except now she found herself in a tunnel, everyone else echoing and far away. Out of a clutch of Clarendon boys, identical in their khakis and blue blazers, their too-long hair curling behind their ears, one stepped forward. Sam, a student in her tiny fall seminar, the Italian Baroque.

"I—I just wanted to say..." Sam faltered. "But he was a great teacher, and even more in the band—" The student-faculty jazz band, he meant.

"Thank you, Sam," she said. "I appreciate that." She watched him retreat to his group. Someone had arranged for Sam and a couple of other Clarendon boys to play during the reception, and she hadn't noticed until now.

"How 'bout we sit, hon." Marnie steered her to a couch. "I'm going to check on Becca and Momma and June—" the oldest of Virginia's two sisters "—and then I'll be right back."

"Right." Virginia half listened to the conversation around her, people in little clumps with their sherries and whiskeys. *Mainframe, new era*, she heard. Then *well, but Nixon*, and *a few problems with the vets on campus*. She picked up President Weissman's voice, reminiscing about the vets on campus after the war thirty years ago. "Changed the place for the better, I think," President Weissman said. "A seriousness of purpose." And she could hear Louise Walsh arguing with someone about the teach-in that should have happened last spring.

Maybe Oliver would appreciate being treated like a dignitary. Maybe he'd be pleased at the turnout, all the faculty and students who'd shown up at the Congregational Church at lunchtime on a Friday. Probably he wished he could put Louise in her place about the teach-in. Virginia needed to find Rebecca, and she needed to make sure Momma hadn't collapsed out of holiday party–funeral confusion. But now Louise Walsh loomed over her in a shape-less black suit, and she stood up again to shake Louise's hand. "I just want to say how sorry I am," Louise said. "I truly admired his teaching and—everything else. We're all going to miss him."

"Thank you, Louise." Virginia considered returning the compliment, to say that Oliver had admired Louise too. Louise had tenure, the only woman in the history depart-ment, the only woman at Clarendon, to be tenured. Lou-ise had been a thorn in Oliver's side, the person Oliver had complained about the most. Louise was one of the four women on faculty at Clarendon; the Gang of Four, Oliver and the others had called them.

Outside the long windows, a handful of college boys tossed a football on a fraternity lawn across the street, one skidding in the snow as he caught the ball. Someone had spray-painted wobbly blue peace signs on the frat's white clapboard wall, probably after Kent State. But the Clar-endon boys were rarely political; they were athletic: in their baggy wool trousers, they ran, skied, hiked, went gliding off the college's ski jump, human rockets on long skis. They built a tremendous bonfire on the Clarendon green in the fall, enormous snow sculptures in the winter. They stumbled home drunk, singing. Their limbs seemed loosely attached to their bodies. Oliver had once been one of those boys.

"Come on, pay attention," Marnie said, and she pro-pelled Virginia toward President Weissman, who took Vir-ginia's hands.

"I cannot begin to express all my sympathy and sad-ness." President Weissman's eyes were magnified behind his glasses. "Our firmament has lost a star." He kissed her on the cheek, pulling a handkerchief from his jacket pocket, so she could wipe her eyes and nose again.

At the reception, Aunt June kept asking Rebecca if she was doing okay, and did she need anything, and Aunt Marnie kept telling Aunt June to quit bothering Rebecca. Mom looked nothing like her sisters: Aunt Marnie was bulky with short pale hair, Aunt June was petite, her hair almost black, and Mom was in between. Rebecca used to love her aunts' Tidewater accents, and the way Mom's old accent would return around her sisters, her vowels stretching out and her voice going up and down the way Aunt June's and Aunt Marnie's voices did. Rebecca and Dad liked to tease Mom about her accent, and Mom would say *I don't know what you're talking about, I don't sound anything like June. Or Marnie. But* especially *not June.*

Nothing Rebecca thought made any sense. She couldn't think about something that she and Dad liked, or didn't like, or laughed about, because there was no more Dad. Aunt Marnie had helped her finish the Christmas lights, sort of, not the design she and Dad had shared, but just wrapped around the porch bannisters. It looked a little crazy, actually. Mom hadn't noticed.

"Here's some cider, honey," Aunt June said. "How about some cheese and crackers? You need to eat."

"I'm okay," Rebecca said. "Thanks," she remembered to add.

"Have you ever tried surfing?" Aunt June asked. "The boys—" Rebecca's cousins "—love to surf. They'll teach you."

"Okay." Rebecca wanted to say that it was December and there was snow on the ground, so there was no reason to talk about surfing. Instead she said that she'd bodysurfed with her cousins at Virginia Beach plenty of times, but she'd never gotten on a surfboard. As far as she could tell, only boys ever went surfing, and the waves at Virginia Beach were never like the waves on *Hawaii Five-0*. Mostly the boys just sat on their surfboards gazing out at the hazy-white horizon, and at the coal ships and aircraft carriers chugging toward Norfolk.

"You'll get your chance this summer—I'll bet you'll be a natural," Aunt June said.

Things would keep happening. Winter would happen. There would be more snow, and skiing at the Ski Bowl. The town pond would open for skating and hockey. The snow would melt and it would be spring and summer again. They'd go to Norfolk for a couple of weeks after school let out and Mom would complain about everything down there, and get into a fight with Aunt June, and they'd all go to the beach, and Dad would get the most sunburned, his ears and the tops of his feet burned pink and peely...

"Let's just step outside into the fresh air for a minute, sweetheart," Aunt June said, and Rebecca stood up and followed her aunt to the room with all the coats, one hand over her mouth to hold in the latest sob, even after she and Mom had agreed they were all cried out and others would be crying today, but the two of them were all done with crying. She knew that the fresh air wouldn't help anything.

The jazz trio, the only ones who'd said yes to this strange gig, started their second set with a Coltrane-ish "My Favorite Things," Sam playing the clarinet, Stephen on the baby grand and Larry Quinn on drums, half a beat too slow. At least they were out of the way of the funeral guests; Mrs.

Weissman had directed them to set up in the big glassed-in porch, with its view of the town pond.

The other Clarendon guys who'd come to the reception clustered nearby with their plates of food, pretending to listen to their poor imitation of Coltrane, their lame solos. Sam let himself listen too, as Stephen began a Bill Evans number, the slow "Waltz for Debbie," on his own. The front door opened and a scrap of what sounded like "Purple Haze" flew in from across the street, the KA guys already deep into their weekend partying.

President Weissman poked his head into the porch, gave them a smile and two thumbs-up, then disappeared into the blur of dark suits and black dresses. President Weissman liked for Clarendon guys to come over to the president's house, to attend the receptions for visiting lecturers, or to stand around in the big kitchen with its two fridges, eating cookies and drinking hot chocolate. As if their presence could reassure President and Mrs. Weissman that yes, Clarendon was a wholesome school and they were wholesome guys, out snowshoeing on a Friday night, instead of getting wrecked or baked, the weekend having started on Wednesday. But even guys like Sam would get wrecked later.

Go and tell the family that you're sorry for their loss, Sam could hear his mom saying, the kind of thing she always said, and he'd done so during their set break. Just as bad as he'd imagined: he'd stuttered, barely getting any words out, and Professor Desmarais's eyes had welled up. She was teaching his art history class this fall. In class, once she started the slideshow part of the lecture, she grew more animated in the dark. He thought he knew that feeling. If only jazz band concerts could be in complete darkness too. When

Professor Desmarais turned the lights back on, she tended to address only the one exchange girl in the class.

Sam kept playing. There was something wrong with all these people, the other Clarendon guys, the crowd of faculty in the big front parlor, the buzz of voices rising and falling as the faculty talked about whatever they usually talked about, campus gossip, probably. To the faculty, this was just another reception at President Weissman's house.

Sam let himself remember jazz band rehearsals, sharing sheet music with Oliver whenever Sam played clarinet rather than guitar. He'd made Oliver laugh about Schuyler DePeyster's trumpet playing. Oliver had thought Sam was funny, even talented. Oliver had been a friend. The weirdness of being here now was too much. He had to get out of here, he needed a joint, a drink, something.

"Some gig, huh," Stephen said. They were in between songs, and nobody was paying any attention. The other Clarendon guys had left, back to their frats and Friday afternoon beers.

"Let's take a break," Sam said. "Maybe pack it in." They could help Larry take down his drum kit and slip out through the porch door. No one would notice, or care.

Virginia woke in the dark to a sour, fuzzy mouth. She reached across the bed, but the sheets were blank and cool: no Rebecca. This day hadn't ended yet. After Virginia's family and friends had come to the house for ham sandwiches and bourbon, her mother had put her to bed, a cool hand to her forehead as if she were a feverish child, and she'd slept.

As ripples of talk drifted upstairs, Virginia lay there listening. June's voice rose above the others, strident and bossy, and the house smelled like Norfolk, salty, fatty ham and tomatoey Brunswick stew. She made herself get up. Oliver's soft windbreaker lay draped over the armchair, where he'd thrown it a few days ago, and she slipped it on.

Downstairs, she heard the TV—in the den, Rebecca sat with Molly from next door watching *The Courtship of Eddie's Father.* The show's cheerful background music soothed her, and she sank down next to Rebecca, willing her brain to say the things a mother said to her child on a night like tonight, but nothing came. She took in that Rebecca's and Molly's eyes were full, tearing up at Bill Bixby and his darling little boy. Rebecca rested her head on Virginia's shoulder and Virginia put an arm around her. But after only a few minutes Rebecca scooted away. "Can you go brush your teeth, Mom? Your breath is really bad."

"Okay." Virginia pushed up to standing and headed to the kitchen. At the kitchen table, her mother and sisters turned to look at her, all of them smiling too much, and June stood to pull her into a hug. Momma was still in her funeral suit, an ancient black thing with a peplum, a party apron protecting it, and she leaned over a memo pad, pen in hand: when in doubt, make a list.

"Ah, my little baby Ginny," Momma said.

June and Marnie bustled around Virginia's small kitchen, pulling things out of the fridge and the oven. June was small and nimble, and an early white streak ran through her dark hair. Like June, Virginia had Daddy's dark eyes, but her own hair was mousy, not black-Irish dark like June's.

Marnie, bigger and blonder than June, set a plate in front of Virginia—ham, broccoli casserole, rolls, butter—and a cup of coffee. Virginia took a bite of the casserole, pushed the plate away.

"You've got tons of food here," June said. "I've got some Brunswick stew going for the freezer. Between that and the ham and all these casseroles, you'll have dinners for weeks."

Virginia nodded.

June and Marnie started in on Norfolk gossip, filling her in while entertaining themselves. Oh, and had she heard about Jimmy Burwell? "You know he's a lawyer, UVA law, that's right. Well, get this, he left his wife for another lawyer, yes, a *woman* lawyer! Doesn't that beat all!"

Her sisters' gossip washed over her and made her feel sick to her stomach.

"We'll go to the store in the morning and pick up some more supplies, whatever you need," June said. "But why don't you come on home for a while?"

"Jesus, June," Marnie said. "Give her a minute, would you?"

"It just seems like you don't fit in here, Ginny," June said. "Your friends seem—" She paused. "I mean, who *are* your friends?"

"Oh, she fits in fine," Marnie said. "You're afraid of the North, June, that's what."

"I am not," June said. "It's just too cold here. And now it's snowing. There are camellias blooming along the side of my house. Camellias! Blooming. No snow."

"I like the snow." Virginia's voice came out thin and squeaky. She wanted to say something about the snow softening up winter, which made her think of the hard ground, which made her think of Oliver, who'd loved the New Hampshire cold and the snow far more than she did. Tears gathered and stung.

"I will say that it's kind of hard to get here," Marnie said. "That tiny airplane, my God."

"You used to love to watch the cardinals and the orioles," June said. "Remember how we watched them together in the backyard when we were little?"

She nodded. They had birds in New Hampshire too, maybe even better birds. Purple finches, bluebirds, yellow-black-and-white bobolinks swooping over the hayfields north of town.

But she was too tired to say anything. Maybe her mother and sisters could carry her home to Norfolk, and she'd stay wrapped up in gossip and mild weather. Rebecca could go to the academy, where her sisters' kids went; the academy had started admitting girls ten years ago, and her sisters said it was a wonderful school, rigorous and traditional. And Rebecca could go to the beach in the summer and dance to swing-band music at night, as Virginia used to do. Lose a husband, change a life, was that it? Oliver had been fascinated, in a kind of anthropological way, by Virginia's family, and how they did things down there, and how Norfolk couldn't decide if it was a small town or a city. She tried for a second to imagine finding someone down there, maybe one of those lawyers that her sisters had just gossiped about, although Jimmy Burwell—there was nothing to recommend him. One of her brother Rolly's old friends? God, no. She started to cry again; she was thinking about the wrong things.

"Oh, honey." Marnie scooted her chair close, pulling Virginia's head onto her lap.

Virginia let her head rest on Marnie's wide leg, trying to sort her jumble of thoughts into some kind of order. Oliver. Rebecca. Her mother. Her sisters. Her brother. Oliver. Where did she belong? She swallowed a sob, took a breath, wiped her eyes with the handkerchief that President Weissman had handed to her. Weeks ago, it seemed, but the reception had only been this afternoon.

"I—" She was about to say yes, all right, maybe she and Rebecca would come home to Norfolk—but something stopped her.

"It's okay," Marnie said. "It'll be okay."

Virginia heard the plaintive strains of a Simon & Garfunkel song coming from the den; Rebecca and Molly were listening to music on Oliver's hi-fi. Now Simon or maybe Garfunkel sang about how he was gone, how he didn't know where. Virginia wanted to hear more of those shimmery harmonies, but the song had finished.

Chapter Two

VIRGINIA FOUND A PARKING spot across the street from the Clarendon library. She sat in the car, gathering herself, turning her mind to the upper-level class in Dutch and Flemish art she was due to teach next semester. The Northern Baroque. Rembrandt and Hals portraits, how they never flattered, but sympathized. Still lifes full of decay and death. Jan Steen's jolly tavern scenes, talking back to Amsterdam's dour church fathers. Vermeer's utter silence.

She forced herself to get out of the car. Pushing through the library's revolving side door, she trotted down the worn stairs to the basement. She cut through the study room, which ran the full width of the library, to get to the art history department on the far side.

Only a handful of boys were at the study tables this afternoon. To her right, the enormous panels of the González mural, whose monumental figures with burning eyes told the story of the Americas in a way no Clarendon boy would ever think to do. Such a foolish place to display the mural, a basement that smelled of damp and mold. The mural needed restoration; maybe the administration hoped the mural, with its Communist themes, all those skulls and burning eyes, would crumble from the plaster and disappear. For now, those eyes glared out at the scattering of boys who sprawled at the long tables.

A long time ago, Oliver had lured her here with the González mural. *Think of it*, he'd said. *Clarendon can't be all bad if they commissioned a González in the '20s.*

Oliver had gotten only a slim set of offers: Clarendon College, Lake Forest College and two even smaller schools in Wisconsin. Harvard had passed him over, a rejection that had thrown him so badly that she'd turned herself into his cheerleader. What a wonderful town for Rebecca to grow up in, she'd said about one of the spots in Wisconsin, but he must have picked up on her disappointment, judging by the manic way he'd shown her the Clarendon campus. That first visit, her own unfinished dissertation on John Singleton Copley's surfaces never came up because she had Rebecca; Rebecca was her work now. Taking care of Rebecca and getting over the miscarriages.

Upstairs, Virginia leaned into Arthur Gage's doorway, and he stood quickly, motioning her in. He wore a flannel shirt, no tie—exam-week wear. She began to thank him for taking on her class those last weeks, grading all her papers.

Arthur shook his head, waving off her thanks. "Not at all, it was the least I could—but not a problem. Would you like some tea?" He told her how glad he was to see her, and he hoped things were going well enough, all things considered. He didn't leave room for her to get in a word, not that she wanted to tell him how things were going. Oliver was dead, that was how things were going.

"I'm afraid we need to cancel the spring Northern Baroque class." He paused, raked the hair off his forehead. "Not enough students signing up. And perhaps it's a bit too specialized for our men."

She nodded, waiting.

"Though it was well attended last year." He steepled his hands against his mouth, not saying the rest: not enough students had signed up because Virginia wasn't Dan Mason, whom she'd been hired to fill in for while he was on sabbatical in Italy. The Clarendon boys wanted a man, a robust man with a doctorate that they could confidently call "Dr." or "Professor." Not an undereducated woman like her. Or maybe he was only being kind. Maybe word had gotten around that she wasn't much of a teacher. A mere substitute, margarine instead of butter.

"Right." Despite all she knew about Dutch and Flemish art, more than enough to teach a handful of boys and one girl on exchange from Mt. Holyoke, she hadn't finished, never mind published, her dissertation. At home, on the floor next to her desk in the bedroom, the stack of books and monographs on John Singleton Copley bristled with the scraps of paper she'd marked them with years ago. Now and then she shuffled her index cards, typed a few more sentences. Sometimes she drove to Boston to look again at the Copleys, and Copley's *Paul Revere* gazed back at her, chin in hand, daring her to write something when too much had already been written. She felt her fists balling in her lap. She unclenched them and smoothed her skirt; she hated this skirt, wool plaid, neither long nor short. It was the kind of thing June would wear, if June lived in New Hampshire.

"I heard the English department is desperate for help," he said. "Administrative work, but it's been a mess there since Chapman left and Mrs. Smith retired."

She nodded, as if she'd want to take the place of jowly, ancient Mrs. Smith.

"At any rate, you'll have more time to spend with your... daughter?"

How dare he bring Rebecca into this? Virginia pushed back, stood up and left his office without answering. *You've forgotten your manners, dear,* she could hear Momma saying, as she hurried back down the hall, down the stairs and back through the library's study room. If only she had the glaring, magical power of those huge Aztec gods in the mural, she'd cast an angry spell on smug Arthur Gage, let him be tormented for a while.

At home, when Momma asked how the meeting had gone, Virginia answered that it had gone as expected, feeling a flush of rage and embarrassment at the way she'd run off in the middle of it.

Once again, Momma was in New Hampshire, and for a week now she'd bustled around Virginia's kitchen, packing Rebecca's lunches, rinsing out tinfoil and sandwich bags to reuse, and taking Rebecca to piano lessons. Momma pestered Virginia to reply to all those pale condolence notes and to get through the stack of Oliver-related paperwork, but also to rest as much as possible. Momma had insisted on taking Virginia to the doctor, *to get you looked over,* as if she were six years old. At the doctor's office, Momma asked

about a prescription for something *just to tide my Ginny over.*
Tide her over till when? Until Oliver came back?

"I forgot to tie up the pot roast," Momma said. "Who
knows how it will turn out."

Before Virginia could reassure her, the phone rang: Louise Walsh. "We're trying to get Shirley Chisholm up here,"
Louise Walsh said, with barely a hello. "The new congresswoman, from Brooklyn? She's doing good work with Bella
Abzug. There's already been some talk about her running
for president. Extreme long shot, but I'm sure you heard
that speech she gave in Congress about the equal rights
amendment a couple months ago? It was so electrifying
that we thought we'd raise some money to help her come
up here for the primary—"

"I'm sorry, but that's not my thing," Virginia said. No,
she hadn't heard Shirley Chisholm's speech about equal
rights. If politics had ever been her thing, it certainly wasn't
right now. "I'm a little out of—"

"Right, but I thought that since you're—I thought you
might—" Louise stumbled over her words.

You thought wrong, Virginia kept herself from saying.
"Maybe some other time." She hung up, fueled by irritation.

Louise Walsh. She strongly disliked Louise by the tran-
sitive property. Oliver used to get red in the forehead and
temples when he'd talk about Louise, how Louise hijacked
meetings with her crazy tangents, and how nobody ever
stopped her, just let her go on and on. He was the only one
who ever tried to keep meetings on track.

The faculty had almost gone to war with itself last year,
when a handful of Clarendon boys, inspired momentarily
by more activist schools, had taken over the administration

building to protest ROTC recruiting, Virginia remembered. The national wave of sit-ins and takeovers had rolled onto the Clarendon campus, and some of the faculty had wanted to cancel classes in solidarity with the protesters. Louise was on the side of the protesters, Oliver on the side of practicality; cancel classes and too many boys would get drunk and start breaking things. Louise was always agitating about something, Oliver used to say.

"… But he's a good man, honestly," Momma was saying. "And from a good family."

Virginia willed herself to listen to Momma's chatter about Bryce Watson, Daddy's banker. Momma still referred to Bryce Watson as Daddy's banker, even though Daddy had been dead for fifteen years.

"I'm sure it will all turn out fine, I'll just have to trim my sails a bit," Momma said, about something to do with her investments and needing to budget better. The softness of faraway Norfolk hovered like a cloud around Momma. Those early-spring days, the redbuds and azaleas and dogwoods a haze of blooms.

Momma was still talking; now she'd moved on to her friend Liddy Reynolds. "Did I tell you that Liddy's moving to the Outer Banks?" Liddy was the mother of one of Virginia's childhood friends, Sandra. Sandra Reynolds had died in a car crash sophomore year, driving back from a frat party at Washington and Lee. Ah, Sandra.

Virginia's girlhood friends had stayed close to home for college, while Virginia had headed north, to Smith. Long ago, home from college for the summer, Virginia could hear her old friends' accents which until then she'd never noticed. "You wear too much black," one of her friends said. "She's trying to be mysterious," another said. They'd all laughed, Virginia too, but she felt this wall rising up between herself and her childhood friends.

Then there was Archer, who she'd gone on two dates with that summer. Arch Tazewell, with those dimples and long eyelashes and football shoulders—he played quarterback for Hampden-Sydney College. On their second date, he drove her to the crab place down at Lynnhaven Inlet, and they sat in the back room, a screened porch where they could look out at the Chesapeake Bay, flat-calm and silvery in the distance. She'd already asked him about football and lacrosse, about his summer ROTC duties. Now she pretended interest as he droned on about Hampden-Sydney's traditions—was she aware of all the Virginia governors who'd gone there, back to the Revolutionary War? She wasn't. She picked out the yellowish mustard from her third crab.

"It wouldn't be natural to admit him, of course." Arch was talking about a black man who'd applied to Hampden-Sydney last year; she snapped to.

"Who would he socialize with?" Arch said. "It's like a bad joke."

"A bad joke," she repeated. "Why?"

"Don't pretend you don't know what I mean. You can't have white and colored students together like that." He chuckled, as if she'd said something stupid and now he'd have to correct her. "You know that we can't be wrecking our traditions that way."

This accompanied by his trademark smile, and those dimples. Of course she'd heard older men talk like that, some of Daddy's friends, but never with the sense of glee she saw on Arch's face now. "I just need to run to the ladies'—" And she'd even smiled back as she untied her crab bib.

At the pay phone outside the restroom, she wiped her

buttery fingers on her dungarees, then called home. She walked out of the crab place, then put her head down and darted across the two busy lanes of Shore Drive to the marina on the other side, where she waited for Marnie.

Marnie—thank God she'd been home doing her toenails—was laughing out the window when she got to the marina, barefoot and in shorts. A minute later, they sped over the Lynnhaven Bridge, the warm night air rushing through the car, and Virginia felt sick, guilty and exhilarated all at the same time.

When Arch called the house an hour later, she'd refused to talk to him. After that he spread horrible rumors implying that she was a slut, and she'd had to say over and over that nothing had happened, that he was a conceited dolt.

What a coward she'd been, slipping out of the restaurant like that, afraid to tell him that he was not only arrogant and braggy but terribly bigoted. What a coward she still was—she'd run out of her meeting today. Still, that long-ago incident had cemented her understanding of herself as different, as a New Englander, temperamentally at least. She supposed she should write Archer a letter and thank him for that. And yet here she was, twenty years later, listening to her mother yammer on about Norfolk and thinking about returning there with Rebecca.

But was the North any better, even now, in 1970? Almost 1971, but you could hardly call New Hampshire progressive. She imagined an auditorium of Clarendon boys, full of themselves and perhaps just as bigoted as Archer. And how many black Clarendon students were there even now? Oliver had liked to talk about how the Clarendon frats had severed ties with their national organizations ten or fifteen years ago, turning themselves into local clubs to protest the national fraternities' segregation policies. That was after Oliver's time, but he'd been as proud as if he'd been part of those decisions.

"We were in Carter Junction today," Rebecca said at dinner. "What a dump."

"*Rebecca,*" Virginia said. After her humiliating meeting with Arthur Gage, Virginia had spent the afternoon looking through her dissertation notes, trying to pick up the thread of Copley before he went to London, of his first portraits, assured and vivid. "What were you doing in Carter Junction?"

"Just took a wrong turn somewhere." Momma gave a little laugh. "And then we weren't at all where I thought we were going."

"Ah," Virginia said. Being out of her element, being stuck in strange New Hampshire with its cold, the snow-banks already lining their street, was tuckering her mother out. Momma might be brisk and energetic, and she kept up appearances with her constant red lipstick, but she was getting old. Momma *was* old. She was drooping: her eyelids, the skin on her jowls and neck. "You need to get home, Momma."

"Christmas is coming," Momma said.

"We'll be just fine," Virginia said. "Won't we, Bec?" She reached for Rebecca's hand, but Rebecca had already pushed back her chair and stood up, all in one motion. Rebecca left the kitchen without a word.

Virginia got up to follow Rebecca, but Momma raised her hand. "Let her be," Momma said. "It's just going to take some time."

She nodded. Another day, another round of tears, that

was the way it was. That and the memories, the endless memories that pressed on her. Some of them shouldn't have stuck in her head, but they had, and now they scrolled one after the other. Like last Christmas, after Christmas Day but before New Year's, she and Rebecca and Oliver had been home together watching TV, *The Carol Burnett Show*. Harvey Korman and Tim Conway, playing nineteenth-century explorers, had encountered Carol Burnett dressed in skins, and Harvey Korman had started laughing as Tim Conway crawled around on the floor looking for something. Harvey Korman couldn't contain himself, which made Tim Conway start laughing. Only Carol Burnett stayed in character, until she too, broke up into laughter. And Virginia and Oliver and Rebecca had cracked up at the chaos on TV. Virginia couldn't remember when she'd last laughed so hard. Oliver wheezed and then took off his glasses to wipe his eyes, and Rebecca had watched her dad, charmed by his wheezy laughter and his tears. Harvey Korman was kind of old, Virginia had thought; he needed to take better care of himself. Oliver was getting older too. He needed to lose weight, drink less, stop smoking that pipe. She needed to tell him that. But she never had.

Chapter Three

HOME FOR THE THREE weeks of Christmas break, Sam and his old friend Tommy wandered the Village, checking out the head shops and record stores. They'd gotten high at Tommy's apartment, like they always did before they headed downtown. The city was cold but sunny, and no wind, not so bad for poking around downtown; on days like today the trash and grit stayed on the ground, instead of getting whipped up into their faces. That briny-sewery smell that wafted from the rivers was stronger down here, but Sam didn't mind it.

In a basement record store, Sam and Tommy flipped through albums in the bins the way they used to do, only now they mostly hunted for the old and the obscure. The Beatles' *Revolution 1* floated out of the sound system, and Sam sang along with McCartney's slow "shoo-be-doo-wop" backing vocals.

Everyone had a signature band, the band whose albums

you owned every one of. (Not the Beatles. Beatles didn't count.) Tommy was into Creedence—a lot of the guys in Sam's frat liked CCR, its clangy guitars backing up Fogerty's freaky voice. Sam liked Crosby, Stills & Nash and Three Dog Night, and he pulled out Three Dog Night's new album, *Naturally*.

Tommy sang about lonely numbers, butchering Three Dog Night to irritate Sam. "They hardly write any of their own songs."

"Uh-huh, and Creedence is authentic Southern roots music," Sam said, like he always said back. "Imposters from California."

Tommy shrugged, not agreeing or disagreeing.

Nothing anyone listened to was authentic; everything was borrowed or stolen. Elvis and the Beatles and the Stones borrowed from black rhythm and blues singers. At least Three Dog Night gave credit to the people who wrote their songs, didn't try to pretend they were something they weren't.

"So lay it on me," Tommy said, when they were back on the street. "What's the latest?" The latest about girls, Tommy meant. Sam never had anything to share, but he'd never corrected Tommy's impression that Clarendon guys had all the fun *and* got all the girls. Swarthmore, where Tommy went, was coed, and Tommy even had a girlfriend now, Jane.

Instead of making up fictional girl-details, Sam usually talked about his frat, which had an okay mix of guys. Guys in the jazz band, a few Nordic skiers, a bunch of runners. Sam was the only Jewish guy in Lambda Chi, and he hadn't told Tommy that they'd made him chaplain, a supposedly hilarious reference to his Jewishness. He didn't talk about the way he got made fun of at house meetings, the whole Jewish chaplain thing, or the humiliating rituals, like the night of the peckerwood ruler, when the pledges had to strip and look at *Playboy* centerfolds and get measured, and he'd had a hard-on for the wrong reason. He'd been terrified that the upperclassmen would somehow know.

They backtracked, Bleecker to West Third. Sam felt a grass-induced rush of love for the crazy mess of downtown streets, arrows pointing in too many directions, where even the old people looked like hippies. They hadn't crossed Christopher Street today, but that flyer he'd seen there last year—an ad for a new club, a photo of a guy in a tight T-shirt looking away from the camera—had stayed with him. He wondered absently whether the club was still open. Where it was. Whether the guy on the poster was a model or someone who might actually go there.

On the sidewalk outside the place that used to be Cafe Wha?, two vets camped, with flattened cardboard boxes for their beds. One was missing an arm, his jacket sleeve hanging loose. It was better not to look, so Sam focused on the awnings above, the glow he'd felt a few minutes before gone now.

They ducked into their coffee shop on Waverly Place, and slid into a booth at the back. They'd been coming here for fries and sodas since they were twelve; they could sit and watch the NYU kids, the hippies and the folkies, the guys who wore all black and grew pathetic beards and mustaches, and the beautiful girls with their miniskirts and long hair that fell to their asses. Everything had happened right here: the peace marches and the demonstrations, the music in Washington Square Park, the pervasive sweet-sharp smell of grass smoke. If only he'd gone to NYU, he'd have something to say. He should never have listened to his mom about colleges.

Tommy pulled a photo from his wallet and slid it across the Formica. A photo from a formal dance, Tommy with Jane. Big smile and big dark eyes, and petite, which Tommy, at five foot six, must have appreciated. At least Sam had his height. And his eyes: he had beautiful eyes, according to Cynthia, the Wellesley exchange girl from his American Diplomacy class. He'd managed to talk to Cynthia at a Lambda Chi party in October. Cynthia had danced two songs with him, and when he'd returned from the basement with more beers for the two of them, she'd started dancing with Bruce, a senior, and Sam hadn't had the heart to try again. He could see why she'd rather dance with Bruce than with him. Cynthia had probably left Clarendon with an engagement ring on her finger.

"Nice," Sam said. "She's very—"

"I know, I'm the luckiest guy," Tommy said. "Hey, can you get me something from Red Wagon?" Sam's dad's company. "Jane likes jazz."

"Sure, I guess." He'd only seen his dad once this break and not at all during Thanksgiving. His dad had gone to Minnesota with Patty, his new wife, to see Patty's family. "What are you looking for?"

"I don't know, Coltrane?"

"Coltrane was with Impulse."

"Oh. Right."

Tommy had an elaborate memory for rock bands, but he couldn't keep jazz musicians straight. Maybe Tommy didn't even know that Coltrane was dead four years already.

"Stones are doing a US tour this summer," Tommy said. "Did you see the thing in the *Voice*? Want to go?"

"Sure, maybe. I don't know what I'm doing this summer."

Tommy said he was applying for a summer job at Chemical Bank, and maybe Sam could work there too. Working at a bank sounded deadly, but Sam didn't say that.

"Too bad you don't want to work at Red Wagon," Tommy said. "At least your dad's not as big a stuffed shirt as mine is."

Yeah, too bad. Dad was a jerk, and Sam hardly talked to him anymore. And yet why not? He knew music. He knew the standards, he even knew some of the musicians, a little. *You have to make something of yourself, Sam*, he could hear Dad saying. *I did all this on my own*—not true, his dad had had partners and a loan from Zayde Waxman—*and my father came here with nothing, absolutely nothing, and made something of himself. You, on the other hand. The way you mope around—and art history? What the hell is that?*

Math, Sam would remind him. Dad made all this noise just because Sam had taken a few measly art history classes. Sam hadn't even mentioned the computer stuff, because his dad would only say something negative. *Computers, eh, why bother*, his dad would say. *Some kind of fad.*

Irritation rose up inside him. In the next booth, two couples rehashed the never-ending subjects of draft deferments and the lottery. "At least we're not freshmen," he said, trying to shake his mood. He and Tommy had drawn high lottery numbers, possibly because they were both born in the fall. They'd compared numbers, trying to puzzle out the odds, since people said the supposedly fair lottery wasn't random at all but a plot to grab the guys with spring birthdays. Still, this year's freshmen had it worse—they all got I-A, *available*, instead of II-S, student deferment, which made no sense if the war was winding down. Maybe the war wasn't winding down and would keep scooping up guys like him. The image of the two vets on their cardboard beds, their long oily hair under their knit caps, and that empty sleeve, intruded and wouldn't leave him. Those two vets weren't dead, at least.

"Yeah." Tommy let out a sigh.

"Man, I wish they still had the Tenth Mountain Division," Sam said, trying to joke. "If you have to go to war, that's the way to go."

Tommy laughed, aspirating his coffee. He coughed and smacked his chest. "Yeah, you'd be a lot of help on your skis in My Lai."

"Water skis," Sam said. Every guy at Clarendon knew about the way the Tenth had taken Mount Belvedere in northern Italy because of all the Clarendon men on skis in the division. The waitress brought their fries, and one of the girls in the next booth started to cry.

Me too, he wanted to say to the girl in the next booth. It felt weird to be sad about losing someone he didn't know all that well. Yet Oliver was—had been—a friend; at jazz band, Sam felt like he belonged, and Oliver was a huge part of that feeling. And then Sam had misinterpreted something important, and that felt weird too. *That's not me, man*, he'd thought of saying, *you got the wrong guy*. But a deeper part of him figured that Oliver had his number.

"So this professor at school, Professor Desmarais, he, uh, he died a few weeks ago."

Tommy looked at him blankly. Like why would Sam bring something like this up, what was interesting about that? "An old guy, huh?"

"No, maybe late thirties or early forties."

"Old guy," Tommy repeated.

Sam shrugged. There was nothing more to say. "When do you go back?"

★ ★ ★

That night, Sam and his mom went to dinner at the French place where his mom was a regular, four blocks from the apartment. He liked the restaurant's old-fashioned lighting, and the way the waiters greeted him, as if they knew him.

But the waiters were also a million years old and most of the other people in the restaurant were either old or people his mom knew, other thin and brittle women, and tonight they all wore the same kind of dress that looked like a short coat with big buttons down the front, and their hair puffed up in the back. When he thought about his parents, he couldn't parse out whether they'd always been so different from one another, or whether their differences had amplified after the divorce. His mom so Upper East Side, his dad still trying to be a beatnik or something at his late age.

"Do you mind if I'm out tomorrow night?" Mom asked. "I know you've only got a few days left at home, and I hate to be out when you're—"

"It's fine, Mom. I'm supposed to get together with Tommy anyway." He didn't want to hear about her latest date with some other old guy.

He couldn't tell if his mom was lonely, or just trying to compete with Dad, who not only had Patty but a baby on the way. When he was a kid, Sam had asked for a little brother, and his mom always said, *We'll see, we're doing our best, honey.* Now at the exact wrong time he was going to get a sibling. Half-sibling. So embarrassing, the way his dad tried to act young, such a dope. If only Sam had known then, he would never have asked for a brother and maybe none of this would have happened. Ha, still thinking like a child, like he'd learned in Psych 1, how children were so self-centered that they thought they had the power to cause all kinds of adult disasters.

One of his mom's friends stopped by the table. Mrs. Bemis. Mom complimented Mrs. Bemis's dress, which was a dead ringer for Mom's, and they spent a few minutes discussing it. Mrs. Bemis mentioned an article she'd read, something about a revival of New York's jazz clubs. "Of course I don't usually read the *Village Voice*, but that's just wonderful that Harry was quoted. He's an expert after all."

Mom smiled and nodded, as if she were perfectly pleased that Dad had been quoted in the *Village Voice* about jazz clubs.

"And, Sam, remind me, you're at…" Mrs. Bemis said.

"Clarendon."

"High honors, math major," Mom added. "Plays two instruments in the college jazz band. And ski patrol." Mom widened her eyes as if the very phrase *ski patrol* frightened her. She asked Mrs. Bemis about her children, and Mrs. Bemis went on at length about the two daughters at Wellesley and the son at Taft, bound for Yale like his father.

"Wonderful," Mom said. "Just wonderful."

Mrs. Bemis patted Sam's shoulder, and wound around tables on her way to the bathroom. Mom's smile disappeared. She pressed her lips together and leaned across the table. "Sylvia Bemis is a horrible person," Mom whispered. "Of course she knows that Harry and I are…" She left the sentence unfinished, avoiding the *D* word. "She's just fishing for gossip about your dad. Or me. God only knows what he's up to. Sheesh. A new father at his age. That's even worse than…" She trailed off and Sam said nothing, not wanting to hear any more confiding.

When Sam was little, he'd been wowed by his dad. Dad would come home late at night and check on Sam in bed, and sing him back to sleep. Whatever Dad yelled about, like the time Sam unscrewed all the doorknobs from every door in the apartment, or had taken apart his alarm clock and left the pieces scattered on his bedroom floor, got washed away with those nighttime moments. And a few times Dad brought Sam to his favorite recording studio, a place on the West Side that used to be a church, and Sam would get to put on headphones and listen to someone practicing drum fills, and then the actual music, until he got bored and went back to his comic books, and then later on, everyone would join him in the lounge to eat pizza and drink Scotch and tell dirty jokes.

Sometimes when Sam was at a frat party, and the smoke got to a certain level and he'd hear a tenor sax line or a quick blurt of trumpets, he'd be transported for a second back to those Saturdays in the studio, and the way his dad was happy there, his nervous energy contained, deferring to whatever the engineers said.

There used to be a photo of his parents in the back hallway, the two of them at Stowe, before Sam was born; in the photo his mom leaned against a fence and his dad held their skis, kind of curving around her, both of them in tight pants and Norwegian sweaters. You could see why they were drawn together, they'd been a good-looking couple, his mom petite and dark haired, his dad bigger, his hair sandy back then. Sam got the worst of his parents: his dad's nose, his mother's mouth. His lips were too fat. God, now he was thinking like his mother, who was way too focused on her appearance, how old she looked, whether she was thin enough.

"Don't worry about her, she's a moron," Sam said, about Mrs. Bemis. He wished he could talk about real things with his mom. He wished he could tell Mom to stop being a moron too.

★ ★ ★

The afternoon Momma flew home to Norfolk, Virginia made herself go out, to pretend that today was a normal day. She would get on with things. A job: she had to find something. She'd paid the bills that had piled up, and she was no math whiz, but she could see that Oliver's pension—she'd gotten the estimate from the college business office—would cover nothing more than the monthly mortgage. A smaller house, sell the car? Maybe she could take a loan against her future inheritance from Momma.

With the college closed for Christmas vacation, little downtown Westfield was quiet, and she stopped at the college bookstore to look for a few small gifts for Rebecca and for her own sisters. She dawdled at the "In the News" table; Kate Millett's tome *Sexual Politics* had been propped up next to *Diary of a Mad Housewife*; and next to them, Shirley Chisholm's biography *Unbought and Unbossed*. Louise had called Virginia about Shirley Chisholm, something about equal rights and chipping in money to bring the congresswoman up to Clarendon, and Virginia had practically hung up on her. But she wouldn't think about that now.

Finding herself in the "New Fiction" section, she picked up *Islands in the Stream*, the posthumous Hemingway that was supposed to be terrible—she'd get it for Oliver; he'd enjoy spouting off about it. With a sharp intake of breath, she realized her mistake, and she circled the store, counting her breaths. She stopped to look at the ornaments in the Christmas-decor section. She was fine. She made herself focus on two girls, late high school maybe, one of them holding an unlit cigarette, the other laughing and lifting a bunch of plastic mistletoe.

At least Rebecca wasn't a true teenager yet. If Rebecca

had been, say, sixteen when Oliver died, she'd be smoking grass or dropping acid. Rebecca's childish pudginess was gone, but she was still willing to wear the matching crocheted vests and berets that June made for her.

There'd been a heroin overdose at the high school last year, a shock because all the unrest and upset, all the marches, the love-ins, the sit-ins, the drugs, the riots, the police beating up protesters, the Kent State killings—all of it remained far away from Westfield. Sure, that group of Clarendon boys had taken over the administration building for a few hours last year, but no one had been hurt, and the drama seemed to pass as soon as it was over. The thirty activist boys had been put into county jails around the state for thirty days, then expelled. *I just thank God Clarendon's not coed*, Eileen from next door liked to say. *Can you* imagine? Eileen's older daughters, a high school junior and senior, were a handful, according to Eileen. Virginia hadn't bothered to point out the obvious, that a coed Clarendon would cut in half the dangerous allure it held for Eileen's daughters. Still, the world's dangers remained exponentially far from Rebecca's orbit, and therefore far from Virginia's orbit too.

On her way to art supplies—colored pencils for Rebecca's stocking—she passed through the textbook section. Above a small pyramid of books, Oliver's name caught her eye:

Professor Desmarais, History
Spring semester Tues.–Thurs.
Early Modern Europe, The Flourishing of the Holy Roman Empire

She wondered if the books would have to be sent back. No, of course someone else would fill in, someone else would run Oliver's classes, lead his discussions and grade his students' papers. Her tears flowed, as usual. She wiped at them and went to buy her books, including the stupid Hemingway, which she'd neglected to put back. She tried to smile at the cashier—a young woman, who looked a little alarmed at the sight of this crying, dripping middle-aged lady on the other side of the counter—and fled to her car.

At home, she found a package in the mailbox. She sat at the kitchen table to open it. From Momma, an unwrapped book that Momma must have mailed the second she got home to Norfolk. "How I miss you girls! Found this for you both," Momma's note said. "Thought you might like it." *Heloise All Around the House*: a whole book's worth of housekeeping hints from Heloise. God, did her mother need to find yet another way to remind her that she was a bad housewife? Bad housewidow.

Rebecca had always been too much of a neatnik, and she had this strange habit, a kind of compulsion, to clip out Heloise and Dear Abby columns, practical hints and recipes and little spiritual sayings, and paste them into scrapbooks. An analyst would say that Rebecca was trying to make up for her mother's lackadaisicalness. And now Virginia's own mother was telling her the same damn thing. *Stay home, Virginia, and take care of your child, your house, yourself. Or better yet, think about coming back to Norfolk, starting back where you belong.*

Momma was only trying to help, but it felt awful. Her fingers traced the metal banding around the kitchen table. She put her head down on its cold laminate top and let herself cry until she heard the back door open and felt the puff of cold air enter the house—Rebecca home from school. She shoved the book in the junk drawer, then ran for the bathroom to rinse her face and wipe her eyes.

Chapter Four

SKI DAY: REBECCA REMEMBERED before she was fully awake. Last night after dinner she'd asked Mom to drop her off at the Clarendon Ski Bowl this morning, because they were more than halfway through January and she hadn't skied even once this winter.

"Skiing?" Mom had said in a surprised voice, like she'd forgotten that skiing even existed.

"At the Ski Bowl. I just need a ride tomorrow."

"Sure, hon." But now Mom was talking about her own skis and how cold it was going to be, maybe too cold, and how she hadn't skied at all last year. Mom wanted to ski too.

"I'll find someone to bring me home, you don't need to go," Rebecca said. But Mom had decided, and now Rebecca was stuck—she'd have to ski with Mom.

Every day, another first. First time going skiing since Dad died. It wasn't like they'd skied every run together, it was just that skiing was her and Dad's thing. And Mom only sometimes came along.

When Rebecca got to the kitchen, Mom stood at the far counter laying out bread and ham for sandwiches. Mom was half-dressed for skiing, long underwear and slippers on her bottom half, red turtleneck on top, and she smiled at Rebecca in that way she had now of pretending to have a good time. "Eggs or cereal?"

"Cereal." Rebecca reached for the Cheerios, poured them into the bowl Mom handed her. She didn't know why she felt so provoked just now. "I wish you weren't so sad all the time," Molly had said at morning break yesterday. "I mean, you didn't even hear what I was saying," Molly complained, her voice scratchy with irritation. "Do you even care?" Molly had been talking about Todd, something about Todd's hockey team. Molly and Todd were going together now.

"We don't need to rush to get out there, because it's really cold this morning," Mom said. "Here's the paper." Mom had left the newspaper folded open to the women's page. It used to drive Mom crazy that Rebecca had to cut things out of the newspaper—she'd heard her parents arguing about it. Dad thought Mom was overreacting, *Becca's just interested in the world*, he'd said, *and an organized kid, nothing wrong with that.*

Rebecca couldn't remember why she'd started clipping things out of the paper. It was weird, she knew. Maybe it was because Dad had been so happy that she could read when she was little, and they'd sounded out newspaper headlines together at breakfast. Or maybe it was a way for her to keep track of all the things she might need to know when she was older. But ever since she was six or so, she'd loved how Heloise could make something out of nothing. Heloise wrote about how to turn old pantyhose into scrubby-sponges, how to use a piece of bread to rub fingerprints off wallpaper. Things you'd never think of.

And Dear Abby, she loved Dear Abby too, for Abby's snappy answers, especially to obnoxious or stingy people. Anyway, Rebecca used to cut out hints, recipes, comics, bits of advice columns, then go through all her clippings once a month, pasting her favorites into scrapbooks. She liked getting the dots of glue just right: too little and things wouldn't stick, too much would bleed through and make the pages stick together. She had four full scrapbooks and three empty ones because Mom and Dad always gave her a scrapbook for Christmas. Those scrapbooks were stupid; she was too old for that kind of thing.

Out the kitchen window she could see Molly's backyard, and the snow fort that Molly's brothers had made last weekend—it was still holding up. She and Molly used to play that way, turning Molly's porch roof into a rocket ship and themselves into astronauts. She missed those days. She missed playing with Molly, their long games of pretend and wandering around on the Clarendon campus. Now they just sat on Molly's bed and listened to Molly's sisters' Rolling Stones albums. And Molly wanted to talk about Todd, or else she wanted to call Todd's house and hang up and then call again.

Rebecca missed Dad.

She missed all the things she used to do, like walking over to Dad's office in Clarendon Hall on half days. When she was little, she'd sit with Miss Hazel and draw pictures while Miss Hazel banged and dinged away on the typewriter.

One time about a year ago, Dad had a committee meeting, and she and Dad walked across campus to the English department. The English department had its own little library, with bookshelves dividing the library into alcoves, and an upstairs gallery with a matching set of alcoves, a kind of balcony that circled the room. Each alcove held a comfortable chair and a lap desk. It was the kind of place where the Pevensie children would have done their homework, once they left Narnia and became kids again in London.

"Okay, Bec," Dad had said. "Where do you want to sit, up or down?"

"Up," she'd said. She'd seen this place plenty of times but had never actually hung out here, since it was on the other side of campus from Dad's department, and she felt a tiny thrill mixed with embarrassment. They climbed a miniature spiral staircase and shuffled along a narrow gallery, where Rebecca picked an alcove with a red leather chair. Through the window she could see the Clarendon green, its crisscrossing paths. If only she could live here. Molly would love this too, she'd thought, but then stopped herself. She was way too old for pretend.

"And look, here's Dickens if you get bored," Dad had said, pulling an old leather-bound book off a shelf. She sat down, and Dad set the lap desk across the chair's arms. He handed her a Coke, and left her there.

She started her math homework. Outside the window, two men in blue military uniforms crossed the green. She wondered if they were cold—they wore no coats over their uniforms. A minute later, one college boy darted up behind another and gave him a shove, so the other one tripped and had to break into a run to keep from falling. God, they were acting like sixth graders.

After a while another student entered the library, then a few more. One of them lifted an eyebrow, noting her presence. He was tall; he reminded her of a bird, and he had dark hair, longish and feathery. He smiled up at her as if he knew her, or as if the two of them shared a secret—*hey, I still like the Narnia books*, he might be saying—and plopped down on a couch. Hunched over a coffee table, he opened a thick book, scrawling in a notebook as he read.

The next time she looked up, Dad was greeting the bird-like boy, then motioning for her to come downstairs. She could hear a shrill hiss; a woman had come into the library and was setting a tray of cookies on a table near the French doors. Behind her, a big brass urn was making that hissing sound. The library had filled up, boys throwing their books on chairs and lining up for tea.

"Tea, Bec?" Dad said. "They serve tea here every afternoon."

"Five cents a cup," the birdlike college guy said, and Dad made introductions.

The college guy's name was Sam. He was a sophomore from New York. "Jazz aficionado," Dad said.

Rebecca followed Dad and Sam to the tea table. She picked Earl Grey tea and a sugar cookie while Dad spoke to the tea woman, dropping some coins into a money box. She followed Dad to a couch near French doors that looked out onto the library's snowy lawn.

She drank her smoky tea out of a china cup and took occasional bites from the sugar cookie. The library felt both old-fashioned and serious, smelling of the tea and all the leather-bound books, while outside the sun shone at an angle and made the snow sparkle. It was as if she'd been dropped into a novel. If only Susan or Lucy Pevensie would pop in and take her on some kind of magical adventure on the other side of the bookshelves. *God, don't be so stupid*, she scolded herself. This was just what college was like—tea and studying in the afternoon, and talking to professors as if you were all close friends.

Dad took off his glasses to clean them with his hankie, and the glasses left red indentations on the bridge of his nose as he said something to Sam about the jazz concert next weekend, the student-faculty jazz band. Maybe that was where she'd seen Sam before. Sam was talking too fast, and he blushed, as if he knew he was talking too fast but couldn't stop himself.

The student-faculty jazz band was okay. At the concert in the fall, Dad had held his clarinet ready, even when he wasn't playing, head nodding and toes tapping. Dad's stomach jiggled as he tapped, his cheeks pink, sweat glistening around his temples.

But all of that was such a long time ago.

She missed Dad. She missed him every breakfast when he wasn't there to pass her the paper, the smell of his leftover pipe smoke blending with the other morning smells of coffee, shaving cream and starched dress shirts. There was no one to talk to about how much she missed Dad, except Molly, who was sick of hearing about it. Molly had a boyfriend and she was moving on.

And today Rebecca would take her first downhill run of the season, and Dad wouldn't be there to remind her to lean forward, to wave at her with his pole when she got ahead of him. Even good days were bad days now.

Foolishly, Virginia had taken the back way to get to the college's little ski mountain, and the car slipped and fishtailed along the road's curves. In the passenger seat, Rebecca kept her arms crossed over her chest, frowning and grim.

There was nothing Virginia could say to make Rebecca feel better. They'd gotten through Christmas; they'd driven down to Concord for a sad lunch with Oliver's brother Charlie and wife and college-age son. And she and Rebecca had gotten through school vacation. One afternoon Virginia had felt compelled to make pound cake and they ate that for dinner with glasses of milk. When New Year's Eve finally arrived, Rebecca went next door to Molly's to spend the night, while Virginia sat in bed with Rebecca's copy of *Jane Eyre*. She and Oliver had always made something French for New Year's Eve dinner, a Burgundy wine with dinner (a Roy Rogers for Rebecca) and champagne afterward. Just their little family. Never a New Year's Eve party.

She and Rebecca had made it all the way to the middle of winter, but now everything Virginia did felt like a mistake. No point in saying again to Rebecca that she was so very sorry that Daddy was gone, sorry he hadn't taken better care of himself. She was sorry they'd been so late having kids; she was sorry that Rebecca would never get a sibling. Things hadn't been perfect but Virginia missed Oliver in ways she couldn't put into words, and she was undone and trying to put herself back together, and surely Rebecca knew at least some of that, but of course Rebecca was even more undone, and that was what made her so grumpy and prickly.

"I'm sorry, we should have gone the other way—" Virginia began.

"I heard you fighting," Rebecca said at the same time.

"What?"

"You were fighting, the week before. You weren't being nice to Daddy." She could hear the blame in Rebecca's voice. *Your fault, Mom.*

"We might have had a little fight, Becca, but that's just part of marriage. It wasn't anything—" But she could have been a better wife. She could have done more to support Oliver's career, like her friends Eileen and Gerda did. Gerda's husband was dean of the faculty now; he'd leap-frogged far ahead of Oliver. "Let's just think about skiing this morning," she said, and Rebecca made a harrumph-ing sound.

Well. Rebecca had a right to be angry. Especially today, since skiing was Oliver's area. He'd taught Rebecca how to hold onto the J-bar and ride the ski lift when she was a little thing, and every year he took her to watch the collegiate ski races during Winter Carnival weekend.

They parked, lugging their skis and poles and boots up-hill to the lodge. Inside the lodge, Rebecca slipped away, stopping to talk to two of her classmates and sitting down with them to buckle on her ski boots instead of finding a table with Virginia.

At a table a respectable distance away from Rebecca, Virginia worked to get her feet into her heavy, barely used boots. The lodge always smelled of frying oil and woodsmoke. It was full this morning, other families suiting up, and Clarendon boys shouting to one another across the room. Two Clarendon boys tossed a football in the open space between the tables. *Make the best of it*, she told her-self, *just get on with the day.* Still, she felt exposed, as if ev-eryone around her was staring, feeling sorry for her: *Oh, that widow, and my God, that poor child.*

Virginia could see that Rebecca had her eye on the football-tossing college boys across the lodge, and Rebecca's school-mate Sydney leaned over and whispered something that made Rebecca blush and laugh.

"Ready, Mom?" Rebecca said a minute later, in front of Virginia now, booted, hatted and smiling, as if she hadn't just accused her mother of contributing to her father's death.

As she and Rebecca went up the new chairlift, Virginia scanned the trails. The snow cover on Martin's Ledge looked thin, despite the two snowstorms last week. She could see icy patches near the top of the trail, and the lift made a scary squeaking sound as they went upward. "Let's just take it easy at first, okay?" Virginia said. "I'm a little out of practice."

"Sure, okay." Rebecca kept her eyes on the skiers below them, probably looking for kids she knew.

Virginia followed Rebecca's lead, sliding off the lift as the summit rose up to them. Virginia stopped to adjust her goggles and Rebecca took off, heading straight down the expert trail that ran under the lift. Virginia let out a sigh and followed, trying to keep up with Rebecca, hugging the slope's left side to avoid that big ice patch in the middle.

Rebecca zipped around a curve and disappeared. Virginia sped up, tried to find a rhythm. *Keep your skis together, Ginny, now put your weight on the outside ski*, she could hear Oliver instructing her. Okay. This wasn't so bad, and at least it wasn't windy today. And the sun had come out. So what if she and Rebecca weren't skiing together, so what if Rebecca was angry at her. That was all normal. Even kids who had two healthy parents got angry and pouty during adolescence. And at least they were out, attempting a little of a regular winter. They could do this every weekend until March. Yes. Everything would be okay.

Something hit her head, knocking her ski hat loose. It didn't hurt; it was just a bouncy hard something that had glanced off the side of her head. As she turned to see what had hit her, her ski caught an edge, and she lost her balance. She worked to get her balance back, but her other ski shot out in front and she went down hard, tumbling and tumbling, her shoulder banging hard into the snow, then her hip. She was going to die in a minute, and Rebecca would be an orphan.

At last she slid into a heap, one ski off, poles gone. She'd stopped moving, at least, and she was still on the trail; she wasn't dead and she hadn't gone over the edge. She listened to her breath for a minute, then rolled over and pushed up to sitting. Was she hurt? She tried to assess. Hip, knee, ankle: they all throbbed and pinged with pain. Suddenly she was surrounded by college boys, those same boys from the lodge. One boy had gathered up her lost poles and ski, another was yelling for the ski patrol, and two others knelt next to her, peering into her eyes. "Are you—are you—"

"I'm fine," she said, annoyed now.

"Jesus, Squirrel, you jackass," one of them said.

"Hey, I'm sorry, I never in a million years would have—"

She tried to understand what they were saying. Two more had skied close; they wore red ski-patrol jackets, one towing a sled behind him.

"We sometimes play football on the way down," another boy apologized. "You know, to make it more of a challenge. The skiing's not—"

"Move it, Squirrel," one of the ski-patrol boys said. "You're going to get kicked out of the Ski Bowl for the rest of the season if you don't rein it in. Shut up about it."

If her foot didn't hurt so much, if she didn't feel so humiliated and out of place, she would have laughed at the strangeness of being surrounded by frightened boys in their old-fashioned wool trousers, two of them hatless despite the cold. The two ski-patrol boys asked her name and age, and was she having trouble breathing, and what hurt? Her foot, or maybe her ankle, she said. And her knee and hip. She thought she'd answered normally, but she heard one of them saying something about shock into his walkie-talkie, and the other one said they'd take her down in the sled, to be on the safe side.

She thought of Rebecca. Dear God, what if Rebecca saw her coming down the hill in the sled? She'd think the worst had happened.

"My daughter," she said, her voice a squeak. She swallowed back a sob. "She can't see me in the—in this thing— she lost her dad last month, my—"

"Ohhh," one of the boys said. "Are you Professor Desmarais's wife?"

She nodded.

One of them said they'd all ski in a tight group around the ski-patrol sled so no one could see who was in it. And down they went, Virginia strapped into the sled and covered with a scratchy wool blanket, headfirst and upside-down, bumping along, tears streaming from the cold. It was even more uncomfortable and scary than she'd imagined, and she tried to focus on the blue of the sky, the clear morning, on the trees whizzing by above her.

Rebecca was flying at last. She loved the first drop of Martin's Ledge, a quick sharp plunge down that steep section that always had ice underneath, where you had to let yourself just *go* or you'd completely lose it. Plus you'd lose it right under the lift, which would be so embarrassing. For the first time in so long, she felt like herself. First day of skiing was always a mix of the familiar and the unfamiliar: in the lodge, the friendly sounds of people banging their boots on the floor to get their heels settled into them, and the smells of wet wool and hot chocolate. And that sense of being too bundled up, and then once you got outside and skate-skied over to the lift line, waiting your turn, the cold on your face and that nervous-but-good feeling before the first run.

On the lift, Mom had asked question after question about the trails and the conditions, worrying about every little thing. Rebecca wanted to say, *don't worry, just ski and it will all be fine*, but she didn't; Mom was so touchy about everything, the most random little things made Mom cry. Well, Rebecca knew how that felt. The gray blankness of missing Dad lurked beneath the weirdness of being here with Mom today, and not Dad. She couldn't remember why she'd been so mad at Mom a little while ago; maybe she should wait for Mom, tell her she was sorry.

But she wanted to catch up to Sydney and Josh, who'd gotten on the lift when Rebecca was still waiting for Mom to catch up and get in line. Molly wasn't here today, but skiing with Sydney and Josh would be okay. If she just skied a little faster down the rest of Martin's, she could catch up and ski the rest of the morning with them. She'd yell down to Mom from the lift, and say she'd see her for lunch.

In the lift line—it had taken her two runs of skiing fast down Martin's to catch up with Sydney and Josh—she was about to get on the lift when she heard someone calling her name. She turned to see some Clarendon guy in a red ski-patrol jacket. He'd just come out of the lodge and he wasn't on his skis.

"Oooo, Rebecca's got a boyfriend," Sydney said, sing-song, making a stupid joke. Then Rebecca knew, she just *knew*, that Mom had had an accident, that the injured person she'd seen from the lift a few minutes ago, strapped into the ski-patrol sled and getting towed downhill by the ski-patrol guys, was her own mother.

Rebecca ducked under the rope, sliding toward the ski-patrol guy, tears stinging her eyes. Sydney was calling something to her, but she couldn't answer.

What if—what if—

"Rebecca?" the ski-patrol guy said. "Come with me, your mom asked me—"

"Is she—is she—"

But he'd already turned and stomped away, expecting her to follow. She skied to the ski rack, struggled to unlatch her bindings, her fingers shaking, not working right, and then she ran after him, skidding down the slippery hill and into the first aid room.

"Virginia, right?" It was one of the moms from Rebecca's school on volunteer duty in the first aid room. Barbie, yes, that was her name. Virginia's head hurt, and it was too hot in here.

"You look awful," Barbie said, then clapped a hand over her mouth. "I'm sorry, I didn't mean—it's just that you're a little green—" She stopped. "Let's just get your boots off and see."

As Barbie tugged at Virginia's left ski boot, the pain in her foot sparked and shot up her leg, making her growl as the boot came off.

"Something's sprained," Barbie said, lifting the swollen ankle. "Maybe broken. You'll have to go in and get it looked over."

Rebecca was in the door a minute later, her hat off, hair every which way, with two more college ski-patrol boys. Rebecca's eyes were too big and she started to cry, clomping forward in her ski boots. Virginia smoothed Rebecca's staticky lank hair, Rebecca leaning into her and snuffling into her jacket.

"I thought you were—" Rebecca said. "I thought—"

"Shh, I'm fine," Virginia said. "It's probably just a sprain. Nothing big. I got hit in the head with a football and I lost my balance. Crazy, huh? Those crazy boys."

"Those Phi Rhos, they think they're Kennedys or something with that football," one of the ski-patrol boys said.

It was Sam Waxman, from her fall class, Italian Baroque art. She couldn't avoid her failure as a teacher; wherever she went, it followed her. "I didn't know you were on the ski patrol," she said, to stop her stream of thoughts. "Thank you for your help."

"Just once every two weeks now. I don't have as much time this year as I used to."

"Could you do us a favor?" Virginia asked. "Could you find someone to drive us to the hospital?"

"Sure. My shift's about done, and I can drive your car if you want. Be right back." Sam turned and clomped out of the first aid room.

"Mom," Rebecca hissed, "I don't want to ride with a college guy! Why can't we get a mom to drive us?"

"It's fine, Bec." She kept doing the wrong thing.

Chapter Five

CLARENDON HALL WAS A plain and drafty building—
the offices on the north side needed space heaters in winter. Two hundred years ago, Clarendon Hall had housed
the entire school. Now it was home to history, sociology,
anthropology and government, the four departments shoe-
horned into cramped offices on the upper floors.

As usual, Louise was five minutes early for the department meeting, and as usual the others were late. Garland
had put off their December meeting, what with Oliver's
death and everyone having to scramble, and then the holi-
days. The others dribbled into the seminar room, taking
their usual spots, and leaving Oliver's chair empty.

Garland passed around the carbon copies of the agenda
and called the meeting to order. "A moment of silence for
our departed colleague, Oliver Desmarais," he said.

Louise bowed her head, her eyes coming to rest on the

x's and *v*'s that some Clarendon boy had scratched into the wood of the Harkness table. A renovation from decades ago had tried to give the seminar room an Oxbridgian look, with dark paneling and leaded glass, all wrong for this clapboard and brick building. In the silence, she gazed around: Garland was wiping his nose with his hankie; Fred leaned on an elbow, hand lifted to cover his eyes; Randolph had bowed his head, eyes closed, seeming to pray. It was as if the others had only just noticed that Oliver was gone.

Garland cleared his throat with a rumble, cleared it again. "Sore throat. Say, Louise, would you mind?" He tapped the agenda, and she took over, asking if everyone had read the minutes. Any changes?

Louise asked Randolph to discuss old business, her mind drifting. She regretted the way things had gone with Oliver. They should have been friends—they'd been hired around the same time, and they shared the same politics, more or less. They'd had a kind of sparring relationship, Oliver sputtering and reddening whenever she called him on an inconsistency. A year or two ago, Oliver had asked her if she'd mind reading some pages for him, flattering her. He needed an incisive, fresh eye on his work, he'd said, not a muttonhead like Randolph. Oliver's work felt outdated, since he was still working over a book he'd started too many years ago. But he was a clear writer, and she'd been tempted to say that his subject—da Vinci's last days, spent in the company of the young French king, overseeing a fantasy of a hunting lodge—could make a terrific novel. Instead she'd only tinkered around the edges, found a few things to compliment, made some suggestions. She'd felt obligated to return the request, to ask him to read her own pages, but she hadn't wanted to. In the end, she'd chosen a short article about breaking the color bar in the trade unions, and his comments, though sometimes fussy and focused on tiny things like serial commas, were helpful enough.

The meeting moved on to the business of hiring Oliver's replacement. *Search committee*, Garland's agenda noted. As usual, no one volunteered. "No one?" Louise asked. They all looked at her, eyebrows raised and expectant, as if she were their mother. This was how you got ahead if you were a woman: you volunteered for every stupid assignment, every single subcommittee and you did it all well. Flawlessly. Then soon enough you found that your colleagues expected that you'd do it, whatever *it* was. Naturally, she volunteered, and when Garland stared at Fred, since he was the newest one in the department, Fred slowly raised a hand. "Er, and perhaps Mrs. Marshall?" Garland asked. "To help with the mailings and such." Fine, Mrs. Marshall, who was an overeducated secretary. Two women and a man. An opening, Louise realized. Maybe they'd hire a woman this time, maybe at last she'd have a friend, a true equal, in the department.

Boxes, volunteers, Garland's next item on the agenda. A few more boxes needed to go to Oliver's widow. Louise debated whether to assign this task to Randolph. Randolph had hired Oliver, and he was the most senior of their little department. She wondered if Randolph had any idea how much she detested him, how she counted the days until his retirement, how she wished he would drop dead. She wondered if he retained any memory of that night, ten years ago now. "Randolph?" she said, aiming for a sweet tone, or something approximating it. But Randolph didn't answer her, just stared at Fred, much as Garland had done a few minutes before. "Bruce and I will do it," Fred said.

"Sure," Bruce said. "No sweat."

The slow pace of the meeting was excruciating. They managed to get the minimum done, pushing other business back to next month. If Louise were in charge, she'd run everything differently. Before she took over, though, she'd find a way to tell them a few things. She'd tell them that she could feel them working hard to be cordial to her, and that it wore on her, the way they didn't bother to hide their continuing surprise at her presence. She could feel them judging her clothing choices, her hair, even her shoes. Wanting to comment on her looks, or lack thereof, and her lack of fashion, while inwardly congratulating themselves for refraining from comment. She could see all that, and it wore on her.

On Wednesday, Corinna Beacon phoned. Virginia hadn't spoken to Corinna beyond a hello-how-was-your-summer at the October faculty parties. She found it easier to talk to the faculty wives instead of the Gang of Four. "I heard about your injury," Corinna said, and Virginia answered that she was fine and they had plenty of meals, but thanks for calling.

"Very good, but we were thinking you could use a night out," Corinna said. "With us—Helen, Lily, Louise, me. Take your mind off things."

"Ah," Virginia said. Dinner with the Gang of Four. "Thanks, it's just that my ankle is still a little—and I hate to leave Rebecca—"

"We were thinking a week from Friday," Corinna said, ignoring Virginia's half-hearted excuses.

Virginia had no real reason to refuse, since Rebecca had started babysitting on Friday nights for the Paretskys' girls. She couldn't say, *Louise has a swelled head and I'd rather not have dinner with her.*

"I'd love to," she said. "Thanks, Corinna."

"Great, I'll pick you up. Six thirty."

Louise had been promoted too soon, Oliver used to say, and her areas were a hodgepodge—Southern rural history, plus urban history and now, apparently, women's history, which, it went without saying, made no sense for a school like Clarendon. Being the only woman at Clarendon with tenure had gone to her head, Oliver said.

But Oliver wasn't in competition with Louise, Virginia had reminded him—they couldn't even teach the same survey classes. Louise was just prolific, that was probably what got Oliver's goat. She'd published more than the others in the department. She'd gotten grants to spend the summer in historical societies in Mississippi and Alabama. Last year, she'd won the teaching award; Oliver said it was because the American survey course was a reliably big class, and one of the required distributive classes. Virginia imagined Louise taking charge of Clarendon Hall, the sixty boisterous young men silenced by the sheer force of her personality.

"And frankly, she's a show-off," Oliver had said, about the award. "It's because of Michigan and Berkeley. If she'd gone to Harvard she wouldn't be grandstanding in front of students like that. She'd have more finesse."

Virginia had forgotten all about Louise then, had only been annoyed at his narrow-mindedness. "Your snobbery is showing." She'd turned to head upstairs.

"That's not—you're misunderstanding—" The phone rang while he was still talking, and Virginia sat in the upstairs phone nook and pretended to listen to Momma chattering on about the delightful new young rector at St. Luke's. Virginia glared down the stairs in case Oliver happened to wander by.

Well. Oliver hadn't apologized for his snooty statement, hadn't said, *I know that women can't be Harvard men, I realize that a Radcliffe degree isn't the same.* She'd let it go, though she'd played out the argument in her head a few more times, rehearsing how she'd answer if he brought it up again.

She'd been right, but she'd also been petty. She hadn't bothered to consider how much pressure Oliver put on himself, how it all weighed on him, his late start in academia and that second book he couldn't finish. And yet he'd never admitted that Louise probably deserved her promotion and that award. Still, Virginia wasn't going to be friends with Louise, dinner or no dinner.

At the Lamplighter Restaurant, Virginia and Corinna sat at a low round table in the bar. Nearby, two couples stood waiting for a dinner table, and a few men sat hunched over their beers, watching hockey on the corner TV. Virginia had asked Corinna about her summer research at Woods Hole, and now Corinna was rhapsodizing about single-cell algae, beautiful little things that moved about in the water with tiny forked tails. Corinna's blond hair was serviceably short, and Virginia could imagine Corinna standing in a pond, in rolled-up khakis and a fisherman's hat, nose sunburned and peeling, gathering those beautiful little things in a jar.

"You all know each other," Corinna said a few minutes later, as Helen and Lily seated themselves. "And of course you know Louise."

"Old friends," Louise said.

"Yes, of course." A wave of unease slipped through her. She'd been rude that time Louise had phoned her, about Shirley Chisholm. She recalled that bookstore display, Kate Millett's enormous book about sexual politics and Shirley Chisholm's biography. She was a dolt; she never should have accepted Corinna's invitation.

"How's your teaching going, Virginia?" Helen asked. Helen's wavy red hair was threaded with gray, and she'd twisted and pinned the front part of it up into an old-fashioned yet appealing style.

"Arthur Gage was kind enough to finish out the semester for me," Virginia said. "But they canceled the class I was supposed to teach this semester."

"Aha," Louise said, inexplicably, and the other women made sympathetic sounds.

"Art history's in trouble, isn't it?" Helen said. "Science and economics—that's all the administration wants to think about these days."

Virginia frowned and nodded, as if she too knew what the administration wanted to think about these days.

"You're lucky, Corinna," Louise said. "There's always going to be money for bio and chem."

Corinna shrugged. "Maybe. Word is, we need to be more self-sustaining, get more grants."

As the other women grumbled about Clarendon, Virginia relaxed a little. She'd been both grateful and irritated about the way her neighbors Eileen and Gerda and the others brought casseroles and soups, clucking at her—"Wow, you've had such a time of it, Virginia, your ski accident on top of…everything else," or "I'm just *so sorry*" for the hundredth time—so she couldn't help but tear up.

But tonight she wasn't with other wives, she was out

with the Gang of Four, drinking Chablis, and no one was clucking at her, or saying it was for the best that the spring Northern Baroque class was canceled.

"Stuart Jaquith told me that applicant numbers are down again." Louise passed the stuffed mushrooms. "The writing's on the wall. If Clarendon wants to keep up, they'll have to go coed."

"That's what we keep hearing, but coeducation has been on the agenda at trustees' meetings for years now and I don't see any sign of them giving in," Helen said.

"Yes, they always find another reason that it's too soon," Louise said.

"But if we can hang on a little longer, sooner or later they're going to need us even more, to teach all those girls," Lily said.

"Eh, I can't see it," Corinna said. "The alumni will drop a bomb on this place before they let that happen." The rest of the appetizers arrived and they served themselves crab dip and meatballs.

Virginia's own college years rushed up at her, before her grad-school years at Harvard, before her doomed dissertation. Before Oliver. She tried to picture Smith as coed, but she couldn't do it.

Lily said something about English-department openings at Wisconsin and Northwestern.

"I should be applying too," Corinna said. "But I don't want to start all over. The algae and seaweed don't care that I'm a woman, but to everyone else it's inexcusable, or at least problematic." She laughed, but slumped a little as she speared a meatball.

Louise said nothing, Virginia noticed. Of course: Louise had tenure; she didn't need to look for better work elsewhere. Louise hadn't taken Oliver's job, Virginia thought now. She'd just gotten promoted a couple of years faster. If Oliver had finished his book on Francis I, he'd have had tenure too, and eventually, maybe, an endowed professorship. But what if Oliver *had* gotten tenure first? Maybe his aneurysm would have stayed a tiny, innocuous balloon, unburst. God, when would she ever stop ruminating?

"Your ankle bothering you, Virginia?" Corinna asked. "You look a little pale. Drink your wine, it'll help."

Virginia took a sip of her wine. "It's fine." She took another sip, bigger this time.

"Looks like something just occurred to you," Lily said.

"Don't put her on the spot like that, Lily," Helen said. Then, to Virginia: "She can't turn off the teacher part of her brain."

"Oh, I was—" Virginia cast about for a topic that had nothing to do with Oliver or Louise or aneurysms or tenure. "I was thinking about Smith College." She felt a sudden homesickness for Smith, not for the big rituals, like Ivy Day, but for the smaller moments, the endless hands of bridge between classes, their heads wreathed in cigarette smoke, and the candlelight dinners where they solved the world's problems. They'd been brave, obsessed, hilarious together. At Smith, she'd felt powerful for the first (and last) time. "I was remembering college, and I didn't mind that it was all girls—er, women—what I mean is that our professors took us seriously, that it was the first time anyone had ever taken *me* seriously. And we cheered each other on. I'd hate for all of that to go away. Although come to think of it, almost all our professors were men."

Helen nodded. "Lily and I went to Smith too. I always loved Mountain Day."

"Radcliffe," Corinna said. "But I never fit in there."

"Michigan," Louise said.

The others talked over one another about the Seven Sisters going coed, how soon that could happen and whether any boys would ever apply.

"I can't believe we're having this conversation, in this decade," Helen said. "The dorms are coed at UConn, even dorm *rooms*—"

"And Oberlin and Stanford, all those teach-ins and protests—" Lily said. "I mean, we've never—"

"On every other campus, it's anything goes," Louise said. "And Clarendon is stuck in the '50s. Or the last century."

"Maybe best to just get out of here," Corinna said.

"Oh no, don't leave," Virginia said, surprising herself. "You can't leave—"

The others burst out laughing, and Helen patted Virginia's hand. "Don't pay any attention to us," Helen said. "We always have some version of this same tired conversation, don't we, ladies?"

Louise let out a sigh. "The world is passing us by."

Virginia got a glimmer of Oliver calling Louise *that strident, pushy woman, she's always angry about something.* She wondered what Oliver would think about their conversation tonight. He'd say, *These things take time, Virginia, you can't force change.*

She was angry. Angry at Oliver, for dragging her into this life in Westfield, and then dying like that, disappearing in the middle of things. She was angry at President Weissman too, for pretending to have nothing to do with Oliver's pension. And Arthur Gage, she wanted to sock him right in his thick, smug lips.

"I never finished my dissertation," Virginia said. She'd

just said that out loud. What else had she said out loud to-night? Lily and Corinna were still exclaiming about the anti-war classes at Berkeley, and how at Stanford, a student committee had finagled approval power over the *entire curriculum*. Only Louise heard her lament.

"Well, you're clearly too old now," Louise said.

Yes, she was too old; of course she was too old. Louise wasn't afraid to say the sad, bald truth. Virginia wasn't a has-been, she was a never-was, a won't-be.

Louise barked out a laugh. "Don't look so defeated. That was a joke, Virginia. You can finish. Just go do it. Go to the library, check into a motel. Just map it out, write it out, and a couple of us can read it and proof it for you."

This night wasn't going as she'd expected. No one had bothered to ask her how she was holding up, because they all had their own, legitimate woes. And now she'd gotten drunker than she'd meant to. But she was having a good time. For the first time since—for the first time since she'd lost Oliver, she was having a good time. No, she thought. She was having a great time.

Awake in the middle of the night, Virginia thought about the four women. Louise, Helen, Lily and Corinna were the women that she and her fellow Smithies had once dreamed of becoming, more or less. None of the four were mothers. Possibly they thought she was freakish for having a child, the way Eileen and Gerda thought she was freakish because she sometimes sat staring at the typewriter, not answering the phone.

Her thoughts roamed back to her own grad-school years. Especially that first year, how she'd felt turned loose. There were only two women in her program year, but as she sat with Rembrandt etchings and Sargent drawings in the Fogg

Museum's storage files, and as she cataloged photographs for her work-study job, she'd had visions: she'd end up a curator for one of the New York museums, part of the American staff. Deciding for everyone else what counted as Art. And maybe making some wonderful discovery about one of these artists.

Later, after all her PhD coursework, she'd lost heart. She'd been working in Houghton Library's reading room, a room that had been opened to women only a few years before. She sat copying out Copley's letters home from London to use for quotes, the bound letters on their protective cradle, her friend Linda across the table doing her own work. There was a man from France at their table, and at the next table, one from India. All the world was in this high-ceilinged reading room, resplendent with antique books tucked inside the fluted woodwork. Plus her and Linda, two young women moving into the future together, their pencils in hand, exchanging mirthful looks when the librarian left his desk to tell the Indian man—again—to put away the fountain pen, pencils only, please. Those were the rules.

The portrait of Teddy Roosevelt, its glaze darkened with age, had glared down at her then, as he always did.

Half an hour later she felt it. She looked down at her notebook, her scratchings, and she lost her confidence. *I have nothing to add*, she thought. It was a sudden but quiet realization. *All the good things have been said, and whatever else I say is going to be too far-fetched, so I might as well stop now.* The sensation filled her body: she'd been sliding along in the slipstream of every other art historian, and now she didn't know how to reach an original yet scholarly enough conclusion. She had nothing worthwhile to contribute.

Chapter Six

AFTER MOM BROKE HER ANKLE, the meals started arriving again. Chicken divan, beef stew, Mrs. Koslowski's pierogies. Disgusting salads with disgusting dressings. Other moms would let themselves in the side door, stomp off the snow, and set a dish on the kitchen counter or slide a pan into the oven, and Mom would hobble into the kitchen, and they'd talk for a few minutes in those loud, cheerful voices moms used with each other. It was good to have something for dinner and cookies to snack on, but it felt like the first week or two after Dad died, like they'd gone back to square one.

On the way home from school on Friday, Rebecca was walking with Molly but not listening because Molly was talking about Todd, and maybe going to his hockey game on Saturday. The clouds were low and heavy looking, and the air felt like it might snow, and Rebecca was thinking about this stew Mom made sometimes, Brunswick stew. It was one of Grandmomma's Norfolk recipes, and Mom didn't make it all that often—Dad didn't like it because it had lima beans in it. Maybe Rebecca could make a pot of Brunswick stew herself. She had her cooking badge from Girl Scouts, and she'd made bread with Molly's mom last summer. She said goodbye to Molly and went in through the side door.

Mom was at the kitchen table reading an art book, judging by the old-fashioned portrait of a colonial man on the cover, and writing in a notebook, one foot propped on a chair. Mom's hair was dirty, pulled back in a messy ponytail, as if she were a fourth grader who hadn't learned to wash her hair.

"Can I make Brunswick stew?" Rebecca asked.

"Hello to you too," Mom said. "Brunswick stew? Now? I think we've got a lot of Gerda's spaghetti pie leftover."

Rebecca's nose wrinkled at the memory of that spaghetti pie, burnt black and crusty at the edges. "I can cook dinner until your ankle's better. You can just sit there and tell me what to do. Or give me one of your recipe cards and I'll figure it out." She didn't say, *and also so people can stop coming into our house every night and bringing us their weird meals and all their stupid pots and pans with the labels on them.*

Mom gestured with both hands out—*come here,* she meant—and Rebecca crossed the room to lean down for a hug. "My great big girl," Mom said. "We're going to be all right, you know that? I know you didn't mean anything by what you said the other day."

"Uh, okay." Mom always said things that made sense for a while but then stopped making sense. But Rebecca didn't want to make Mom cry, so she crossed the kitchen to get the recipe folder, and found the Brunswick stew recipe card, with half the ink—was that her mom's neat cursive, or was it Grandmomma's?—blurred by a red splotch. She handed it to Mom.

Mom patted Rebecca's arm as she took the card and scanned it, but then shook her head. "Oh, but the chicken's frozen," Mom said. "Maybe you can make it tomorrow."

A mean feeling seized her. She knew it wasn't Mom's fault that the chicken was frozen, but it wasn't just that. Mom didn't act like a regular mom anymore; she was always about to cry, and she forgot to sign things, like the form for the field trip to the statehouse in Concord. Mom was such a klutz that she couldn't ski even one run without a giant accident. "Forget it." Rebecca grabbed her books and blasted out of the kitchen. Upstairs, she slammed the door to her room.

She pulled a Jackson 5 album out of its sleeve and set it on her record player. Their voices sounded stupid, too bouncy and harmonious, while Michael Jackson sounded too sad. And Molly hadn't even asked her if she wanted to go to the hockey game tomorrow. Everything was stupid.

She started her English homework, but she couldn't focus. Instead, she kept thinking about Molly and how things used to be. Like the magazines she and Molly used to make when they were bored. They'd cut up notebook paper, staple the pages together, and fill them in with games and puzzles and beauty tips. The best part was their advice column. "Ask R.M.," they'd called it, for themselves, with crazy answers to made-up questions from people they hated, like certain teachers and obnoxious boys. *Dear R.M.*, Rebecca thought. *My mom is useless and my best friend is leaving me behind. She likes her boyfriend Todd better than me. Should*

I just show up at Grayson Rink tomorrow like I was included? Sit down to watch the boys play and cheer for Molly's stupid boyfriend?

She thought about all the time she used to spend at Molly's house. Molly's house was kind of a mess. With five kids, how could it not be, even though Mrs. Koslowski was always folding laundry, vacuuming, making pierogies, making soup. Molly's dad worked in the chemistry department, and he spoke with a trace of an accent because he'd been born in Poland. Molly's mom wasn't Polish but she knew how to make Polish dishes, and Rebecca loved the way Molly's house smelled, a mixture of cabbage and garlic and mothballs, delicious and repellent all at once. One time she'd tried to tell Molly about the smell, but Molly didn't get it. She looked kind of offended, even after Rebecca tried to explain that it was a good smell. Then Rebecca had gotten the idea for them to run across the yard to her own house, so Molly could say what she smelled the moment she went through Rebecca's front door. *Hmm. Dust?* Molly had said. *Or no, maybe it's paper, like an old book. And smoke. Definitely smoke.*

Rebecca missed the scent of Dad's pipe smoke, a smell that reminded her of old wet leaves mixed with something sweet, dried apples, even though she'd kind of hated it when he was alive. The front hall closet still smelled a little like him. It was another layer of sadness on top of the others, that Dad's smell would be lost before long, and that she would forget it, and over time she'd forget so much that Dad would be about as detailed in her mind as a hard-boiled egg. She would keep losing Dad forever; she would never be okay. *You won't forget, hon,* Mom said a few weeks ago. But Mom had looked so sad, as if she might start crying again, that Rebecca could tell she didn't mean it. Mom was only trying to stay positive because she was a mom.

Heloise answered a lot of questions about smells and stains in her column. Getting smells and stains out of curtains, carpets, furniture, towels, the leather upholstery in a motorboat. Heloise always had a good answer, no matter how weird the question. What would Heloise say if Rebecca wrote and asked how to preserve her dad's smell? It was the exact opposite of all those other questions. Heloise would have the perfect answer. Or maybe she'd say, *Sorry, can't help you. Try some other advice lady.*

The warm smell of bacon frying wafted into her room. What a brat she'd been, demanding to make Brunswick stew like that. She smoothed her hair, tucked her homework under her arm and went downstairs. At the stove, Mom watched over the bacon, one knee on a chair to keep her weight off her foot. "I can help, Mom." She hadn't meant to be a jerk. She'd only wanted to make things more normal in their sad little house. "I can do that."

"Why don't you crack some eggs and we'll have scrambled eggs for dinner," Mom said, and Rebecca nodded. At least she could crack the eggs and scramble them. Good thing Dad wasn't here, because having breakfast for dinner always made him a little irritable. She let out a laugh that turned into a gasp.

"What?" Mom poured the spitting bacon grease into a coffee can, and as she set the frying pan back on the stove, she looked at Rebecca with her usual big worried eyes.

"I—uh—I just had this thought that Dad would be annoyed if he came home and we had scrambled eggs for dinner. So, at least he won't be bugged."

Mom started to laugh too. She stood near the stove resting both hands on the counter, eyes scrunched up as if she were about to let out a sob, except she was laughing. Mom took a breath, ate a scrap of bacon from the bacon plate and started laughing all over again.

It felt so good to laugh, even if what Rebecca had just said wasn't funny, and was pretty horrible: thank God Dad was gone, so now they could have breakfast for dinner whenever they wanted.

"You're right, hon. We'll have eggs tonight, and Brunswick stew tomorrow night, and then we'll make a great dinner that Dad would love, and maybe he can enjoy it in his own way." Mom shook her head as if to say, well, doesn't that beat all, but now Rebecca was crying. She didn't bother to wipe the tears, just picked up her bowl of eggs and poured them hissing into the frying pan. "I can do it. Let me."

Mom nodded and lurched back to the table, while Rebecca drew the wooden spoon back and forth across the bottom of the pan, the way Mom had taught her.

Sam came in a beat early on the transition, and Professor Henderson held up a hand.

"Sorry," Sam said, even though he wasn't sorry. Larry Quinn was perpetually slow on the drums, and no one ever called him on it. And Professor Henderson's arrangement of "Mood Indigo" and "Do Nothing till You Hear from Me" wasn't working. They started again, ran through the whole thing without stopping, no solos. The jazz band sounded drab and inadequate. Maybe Sam was as bad as everyone else, but still he felt the urge to stand up and scream at Professor Henderson (all the other faculty went by first names in jazz band, but no, not Professor Henderson). Yeah, scream at Professor Henderson about his terrible arrangement and then run out into the snow, and yell some more. But he swallowed the urge, played on. They sounded okay on "A Taste of Honey," even though anyone with half a personality would choose the mournful Beatles version over this Herb Alpert-y syncopation. Jazz band wasn't the same without Oliver.

Two sophomores had dropped out this winter because of their schedules, they'd said, but Sam figured they'd picked up on the weird vibe that rehearsals had now, the way no one joked around anymore, the way Professor Henderson seemed crabby and tired and old. Maybe Sam should drop out too. He'd never taken a class with Oliver; he'd known Oliver as a friend, sort of, not as a teacher. Oliver had made Sam feel like his opinions were worth hearing. Oliver thought Sam's knowledge of the jazz greats was impressive. And that afternoon last spring, Sam had been standing on Main Street not wanting to go back to his dorm or to Lambda Chi, and Oliver had walked by. "Care to grab a coffee?" Oliver said, and Sam followed Oliver down the stairs into the dark-paneled tavern. Oliver ordered a beer and pretzels and Sam said, "Same for me." It felt good to be listened to as if he had something to say—Oliver had a lot of questions about New York and about Red Wagon Records—and it was good to talk about ancient jazz saxophone guys like Coleman Hawkins and Ben Webster, and not get laughed at for general dorkiness.

Back at school early in the fall, he'd walked into rehearsal one night and Oliver caught his eye in greeting. Momentary though the glance was, a strange tremor raced through him. That night he'd imagined the two of them meeting for dinner or drinks—students had dinner with their professors all the time, and the faculty got just as drunk as the students at the parties after band concerts—but every place he imagined felt wrong. He let the story drift to New York, to some dark jazz club, and he realized he was having a fantasy about a guy. Hell. About an old guy. During band practices, he began to wonder if Oliver's jokes at their shared music stand were supposed to be flirtatious, if Sam had been an idiot by responding the way he had, and the strange tremor struck him again. Probably he was thinking too much; probably he was imagining things. Still, he wanted to go back to last spring, when Oliver was a friend who Sam was glad to see, who made Sam feel normal.

After the last practice before Thanksgiving break, Sam headed out of the performing arts center, Oliver a pace or two ahead of him. They passed through a gauntlet of modern sculptures that some alum had installed, a group of unidentifiable but enticingly smooth and curving marble forms.

"Hey, Sam, good work tonight," Oliver said, when they neared the door.

"Thanks," Sam said.

"We'd love to have you come for dinner sometime," Oliver said. "Hear some more of your stories from New York, all of that—"

"Thanks. Sure." He'd interrupted and now he debated whether to apologize for interrupting.

Oliver squinted at the air, as if consulting an invisible calendar. "Or you know what, how about let's go back to the Tavern for a burger and a beer. Maybe after Thanksgiving?"

"Sure," Sam said again, his ears and neck hot. "Thanks."

"You want to say Monday, six o'clock? Or wait until you get back and see how your schedule looks?"

"Monday's fine," Sam said.

"A man's got to eat, right?" Oliver slapped Sam on the back. "Six thirty? Have a good Thanksgiving."

The Monday after Thanksgiving, Sam got halfway to Main Street before he bailed out. He'd say his train from New York was late getting back, he'd say he had a paper due, he'd say he had a family situation to deal with. He didn't have the rest of the words, other than he wasn't that kind of guy. But maybe he was assuming too much anyway. Maybe he'd gotten all of this wrong. He spun around and jogged to Lambda Chi, where he drank four beers and ate part of someone else's leftover pizza, and trudged back to his dorm room to write his art history paper.

The next morning he'd checked his mailbox; he hadn't done so since he'd gotten back to school after the holiday. He opened the letter from President Weissman to the Clarendon community. "I have some sad and dismaying news to share," President Weissman wrote. "Professor Desmarais passed away this weekend. He fell victim to a brain aneurysm."

And now it was the middle of winter and the jazz band sounded lame, and Sam had messed up the friendship with Oliver, except Oliver had gone and died. Sam kept paging through his memories of rehearsals, of that beer last spring with Oliver, looking for the details he'd missed. It always came back to this: Oliver had liked him, in a way he wasn't ready to think about, and that's when he slammed the book of memories closed again. He walked out of rehearsal with Stephen—the snow had picked up, tiny dry flakes, which meant that the Ski Bowl might stay open for another couple of weeks. They'd go to Lambda Chi and have a few beers and get high like they did most nights, and probably talk about the next Granitetones rehearsal—he and Stephen were co-leaders of the Granitetones vocal group this year since no seniors wanted to do it—and maybe no one would care enough to make fun of him around the bar in the basement. He'd get up and go to class tomorrow, do the same thing all over again.

By 8:00 on Sunday morning, Louise Walsh had finished with her work. She'd graded the last paper, and now she set the stack of them on the hall table, the one decent paper on top. Opposition to manifest destiny—the boys had struggled with this set of prompts. She circumnavigated her little apartment, thinking, planning. It was too early to run the vacuum; she'd wake the Connollys downstairs. Too early to call Lily or Corinna. The A&P didn't open until noon, and she didn't want to go to Mo's and sit alone with her coffee and pancakes. The thermometer outside her kitchen window said two below, but it was clear, and there didn't seem to be any wind.

Louise returned to the dark bedroom, banged her shin on the bedframe as she did too often. Limping, she pulled long johns out of the bottom drawer, slipped them on, and then the wool trousers she'd bought long ago as an undergrad in Michigan. She felt a tiny zing of pride that she still fit into them.

Outside, she carried a snowshoe in each hand, paddling the air. She turned left, the houses growing bigger, homes of old alums and chair-wielding professors. She passed Malcolm Ferber's house with its wraparound porch, its deep front yard, the snow-covered perennial beds tended by Priscilla Ferber. She wouldn't think about Ferber or any other men this morning. No, she would think about the weather.

She'd think about the snow, the way each crystal refracted the light so that her eye caught thousands of tiny rainbows each time she glanced down at it. A tiny visual miracle.

It snowed in Willow Springs when Louise was little, enough to make snow ice cream and snowmen, to sled right down Washington Avenue—there was no equipment to clear the snow, other than what people devised with tractors and push brooms. The snow always disappeared after a day or two. There was never a crystal winter day like you got in New Hampshire.

Near the town pond, she sat on a bench to strap the snowshoes over her boots. Out on the ice, five or six men played hockey, and the sounds carried, the scrape-scrape-scrape of the skate blades, a grunt as one guy lunged for the puck, a curse as another dove ineffectually, the puck whizzing past him. It was beautiful, the way these skaters edged to a stop, then turned, gliding away like they were flying. She hadn't skated since her own college years; the skates made her too tall and she'd been terrified of falling into a tangled mess. Terrified of getting laughed at.

She pushed up to standing and left the pond behind, snowshoes breaking through the deeper snow in the town forest. Soon her breath had turned sharp and painful, pulse racing. If she could exhaust herself, she wouldn't hear the words. But sooner or later those wounding phrases intruded. *You're always going to be alone, you know that? What kind of man would have you? You can be ugly and sweet, or you can be pretty and bookish, but you can't be ugly and bookish.* Over the years she'd made aphorisms out of her dad's hateful, acid words, a scabby sort of armor. No one could think worse of her than what she'd thought about herself. *He only wants what's best for you,* her mother used to say, after one of her dad's rants, and whenever Louise would question that, her mother would close off the conversation. *I just don't understand why you can't get along with others, Louise. I don't understand what's so wrong about Willow Springs.* Her mother, so proud of having become a town woman, no longer a farm kid.

Louise felt her armor dropping away only when she sank into her work. Last summer, at the state archives in Jackson, Mississippi, she read deeply and slowly. She read the letters and journals of those Southern women fighting for suffrage, began to understand how they managed not to see their complicity in keeping another group of people down. Her research helped her empathize, even when those women wrote absurdly about God being on their side.

And another wounding phrase, one that she should have forgotten about by now, but that she carried with her. *You should be flattered*, Randolph had said. More than ten years ago now, her first year at Clarendon, at the Garlands' annual Christmas party. Louise had gone upstairs to use the bathroom, fairly tipsy, and Randolph came out of the bathroom as she was about to knock. He took her hand—he hadn't washed his own—then reached up with his other hand, pulling her head down to his level and kissing her on the mouth, hard. She'd been so surprised that she hadn't thought to let go of his hand, even as she pulled away. "Oh, you've been waiting for it," Randolph said, and like an utter dunce, Louise had felt a blush rise out of her chest all the way to her ears.

"What you need is—"

Louise hadn't heard whatever Randolph said about what she needed, because she'd managed to spring away, tugging her hand back and turning the corner to run down the stairs.

She'd grabbed her coat and hat from the den, where Oliver and Virginia Desmarais were also gathering their coats. "Merry Christmas," she heard herself trilling to them, as if the party, and Randolph, had stirred up her holiday spirit.

You should be flattered, he'd said. She didn't need to hear the rest of the sentence to know what he meant. He meant to wound her, put her in her place. She should have punched him, stomped on his foot, run back into the party to tell Randolph's wife what her husband had just done. Her new colleague. And at his age. But everyone would have laughed, and said something like, *Oh, that's our Randolph, all right. Hitting on all the girls, even the ugly ones.* On this frozen morning years later, the hot blush crept back up, as if she were still standing in the Garlands' upstairs hallway, attached to Randolph.

Chapter Seven

THE MATH BUILDING WAS on the far side of campus, inconvenient to everything else. From the outside, the math building looked like any other campus building, worn-out brick, its black-painted shutters faded to gray. But the first floor and the basement felt new and sleek, renovated to make room for the mainframe computer and its terminals. Sam liked it here, away from the frats, Commons and his other classes. In here, he didn't feel so different.

"Pair yourselves up, men," President Weissman said this morning—President Weissman taught a seminar once or twice a year, and this one, Cryptography and Number Theory, covered the algorithms behind codes, ciphers and computer languages. Sam looked around the seminar table for a partner, but the two guys on either side of him had turned away to choose someone else. Everyone had paired off except for him and Jerry. Jerry the vet, with his ponytail and the leather jacket he wore through the winter, instead of a duffel coat or a ski jacket like everybody else.

Jerry didn't look at Sam, only closed his eyes as if bored with all of them.

"Two parts to this project. I want you to build a cipher, using classical or modern tenets, and I want you to create a computer code," President Weissman said. "Your classmates will attempt to solve and use the cipher. As to your computer code, instruct the computer to solve four complex equations." Back when he was a math professor, President Weissman had persuaded GE to practically give Clarendon its own computer. He turned to the board to write an example equation. "Now, then, men. Go to it for the next fifteen minutes."

As the other guys rearranged themselves, Sam hoisted his chair and went around to Jerry's side of the table. "So I guess we're—"

"Build on the Hill cipher," Jerry said, instead of *Sure, I'll be your partner*, or *Get lost, you pip-squeak asshole*.

"Okay," Sam said. The Hill cipher was a substitution cipher from the '20s, one that used simple algebraic algorithms to scramble messages. The Hill cipher always got him thinking about World War II cryptography, when everything in the world was probably simpler. But the Hill cipher was also the first modern cipher, so the other guys in the class would probably use it too. "Maybe add something to it, or use division instead of multiplication," Sam said, and he bent to start writing a matrix key in his notebook.

Jerry was scribbling too, and he held out his notebook for Sam to inspect. "Or we could do one with multiplication *and* another one with division."

"Complicate things, yeah, that's good," Sam said.

President Weissman started lecturing again. Sometimes math was a slog, but this class was the kind of thing Sam's ten-year-old self would have gone wild over, a grown-up version of the secret decoder rings that he used to pull out of a Cracker Jack box once in a while.

On Wednesday, he and Jerry met in the snack bar in the student center to work on their project. Jerry set down his tray without a word and shrugged out of his battered leather jacket, hanging it over the back of his chair. Jerry and his jacket smelled of cigarette smoke and something else, something like mud or manure.

Sam ate a quarter of his turkey club, slurped at his soda. To break the silence, he asked Jerry where he was from, even though he knew from Jerry's accent that he was from one of the outer boroughs.

"Queens," Jerry said.

"Hey, I'm from New York too. Where'd you go—"

"That was a long time ago." Jerry looked down at his plate, addressing his burger. "I'm not like your kind of New York, okay? You went to private school with the other Richie Rich kids, am I right? And that's all you know in the world. That's not me."

"Uh, that's not me, either," Sam said, stung. "That's like Teddy Burnham. Or Schuyler DePeyster. Or any guy in DKE and KA." Most of those guys had gone to boarding school—Andover, Choate, Deerfield. Good-looking and overly polite, in a kind of jerky way, they played hockey or squash or football. He wanted to say, *Hey, I was a complete failure at Dalton and I don't know what I'm doing at Clarendon. And I think the wrong things and say the wrong things all the time.*

"Uh-huh, right," Jerry said. He stabbed a fry into his paper cup of ketchup.

"I just meant, I'm not one of those guys—"

"We're not going to be friends, okay?" Jerry's voice carried a sharp edge. He shook his head and held up a hand like a cop stopping traffic. "Sorry, I don't mean to be rude, man."

"No, it's okay." Sam leaned down to pull out his notebook and pencil, his face burning. Jesus, Jerry didn't need to be so prickly. What was the big deal about asking where he was from anyway? Giant chip on that guy's shoulder, his dad would say.

"So here's what I've got so far." Jerry dug into his jacket pocket for a pack of cigarettes and some folded notebook paper. He smoothed out the paper. "I'm still thinking about a bigger matrix to start with, or maybe two medium-sized matrices. And the multiplication and then division to complicate the key. But then each time we go to solve it it's gonna take—"

"I wonder if that's what Weissman is trying to get us to do, come up with more complicated ciphers and ask the computer to resolve them," Sam said. "I can sign up for a computer time slot. How about tomorrow night? Or Friday?"

"I, uh—see, I'm kind of—well, I don't know how to do that," Jerry said. "I've never done any—"

"I can show you."

"But what happens if the computer is wrong?" Jerry asked. "I mean, is it going to tell us if it's doing something wrong?"

Here was something Sam knew that Jerry didn't. Something that even made Jerry a little nervous. "It can only do what we tell it to do, so if we're wrong, it will be wrong. But we can only find out by trying, right?" Sam attempted

Weissman's old-school lingo and cadence, "And if it doesn't work, why then, you're simply one step closer to the correct path, men."

Jerry smiled, then laughed out loud. He answered back in the same Weissman-ish tone, then mimed Weissman's eyes going squinty when he pulled on his old-fashioned pipe. But Jerry's smile disappeared too quickly as he went back to his notebook, his shoulders slumping as if he were even older than Weissman.

Jerry's superiority wasn't like anything Sam had encountered. He thought of the way Jerry had called him Richie Rich, lumping him in with those other guys who all had a thing. The football players and the ski racers had a thing; and the DKEs and the KAs and the Phi Rhos had a thing. The other New York and Boston guys, with their summer houses in Maine or the Adirondacks, they all had a thing. Sam had none of that. But Jerry had none of that, either. So whatever Jerry's thing was, it was nothing like all the other college coolness things. Jerry's thing was the opposite—he'd been to war. He'd gone to the other side of the world, marched through Vietnam's jungly alien territory. Sam would have died of fright from all the daily unknowns. Jerry had probably gone down into those tunnels underground, might have killed a bunch of Vietcong. But he'd come back alive.

Thinking about what Jerry might have done made all the other guys seem profoundly stupid, as if everyone else on campus was in third grade. He wondered what Jerry thought of him. No doubt Jerry found him severely lacking. And yet! Jerry had shown his nervousness about going to the computer center, of all places. Jerry needed his help. Maybe Sam wasn't so lacking after all.

★ ★ ★

On the bumpy connecting flight from LaGuardia, Virginia had to close her eyes and breathe slowly to hold back the waves of airsickness. But Rebecca was unbothered, making jokes about her aunts and uncles. She tapped on Virginia's arm to get her to look out the window at the towering cloud formations and the shifting hues of the Atlantic, the narrow jut of the Eastern Shore. Traveling made Rebecca cheerful, more like the enthusiastic kid she'd been not that long ago.

June had sent Virginia airplane tickets. "Surprise! Now you can come on home for a few days," June's note read, and the unexpected plane tickets had sat on the kitchen counter, pushy and irritating, like June. *Oh, come on, Ginny, it won't hurt for Rebecca to miss a day or two of school,* Marnie had said, after Virginia had complained about June's tickets. *Why not?*

Clattering down the portable staircase at the Norfolk airport, Virginia spotted Marnie inside the terminal, waving and grinning through the plate glass. That glimpse of Marnie, along with the milky late-winter sunshine and the cottony feel of the mild air, brought tears to her eyes. She was home, lost and found. Back where she belonged.

Inside the terminal, Marnie folded them both into a hug. "Mmmph, so *glad* you're here, girls. Becca, you've grown since—" Marnie stopped, changed conversational direction "—and you look wonderful, so grown-up."

"You, on the other hand—" Marnie grasped Virginia's arms, squeezing them "—you need some potato chips and a vodka gimlet. Were you always this pale and skinny?"

"Thanks, Marnie," Virginia said.

In Marnie's car, they bumped over the potholes of Little

Creek Road, passing a string of sailors' bars, two of them topless-girl bars; Marnie always took the back way across town because getting on the new interstate made her nervous. "I have to warn you, Momma just put her house on the market," Marnie said quietly. "I didn't want to tell you on the phone."

Momma had talked about trimming her sails, Virginia recalled, but at the time she hadn't bothered to listen, and Momma had been all euphemism, too polite to say, *I'm in trouble, and I don't know how I got here.*

At Wards Corner, they sat in a line at the stoplight. To the right, Hays and Denton department store, where Virginia had bought her skirts and twinsets before college, and to the left, Breyer's Shoes, the other shops radiating out from them.

"Mom, can we go shopping while we're here?" Rebecca said. "I need some—"

"We've got everything you need, Becca," Marnie interrupted. "You just name it. You see how busy it is here with all the stores and everything? This used to be nothing but farms, can you believe it?"

"And the barbecue place," Virginia said, as the car inched along.

"Momma's still mad about that," Marnie said, and they both laughed. Virginia couldn't remember the barbecue joint, which had been torn down in her childhood to make room for this congested shopping center, which showed its age. The drug store's royal-blue awning had ripped, and the bare metal frame poked through like the hem of a slip showing.

"And we have plenty of other shopping centers too,"

Marnie said. "But I bet you don't have a roller rink in Westfield, do you, Bec?"

"A *roller* rink?"

"You know, where you can rent roller skates and skate round and round to the music," Marnie said. "The kids love it. Margaret—" Marnie's daughter "—will take you."

"Oh," Rebecca said. Virginia turned around to give Rebecca an encouraging smile, and Rebecca smiled back, eyebrows raised, maybe skeptical about the concept of a roller rink, or about roller skating with her older cousin Margaret, who paid little attention to Rebecca.

A few minutes later, they pulled into Momma's driveway, the house where Virginia and her sisters and brother had all grown up, and Virginia let out a long breath. A mock Tudor among other mock Tudors in a leafy waterfront neighborhood, Momma's house backed up onto the Lafayette River, with its dock where they used to sun themselves on nice days, and take the sailboat or Whaler out any old time. Virginia had had a happy childhood here; she had family who loved her right here. Why had she ever left?

At the end of the front walk, the FOR SALE sign blared Momma's news.

Momma opened her side door and hugged them one after the other. Her nose was red, the skin around her eyes puffed and shiny. "Don't mind me, just a spring cold," she said, wrapping an arm around Rebecca and steering her toward the kitchen. "Let me get my girl something to eat."

"We'll get the luggage," Virginia said, and she and Marnie backtracked to the car. "So what happened?" she whispered, behind Marnie's car.

"It turns out that Daddy's banker lost a lot of Momma's money. Lost pretty much everything. Which means—"

"Everything? But can't she—"

"It's already decided," Marnie said. "And Rolly—" Marnie tended to defer to their brother "—thinks this is for the best." They were leaning against the open trunk now. Marnie waved at an older woman driving past the house, and Virginia did the same.

But their parents had built this house forty-some years ago. "*Everything*? Pension? Didn't she have plenty for her own—and also, I mean, weren't we all going to get something later, you know, when…" She trailed off.

"Well, first there was this mortgage that none of us knew about, and then Bryce Watson took his clients' money and put it into a bunch of oil wells in Oklahoma and the parent company went bust and now they have to—"

"Oklahoma! What was he thinking? Why wasn't anyone paying attention?" Virginia asked. Marnie didn't answer. "But she just has to wait and eventually get her money back, at least some of it, or she can sue, right?"

"I don't know, Ginny. I think it's gone."

She'd been counting on something from Momma, some small inheritance. A nest egg, at least. But she hadn't bothered to pay attention, either. Now it was her own turn to be too polite, to be like Momma, too ashamed to admit that she was in big trouble.

"It'll be okay," Marnie said. "We just have to…adjust, I guess. Momma can move in with Aunt Kitty, or maybe with George and me. Or you and Rebecca, if you move down here."

She was too roiled and mixed up to respond to what Marnie had just said.

Upstairs a little later, in Marnie and June's old bedroom, Virginia sat on one of the twin beds for a minute, hiding from whatever else she'd ignored. Outside, spindly loblolly pines framed the backyard, and in the distance, the briny river glinted brown and gold. It was already spring here. She felt so tired; somehow she'd turned into her mother, her mother who she was supposed to be nothing like. Momma had gone to Sweet Briar College for one year, leaving to get married the day after she turned nineteen. Virginia never would have done that. Yet here she sat, frozen, in her sisters' old bedroom, verging on middle age, or maybe she wasn't verging, maybe it was middle age—at thirty-nine, she'd probably passed the halfway mark. For Oliver, forty-three had been the end of his life—he couldn't have known that his middle age was his early twenties. But he'd achieved something, he'd had his obituary in the *American Historical Review*, while she had little to show for all her education. Momma had her four children and grandchildren, all her causes and clubs, altar guild and bridge group and tennis and her hundreds of distant relatives and friends. Her mother was a widow at the right age; Virginia was a widow at the wrong age.

A memory came to her: Norfolk, maybe her second year of college, around the time of the Arch Tazewell incident. She'd gone for lunch with Momma and Marnie in the downtown Hays and Denton tearoom. Chicken salad, as usual. The tearoom took up a gallery that wrapped around three sides of the store's top floor. You could look across the open space to the other side, where other women sat eating chicken salad or she-crab soup or ham biscuits. Everyone looked so *smug*: nowhere these women would rather be than this tearoom, this tea balcony, in this staid department store whose top-floor windows looked out onto the Bank of Virginia building in one direction, and in the other, the

Elizabeth River, bordered by its prickle of coal piers and the vast Navy base.

Norfolk was flat, worn-out, tedious. These women cared too much what the other women in the tearoom thought of them. Momma wouldn't dare come here for lunch without a seasonally appropriate hat and gloves, even though it wasn't church or the country club or some better place, a real city. Virginia wasn't going to be one of these women.

"This place isn't even nice." Virginia's voice had come out sulky. She sounded like a child, not a college girl, her bad thoughts colliding and trapping the good ones. She rolled her gloves into a ball, the way she used to do when she was little and bored at church.

"For heaven's sake, Ginny," Momma said.

Marnie laughed. "It took you this long to notice?"

"Marnie, honestly," Momma said. "The women here work *very* hard to make a good lunch. They're known far and wide for their pimiento cheese." Momma's voice wavered, her exasperation showing. "Now *stop* it, both of you."

"I didn't mean—that's not what I meant." Virginia had meant to say that she belonged somewhere else; she just didn't know where yet. Well, Boston, most likely. New York, maybe. Not here.

Now she shook her head to clear out that old memory—how many times had she been sulky and rude to her mother? Years ago, Momma must have been relieved that her youngest daughter had stayed in the North. Yet here she was, home again.

Two days later, Virginia stood in the doorway of the academy's new library with Toby Dickenson, the head of the upper school. The spacious library glowed with natural light from skylights, and beyond the tables and rows of bookshelves, floor-to-ceiling windows offered a view of green playing fields. A lonely librarian looked up at them, waved and went back to her work. This campus was modern and sleek, not at all what she'd been expecting.

"Wow," Virginia said. "I had no idea the campus was so—so complete." June hadn't merely been bragging, all those times she'd told Virginia about the school her boys went to, its wonderful teachers and wonderful campus. June had gone and set up an interview for Virginia without telling her first—it was just like June to do something like that. "I don't have a CV with me. No, June, absolutely not," she'd said yesterday. Overnight she'd softened, though, muddled by Momma's troubles and something else, maybe the damp, milky air, or the potted pansies blooming purple and gold on Norfolk's porches.

Toby Dickenson's beard seemed to signal that he was a progressive, a good sign. He wore a bow tie and corduroy trousers, and as they toured the campus, he made self-deprecating and amusing comments about the school, the kids and his own background. They passed the lower-school building, then walked through the gym and out onto a playing field, Toby talking about his graduate work in history at William & Mary, and Virginia talking about Harvard (she heard herself saying *Harvard* again, name-dropping) more than Clarendon. Toby was proud of getting the girls and boys into the same academic building—when they'd first admitted girls, they'd kept boys and girls separate, except at lunchtime, he said. Before long, boys and girls would take all their classes together, if he had anything to do with it.

She laughed. "The powers that be at Clarendon College decided to let in thirty female exchange students from the Seven Sisters, but only for a semester at a time."

"So we're ahead of y'all. Far out!" He smiled at her. "I have to talk that way because I'm around teenagers all day." They'd circled back to the upper-school building and stopped outside the headmaster's office. She didn't want him to leave. She wanted to keep talking; she hadn't had such an easy conversation with a stranger, a man, in such a long time.

"Call with any questions," Toby said. "I'll be around." He smiled and put out his hand for a quick shake, and was gone.

That didn't mean anything, Oliver, she said silently. *He was just being friendly.* She'd said Oliver's name multiple times without tearing up since she'd gotten home to Norfolk. She wondered what Oliver would think about her coming home to teach, to start a different life down here. The headmaster's secretary, a trim woman in a tidy shirtwaist dress, hair blond shading into gray, looked up from her typing. Virginia introduced herself, surprised at how unflustered, how professional she felt this morning. Yes, she could do this, even without her CV in hand.

The secretary clucked at her about Momma's financial losses, and that scoundrel who'd hoodwinked so many people. Virginia made agreeable sounds about Momma and that scoundrel, not sure how to respond.

"You know, my sister's son Billy, such a nice young man," the secretary was saying. "He's about your age. Well, he never married, just hasn't found the right girl. I think he'd like to have dinner with you, while you're home."

"I—I've got family commitments for the next two nights,

and then we fly back," Virginia managed to say. "And I'm not quite ready for any sort of—"

"Say no more, there's no hurry," the secretary said, her eyes crinkling at the edges, delighted to take part in Virginia's tragedies and family embarrassments.

A few minutes later, Virginia sat across from Foster Burgess, the school's headmaster, trying to attend to his telling of the school's long history. He punctuated this telling— Union occupation of the old school building downtown, the growth spurt at the turn of the century—with brief, tiny smiles, and she found herself returning them. He gave her a minute to describe her graduate coursework and her occasional teaching.

"Nothing against Harvard, per se, but SDS and all of that nonsense came out of the Northeast, didn't it?" he said.

She considered whether to correct him, to say that she was fairly sure that Students for a Democratic Society had started at University of Michigan, then decided to tell him that Clarendon was different, that Clarendon's small group of activists had gone to jail after they'd stormed into the administration building and taken over, forcing President Weissman and Dean Gilbert out of their offices; after a day the National Guard had come in. Since then, Clarendon had been silent, no sign of any activists, since those few had been suspended or kicked out. All of which meant Clarendon was going ever more backward, Louise and Helen and Lily would say. But of course Foster Burgess wouldn't want to hear that.

"Ah, well, good," he said. "Then you know firsthand that too much has changed, far too much. Perhaps the best of our culture has been undermined. But traditions and standards still have a place here, you know. We're here to build a helpful bulwark, if you will." He stopped, waiting for her response.

What was she supposed to say? *Yes, I believe I have bulwark potential, Mr. Burgess.* "Traditions," she said. "Traditional standards," she added, nonsensically.

"We have a couple of openings that you might be suited for, teaching in the girls' division. Before we talk about joining the faculty, can you pledge to be part of that?"

"Pledge to be a part of the girls' division?"

"Pledge to work to uphold our traditions and standards." He gave another of those tiny weird smiles. "We need faculty who serve as role models and mentors as well as rigorous teachers. Who don't undermine from within. We maintain a certain standard in morals, ethics and tradition, and in doing so we build the school and protect the culture at large. Now, for instance, a widow would be—"

"Yes, I see," she said. She should introduce him to Arthur Gage, they'd get along fine. Arthur Gage with his suggestion that she work as a department secretary and Foster Burgess demanding a pledge about morals and traditions, a lovely tradition of white men bulwarking their campus and community against Northerners, agitators, noisy women, blacks... She heard herself talking as if she were interested in this school, these potential history department positions teaching middle-school girls, and she took the folder of materials that the secretary brought in for her as if she were pleased to have it. Foster Burgess stood, and she stood, and they shook hands as he walked her out of his office, and she smiled as Momma always had told her to do.

Back in Momma's car, she set the school folder on the passenger seat. *School leadership*, the back of the folder announced. *Board of Trustees. Archer Tazewell, president.* Oh, yes, she saw. Archer, a helpful bulwark with his hideous pride in his all-white frat at Hampden-Sydney College, *the best men around*, he'd said. She'd start teaching here, only to leave the school after a year or two in exasperation, and then she'd have to find something else, some sad secretarial or bank teller work. She'd live in one of those flimsy new apartments out near the beach with Momma and Rebecca, who'd be flattened by her new school's helpful bulwark and the moral culture, with men like Arch Tazewell and Foster Burgess in charge.

Once upon a time, Virginia had thought she could be something. She'd fallen in love with New England, and then with John Singleton Copley, and then with Oliver. Somehow she was going to put all those things together and be a new kind of woman. She hadn't done that. Yet. But if she stayed here, she would turn into her mother, and not even a good version of her mother.

Chapter Eight

FRIDAY AFTERNOON, SAM AND Jerry sat hunched at a terminal in the back of the math building, Jerry reading numbers from their cipher and Sam typing commands with the keyboard. Jerry continued to act like Sam was merely the sidekick, but it was pretty clear that Jerry had no idea how to run commands.

"Okay, so that's—fuck, I did something wrong here." Jerry peered at his notebook and scrawled an arrow at a row of numbers. "Can you back up to a couple lines before, or is that going to be a huge pain?"

"Sure, no problem." It felt good to be the competent one. Sam deleted, backed up, waited. Watched the cursor glowing and blinking at them on the dark screen. It was quiet in here this afternoon, only that new math professor at a terminal by the window, and the faint hum from the big computer in the basement.

During one of Sam's math classes last year, the group of them had gone downstairs to get a look at the new mainframe and talk to Professor Durer, who was in charge of it. It was cold in the basement, heavily air-conditioned to keep all the machinery cool. And spotless, shining clean. Dust was bad for the computer, they'd learned.

Professor Durer had talked to them about the complex equations that the computer could solve and the vast information storage that the computer allowed. The computer could store all the college's records, all the information about the library's books, and all the Westfield town records, possibly with room for more. "And before long our network will allow our students to communicate with each other, and possibly students at other colleges. Instantly." On one of the panels nearby, reels that looked like audio recording equipment turned round and round, stopped, turned again.

"Does it ever sleep?" Smith, one of their classmates, asked.

Everyone laughed. "No need to sleep," Professor Durer said. "Clearly a better worker than any of us."

No need to sleep: the thought gave Sam the shivers. Computers working around the clock, whirring through the instructions they followed. Eventually these big computers would figure something out, start talking to one another. Rebel against their masters. Control all the humans from the cold basement of this unassuming, beat-up building.

"Are you with us, Sam?" his professor had asked.

He'd blinked, nodded. "Yes, sorry."

Sam didn't say anything to Jerry about that visit last year. It was way too wussy to admit to that shivery feeling about computers leaving the humans behind.

He and Jerry did a test run of what they had so far, and

when they looked at the printout, it had done what they'd wanted it to do.

"Smoke break?" Jerry said, after Sam had typed in ten more lines of instructions.

"Sure." Sam pushed back his chair. Once outside, he stretched in the cold. When Jerry offered him a cigarette, he took one, pretending to focus on the act of smoking— no point in trying to start a conversation. Jerry had made it clear that they weren't going to be friends. But this afternoon Sam didn't mind Jerry's prickliness; Jerry was what he was.

"So what else do you do, Manhattan?" Jerry asked. "For fun, I mean."

A surprise. "Uh, you know, the usual. Some music stuff. Student-faculty jazz band, Granitetones. Lambda Chi." For most guys on campus, Sam knew which frat they'd joined, what sport they played and whether they had a girlfriend somewhere. But he didn't know about Jerry. Jerry would take it the wrong way no matter what Sam asked, so what the hell. "Are you in a frat?"

Jerry gave one of his half-smirk smiles. "You know Topos?" Topos, the commune that some Clarendon dropouts had started a few years ago. Last year, after the Clarendon SDS guys took over the administration building to protest ROTC, and after the National Guard came in and put them all in jail, some of them ended up out at Topos.

Sam nodded. "Cool." He wanted to ask what Topos was like, whether there were girls living there, as he'd heard.

"Yeah. It's okay. Lotta work, splitting the wood, clearing the fields, mucking out chicken shit. But good conversations, you know? Sometimes this place, all these dumbasses on campus, it gets to me. No offense, Manhattan."

"None taken," Sam said. "It gets to me too sometimes.

Not that I—I mean, I haven't gone to—so what did you do over in 'Nam?"

"Don't call it "Nam,' you sound like a jackass," Jerry said. "Okay. In a nutshell, base ops, signal corps support, radio operator. A fucked-up place, a fucked-up war, and the other Clarendon vets started out here and can't relate to me. And everybody else on campus hates us. Or else they're sick of being reminded and wish we'd disappear. That's why Topos."

"Ah," Sam said. "I don't hate you."

Jerry gave a quick grimace of a smile, but said nothing.

Back inside, they worked at the code with the computer, wrestled with the cipher's fourth level, ordered a pizza. As Sam tore into his second slice, he thought of something for the fourth level—his mouth was full of pizza, so he typed into the monitor with his free hand, then gestured for Jerry to look at the screen.

Jerry shook his head in admiration. "You're not so dumb, Manhattan. Good work."

Sam leaned back, clasping his hands behind his head as if he did this kind of thing every day.

"Hey, you want to go over to Topos?" Jerry said. "Little gathering there tonight, a fundraiser, and I was supposed to tell people, but..." He shrugged.

"Sure," Sam said. "I mean, Lambda Chi's pretty dead tonight, so why not."

Sam got into Jerry's beat-up Dodge, and they pulled out onto College Street. Topos was a mile or so north of Clarendon; a couple of members hitchhiked to and from campus, and once in a while you'd see a guy getting out of a farmer's pickup truck near the library. He wondered if they talked about farm stuff on the way into town, and whether the farmer would be happy to see a young person trying to work an old farm. Or would he laugh at the hippie and his foolish questions about the land? Jerry clicked the radio on. Graham Nash's thready, high voice floated from the radio, the carousel song, and Sam sang along. He'd loved the Hollies as a kid, and he still liked to hear Nash's vocals in Hollies songs, Nash before he was Nash.

Jerry drummed on the steering wheel along with the guitar. "Nice falsetto, Manhattan."

"Sorry." Sam knew this road, which led to the Ski Bowl. They passed white-clapboard houses, stone walls, fields where snow had drifted into waves and hillocks that remained, even in March. After another few minutes, Jerry turned right onto a dirt driveway bordered by massive maples with sap buckets hanging off them. "You guys make syrup?"

"Nah, we just let our neighbor tap the trees," Jerry said. "He pays us in gallon jugs of syrup. Sweet, huh?"

The car's headlights illuminated a series of buildings—first, a couple of sheds and an off-kilter barn. Then a rambling farmhouse, with a narrow gable-end front section, and a screened porch to one side. Getting out of the car, Sam smelled woodsmoke, and the familiar acrid-sweet scent of grass. Two guys sat on the porch smoking, despite the cold air. Sam nodded at them as he followed Jerry inside, and they nodded back.

Inside the farmhouse, Sam smelled bread baking, more grass smoke, the wet-dog smell of old sweaters. They passed through a kitchen where a man and a woman, way older than college age, sat at the end of a long table, both of them drinking out of mugs, while a guy stood at an old-fashioned cookstove, checking something in a pot. Beyond, in the front room, there were maybe fifteen people, mostly guys but some girls too. People stood around in little clumps talking. Sam recognized the guy with pale wavy hair and frameless glasses who'd just fed logs into the woodstove. Hank something, one of the SDS guys who'd gone to jail after the admin takeover. Hank had been suspended rather than kicked out because he'd only been a sophomore at the time. Sam remembered standing on the green that day with a bunch of other freshmen, taking in the guy with a bullhorn leading chants from a second-floor window in the deans' office. Sam and the other freshmen had kept their distance because state troopers had started to rope off the building. Soon after, a crew of National Guardsmen emerged from an army truck. They carried a log and positioned themselves in front of the admin building's big front door. *Jesus, it's the battering ram*, Sam's friend Stephen had said. It was like watching a war movie.

Sam tried to be cool, to take in the Topos scene without gawking. Once in a while a rumor would start up about Topos: that a busload of hippies stopped at Topos last summer and camped out in the farm's field, a big naked sex party; that there was some guy, like a crazy priest, who led group acid trips; that the members paid their rent by doing carpentry and odd jobs around Westfield; that Topos had a rich benefactor who'd helped them get off the ground.

"There's a basket for contributions," Jerry said, pointing at a side table. "Officially we don't believe in money, but we gotta pay the bills."

Sam went and put a dollar in the basket. On the wall above the table, a carved wooden sign read EU TOPOS, THE GOOD PLACE. Around the sign, letters and cards had been taped up as decorations: "Greetings from Ere-whon, Keene, NH;" "Greetings from Pie in the Sky Com-mune! Vermont Forever!" And the famous Outposts of the Counter-Culture poster. Next to it another, homemade poster making fun of the famous counterculture poster. The homemade poster showed cartoonish people, the men skinny and bearded, the women plump and wearing headscarves, leaning on a counter, ordering sheep, chick-ens, shovels as if they were in a deli. Sam turned back to talk to Jerry, but Jerry was greeting a girl, so he stood nearby to wait for an introduction. His arms felt too long, his hands too big.

"Elodie!" Jerry had pulled the girl into a hug, holding on to her for longer than your usual hug. When Jerry and the girl separated, Sam recognized her; she'd been an ex-change girl in the fall. Silvery-brown hair in a braid down her back, jeans and turtleneck.

"Yep, I'm back," Elodie said, hands in her jean pockets.

"Still fighting the patriarchy?" Jerry said.

"You know it," she said.

Sam cleared his throat, putting out his hand to shake. Elodie looked down at his hand, smiling, probably amused at his squareness, then took his hand in both of hers.

"Ah," Jerry said. "Sam, Elodie. Elodie, Sam. Sam's a math genius."

"Hardly," Sam said. Elodie's eyes were greeny-gray and smiley, and she held his gaze, as if she wanted to get to know him. This was new. Usually when he talked to a girl at a party he could tell she was looking over his shoulder, trying to find a cooler guy. He felt a new stirring too, felt his mind going blank. He started to blurt out that she had beautiful eyes, but he caught himself—he'd only sound like some lame-ass trying out a line. "You were in American Diplomacy in the fall, weren't you?" he said instead. "You're friends with Cynthia?" He could picture Elodie sitting up front every class next to blonde Cynthia. The exchange girls; since last year, a small group of girls applied to spend a semester at Clarendon. They were of intense interest to every Clarendon guy, but in class all the guys pretended a cool nonchalance, as if they were indifferent to this new occasional presence of girls.

"I wouldn't say we're friends," Elodie said. "Cynthia's the girl my mother wanted me to be. But we both go, went, whatever, to Wellesley."

"How long you here for?" Jerry asked.

She tilted her head one way, then the other. "Maybe a week."

Jerry asked if they wanted some cider and went off to get it.

Elodie introduced him to another girl who passed by, and Sam's heart leaped up at Elodie's friendliness. "Your name, it sounds like—" he said, but she interrupted.

"Ugh, I get that all the time," she said. "It gets a little old."

"Wait, what do you get all the time?"

"I introduce myself and someone says, '*Melody*? Your name is Melody? Like a song?' And I say 'No, *Elodie*,' and even after I say 'Elodie,' still they go and make some dumb joke about my name and songs, like which song would I be, and do I have a good voice, and do I like to sing, because—"

"I wasn't going to say any of that," Sam said. "I only meant that Elodie sounds different, like it's French or something."

"It is. French, I mean." She smiled. "Sorry, I'm a little

touchy about it. I'm named for a great-aunt on my dad's side. I honestly don't know how that happened, since my grandmother is such a battle-ax and most of the women in my family are named Martha, Anna or Louisa. Especially Louisa. Everyone wants to claim a little bit of Louisa May Alcott. Our ancestor. Not directly, because she never had any kids, but you know what I mean."

"Oh," he said. "That's cool. Louisa May Alcott. I was named for a great-uncle." He didn't say. S *for Great-uncle Sol, who did well in the undergarments business.*

"Well, that's a lot simpler."

"So what are you working on in the movement?" Sam asked.

She tilted her head and looked at him, eyes narrowed. "I'm not sure how trustworthy you are, I mean you look okay, but you're probably in a *frat*, or something—" She said the word *frat* like it was a curse word. He'd had to defend himself plenty of times for belonging to a crappy fraternity like Lambda Chi, but never for just being in a frat.

"You think I'm an establishment guy, huh," he said.

"And you're going to tell me otherwise, I take it." She smiled, eyebrows raised, waiting.

He shrugged. "I'm in Lambda Chi. But it's not like KA or Deke."

"It could be worse, you mean."

"It could be worse," he said. "A ringing endorsement. But this is Clarendon we're talking about, not Berkeley." It occurred to him that Elodie must have liked Clarendon enough to come here as an exchange student. But he didn't want to annoy her; he wanted her to keep talking to him. But she'd looked over his shoulder and spotted someone coming down the stairs—Hank the senior, he thought it was—and she excused herself to go talk to him. He watched her go, barely noticing when Jerry handed him a glass of brownish cider.

"Martha and Cyril—" Jerry didn't say who Martha and Cyril were, only set two bottles on the table next to them "—have been trying out different methods. To bottle and sell it, bring in some income."

Sam downed the fizzy-sharp cider in a few gulps. "So, Elodie, is she—" What could he ask: Was she going out with anyone? Was she a radical?

"I don't want to hear it tonight," Jerry said. Sam followed Jerry's gaze across the room, where a group of guys and girls were talking loudly about the wrongheaded Cambodian bombing campaign, the lies coming out of Washington and Saigon. "Sometimes all the talk about the war, the chatter around here gets a little old, man. Nobody has any fucking idea what they're talking about, not the government, not my old man. Not these guys. Nobody."

"For sure." Sam poured more cider. "But it would be good to get some real information. Not what they want us to hear." Now they were sitting on a lumpy couch like old friends, and he scanned the room for Elodie.

"My old man's been sending me stuff about POWs, his Legion post has gotten involved…"

"POWs, man, that's brutal," Sam said. "At least your old man cares, that's something."

"He cares about whatever his Legion buddies care about. Otherwise, he sits in his chair drinking his Rheingold and yelling at Cronkite and my mom."

"My dad has a new wife and she's going to have a baby any minute," Sam said, surprising himself.

"That's a drag," Jerry said. "So you've got to deal with stepparents, not just parents."

"And my mom is dying to get remarried. I'm sure it will be to some jerk."

"Heh. It bugs my old man that my mom works and he doesn't," Jerry said. "She does time cards at Con Ed, and he can't stand it that she goes off into Manhattan every morning. But they need her salary."

"Yeah," Sam said. "What can you do?" The second bottle of cider was gone, and he was feeling good.

"My parents had this kind of mythology about themselves, you know?" Jerry said. "Something about the way they got married so young, how they made it through the war and all."

Sam's dad had served, but he was training in Alabama when the war ended. "At least they're still married."

Jerry shrugged. "They'd be happier if they weren't married, but they'll never break up. Stupid. They don't understand what I'm doing up here, why I didn't settle right down with some girl after coming back."

Sam felt an expansive rush of goodwill toward Jerry, the unexpected way he'd unburdened himself. "You did the right thing. I'm sure they're proud of you."

Jerry turned his palms up in a who-knows gesture. "I guess. But also a little afraid of me."

It had been a long time since Sam had felt this good. After the cider and joints (he couldn't remember how many of either), he was out of it in the best possible way. He'd been hanging out at the Topos party for a couple of hours, and now Elodie sat next to him. They were in tune; they were together. Anything could happen. When she took his hand, a current raced through his body, and he leaned closer. She bumped his shoulder away but kept hold of his hand, studying his veins and knuckles. As she turned his hand over to examine the lifeline, she asked about the frats, and about his frat, what the vibe was there. "What do you love about it?" she asked.

Sam laughed. "I don't know if I love anything about it. It's just a place that feels okay, where the guys are okay."

"You like that word, don't you," she said. "*Okay.* 'The guys are okay.'"

"Well, that's what they are. They're fine, how about that. They'd probably say the same thing about me." At least he hoped they'd say he was okay. Or fine.

"I mean, what if the guys were *incredible*? What if you couldn't live without them?"

He laughed in embarrassment, felt himself heat up as she held his gaze. *What if I couldn't live without you?* he wanted to say.

"I like you," she said, as if she'd read his mind.

"I like you too," he said. But the noisy group that had been across the room was somehow all around them, or had they always been there, and he just hadn't noticed? And Elodie had let go of his hand. He gathered that they were talking about the big protest in Boston a year ago. Everyone except him had been there, and he kept quiet, not wanting to admit his ignorance.

"And God, Abbie Hoffman," one of the girls said. "That speech! Incendiary. Amazing."

"John Hancock was no fucking insurance salesman!" Hank yelled.

"John Hancock was a goddamn revolutionary!" some of the others yelled back, in unison.

"Cosmic day," another guy said. "Completely cosmic. A hundred thousand of us, or more."

"But the riots in Cambridge, the fights, we're not about that, man," Hank said.

"It was cosmic. And beautiful," Elodie said. "And also brazen and awful." Now she was telling about being in Cambridge that night, how she'd seen the riots up close—the guys throwing things, throwing rocks at cops, bricks at cars and buildings. A guy threw a burning log through the Harvard Coop's window. And the police charging, beating people to the ground. She'd gotten knocked over by someone running from the cops, and some stranger had pulled her up to standing, had taken her hand to help her get out of the mayhem of Harvard Square. "I was pretty scared," she said. "But the worst were those Harvard boys looking down from their dorm windows, just *watching* the whole thing, doing *nothing*. Although people in the street were yelling some pretty obnoxious things about them."

Elodie was brave; she was something different, and she made him feel different too. If only he could have been that guy, helping her reach a safer place. He tried to get her attention. "Can I see you sometime?"

"You can see me right now." Her smile let him know that she hadn't misunderstood him. She knew what he'd meant. "I'm only visiting, but I'll be back."

Virginia was sliding backward. The brief visit home to Norfolk had undone her. She'd fled without helping to untangle Momma's financial mess. She'd done nothing. Her brother, Rolly, had said to leave it to him, he'd let her know how things were turning out for Momma. She hadn't admitted to her siblings how dire her own situation was. She had to get a job. She had to get up the gumption to go back to Arthur Gage and beg him for some teaching work. But she needed a salary, not substituting as an occasional instructor for one hundred dollars a term. In the middle of the night, Virginia tried to call forth her school tour with Toby Dickenson, the way she'd felt smart, witty and attractive enough, but Foster Burgess, with his smirks and horrible coded phrases, kept intruding. *Oliver, could you please give me a little something?* she asked. *I need help, I'm sure you can see that.* But nothing came.

At the college employment office, Virginia sat to fill out applications for the two secretarial openings. "You'll have to take a timed typing test for these positions," the woman behind the desk said, and she stood to move around the desk, her nylons scritching against her knit dress, then led Virginia down the hall to a room with two typewriters. Virginia arranged herself at the typewriter, and began to type a document, "Revised Rules and Regulations Pertaining to the Use of Clarendon Hall by Westfield Residents."

Ten minutes later, the woman scanned Virginia's typed pages, frowned at them. "Why don't you work on your typing for a week or so, and then come back and try again."

"I didn't pass?"

"You can use this test if that's what you prefer, but it's better to have a slightly higher score," the woman said. "To give you the best chance against the younger applicants."

The younger applicants; so she was an older applicant. "I have plenty of other skills that could be useful."

"Yes, I see," the woman said. "Nevertheless, it couldn't hurt to improve your score."

The younger applicants. Who were these younger applicants? No doubt *younger* meant unmarried. Virginia was no longer married. Or maybe younger meant attractive. Virginia couldn't understand what people around her were saying; or rather she could understand what they said, but not what they meant. Virginia imagined the younger applicants streaming into the employment office, fashionable and high-heeled, even though you couldn't navigate a late-winter sidewalk, never mind a snowbank, in heels. Once these younger applicants sat down at the typewriter, their fingers would fly across the keys.

In the A&P that afternoon, she grabbed bananas, oranges and carrots, and ground coffee into a paper bag. *Younger applicants*. She wanted to reshape the typing test into a funny story for Oliver, to make him laugh as they did the dishes. She missed his presence, his solid portliness close to her in the kitchen or in their bed; she missed his belly that pulled at his shirts. And meanwhile all these other tiny details that had made up her life had disappeared, like getting the Clarendon gossip, hearing from Oliver about the latest scandal. She stopped at the butcher counter, and one of the young butchers leaned over the glass case. "Rib eye or porterhouse?" He gave a quick wink, his dimples showing.

"I—uh—some stew meat…" Her face went hot and blotchy. She couldn't afford a steak; she couldn't get a job as a damn secretary. He turned away, and she wiped her eyes and caught her breath. A minute later the butcher handed the package over carefully, as if he'd been holding a baby.

She spun her cart around, intending to escape. "Hello," a man's voice called to her, and she looked up, but couldn't place his face. Someone on faculty, someone new.

"Henry," he said. "Henry Jernigan."

Right, Henry. He rented the upstairs apartment from

the Gompers, four houses down. He taught math or maybe economics, and she'd met him in the fall when Mrs. Gompers had taken him around to meet the neighbors. She managed to ask how he was, keeping her gaze on his springy, flyaway hair. If she made eye contact, she'd fall apart.

Pulling out of the parking lot, she spotted Malcolm Ferber, a retired English professor who was a fixture on the campus green on nice days. He was at the wheel of his ancient Oldsmobile. Wispy hair, driving cap, pendulous ears. Why did old Malcolm Ferber get to live so long? "You useless, stupid old man," she said to the windshield, glaring at Malcolm. "You should be dead." Malcolm smiled and tipped his cap to her.

On the way home she tortured herself with memories of long-ago fights, the memories too well-preserved. Like the time when Rebecca had started reading the women's pages in the newspaper. That was Virginia's doing because little Rebecca had been sounding out headlines with Oliver, which were invariably about Vietnam body counts or Soviet missile launches. One morning Virginia had handed Rebecca the women's page, and after that Rebecca read the household hints from Heloise and Dear Abby's advice to the lovelorn every morning. "Our little hausfrau in training," Oliver had said.

"Unlike her mother, you mean," Virginia said.

Oliver laughed. "Well," he said.

Virginia's laugh died. "Where is it written that only I have to do all this stuff, the cooking, the shopping, the laundry, the mopping. Your mother used to get onto me for not ironing the sheets. Sheets, for God's sake." The stab of fury had been inside her, ready to pour out.

"*I* cook." Oliver put his hand to his chest as if protecting the hurt inside. He did cook a little. He made pancakes on Saturday mornings, and once in a while, hamburgers fried in butter. "And I don't mind, you know I don't mind if—" He stopped. "But I *work*, you know. It's a lot of pressure, trying to move ahead, get along with some of these morons, never mind the deans." Every week a new headache, like that cheating business last spring, never mind his research and publishing, which were imperative, she had to know that. *Imperative.* "And it's not like we have five kids, we're not the Koslowskis," he said. "It's—the thing is, it's not easy when your wife has professional ambitions," he said. "People get ideas…" He trailed off.

"Well, I'm sorry you didn't marry the right kind of woman," she said.

I'm sorry, Oliver, those were such dumb fights, she thought now. *I was full of anger and foolishness. I didn't—I don't—know how to be the right kind of woman.*

Monday morning, she hadn't heard anything from the employment office. In the bedroom, her old typewriter mocked her with yet another task she hadn't completed. Instead of sitting down to practice, she stripped the sheets off the bed and went to the basement to start a load of laundry. On her way back upstairs, the woodstove called to her— she hadn't touched it since Oliver—he'd always stacked the wood, kept the stove going on weekends. She opened the little door and peered inside: piles of cold ash made a tiny, desolate landscape. She reached inside to sweep it clean, and as she tipped the dustpan into the trash can, a cloud of ash flew up around her, leaving a layer of fine pale dust on the carpet and the wood trim. She would not let the dust remind her of Blossom Hill Cemetery down in Concord, where they'd put Oliver's ashes. She'd clean and freshen up the house.

At Sears, she bought a stack of fresh green towels and a bright new bedspread for Rebecca's bed. Through the afternoon she vacuumed up ash, wiped down baseboards and chair rails with damp rags, mopped the kitchen floor. She tidied Rebecca's room, put the new bedspread on the bed.

She got a stew going, and she drank a glass of Cognac as she browned the meat, since the stew called for it. She had to open a bottle of wine to add to the stew, and she poured herself some wine, too. It tasted wonderful, a little floral. She slid the stew into the oven, poured a third glass of wine. She was doing better, yes, she was! She decided to make a special dessert: Queen of Sheba cake from Julia Child. She separated the eggs, whipped the whites and the sugar, melted the chocolate and the butter. No almonds in the cabinet. Walnuts? She poured the walnuts into a paper bag and crushed them with a rolling pin—she should do this more often, bang the rolling pin hard on the walnuts, crush things to powder.

She heard Eileen's car rolling into the driveway, then the slam of the car door—Rebecca, home from Girl Scouts. The wine bottle was empty and she was a tiny bit tipsy. Wait, how had that happened? Thank God it hadn't been her turn to pick up the girls. She hurried to the bathroom and splashed her face with water. At least the stew smelled good. She opened the oven to peer at the Queen of Sheba cake, which lay flat and gray in its pan. She'd left out something critical. Or maybe she'd baked it at the wrong temperature.

At the table, she ladled out stew for Rebecca and herself,

spilling a little. She asked Rebecca about Girl Scouts and the newspaper collection drive they were planning. She was saying what a good idea the paper drive sounded like when Rebecca interrupted.

"Mom, are you—are you drunk?"

"No, of course not," Virginia said.

Rebecca squinted at her, took a bite of her stew, then another two bites. Set down her spoon, pushed back her chair and stormed out of the kitchen.

Oh, God, she was a mess. She needed—what did she need? She needed someone to talk to. She couldn't call Eileen; Eileen had already helped too much, picking up Rebecca, taking her in, taking Rebecca skating and to Girl Scouts, making countless meals for them. And Eileen had five children, five! Virginia called Gerda's house, but Gerda was at the PTA executive committee meeting, Dwight said.

She called Corinna. No answer.

She called Helen and Lily's apartment. No answer there, either.

She didn't want to think about how few friends she had, and she found herself dialing Louise's number. Louise, who she didn't even want to see. When Louise said hello, Virginia felt herself starting to cry. "I just—could you—I seem, to be a little…"

"I'm on my way," Louise said.

Virginia let her elbows splay out on the kitchen table, leaning her head on her hand while Louise boiled water for tea and ran soapy water into the stewpot. Virginia heard herself talking, talking, talking, droning on about her family in Norfolk, how they wanted her to come home and help out, but she didn't think she could ever go back there.

About the meeting with Arthur Gage before Christmas, and then Foster Burgess at the academy. About the other wives in Westfield, how she didn't belong anywhere. She was going to be a secretary or a shopgirl because she hadn't finished her dissertation, one misstep leading to another. But she was too embarrassed to admit that she'd flunked a typing test, that she hadn't put her best foot forward, that no one would hire her because she was old and slow.

Louise leaned against the counter, listening, as she waited for the tea to steep. At the table, she poured a mug for each of them, pushing one across the table. "I think it's going to be tough for a while. And Gage is a pompous ass, but you knew that already. I can't speak to Foster Burgess, but I'm pretty sure I've seen his kind before. Way too many times before."

Rebecca clomped into the kitchen with her French homework, and Virginia introduced Rebecca to Louise, then cut her a piece of the misformed Queen of Sheba cake.

"I worked with your dad," Louise said. "He was a wonderful teacher. He loved his subject areas and his students."

Rebecca nodded, taking in this angular woman with her Dutch-boy haircut and straight-across bangs.

Oh, no, Rebecca surely had heard Oliver complaining about Louise, and now she'd blurt out something. Virginia tried to catch Rebecca's eye, but Rebecca wouldn't look at her. "Isn't that—" Virginia began.

"He would have gotten it," Rebecca said, gazing down at the table, tracing the edge of her plastic place mat with her finger.

"Gotten what, Bec?" Virginia said.

"Tenure. He's very smart, you know. Was. Very smart."

In her mind's eye, Virginia saw Rebecca sitting in Oliver's little home office on a Saturday afternoon, reading while he graded papers, and listening to his comments. He'd told her a lot about his work, probably too much, and she'd taken it all in.

"You're absolutely right, Rebecca," Louise said. "He would have. He deserved it."

"Do you need help with your French, hon?" Virginia asked, afraid of whatever Rebecca might say next.

"I thought I did, but I think I know what to do now," Rebecca said. "Nice meeting you," she said to Louise. She gathered up her book and notebook and left the kitchen. Virginia closed her eyes, rested her head in her hand again.

"I wonder if—" Louise stopped. "Never mind. I'll try to think of something."

Later that night, Virginia realized that Louise had never said, *Buck up and stop the self-pity act*. Or, *Why not practice your typing?* Or, *Finish your dissertation already. It's ridiculous that you haven't. Go and do it and then you'll have that backing you up. No one can argue with that, even if you are a woman.*

Still, she vowed to do so.

She cringed at the way she used to talk to Louise in her mind, back when everything she knew about the woman came from Oliver's complaints. She'd imagined that Louise would look down on her for spending so much energy on shopping and cooking, on her piecrust, her boeuf Bourguignon, following Julia Child.

But maybe Louise cooked from Julia Child too. Or maybe she ate soup from a can every night because she was swamped with her research and her teaching. Louise had complimented the sad Queen of Sheba cake, but only ate half a piece.

She wondered if Louise was as lonely as she was.

In the middle of the night, she woke from a dream of

numbers and department meetings, as if Oliver's old wor-
ries were streaming into her head. A frightening yet tedious
dream. But in another part of the dream, Louise sat at a
conference table, hands folded on a stack of paper. *I'm sorry,
Virginia. You're not one of us. You'll never be one of us.* Next
to Louise was Eileen from next door, who shook her head
sadly. *Not one of us, either. Can't sew a curtain. Can barely sew
a Halloween costume. Never dusts the baseboards.*

She wanted to tell them all she was trying, but the dream
had evaporated.

Chapter Nine

"LISTEN," LILY SAID, ON the phone. "Helen and I are hosting a get-together. Next Saturday, six thirty. Just Louise, Corinna and us. Can you join us?"

Louise must have told the others what a complaining mess Virginia had turned into. And how amusing, that she couldn't even get work as a secretary. They didn't have to include her out of pity, Virginia wanted to say. "Umm, did Louise—"

"Yes, and I thought about going too, but Helen's sister was visiting."

"Ah." Instead of asking where Louise had gone, Virginia exhaled, then asked what she could bring. A salad, Lily said.

Lily and Helen's apartment took up the second floor of a big house near the town pond. Along with packed bookshelves and stacks of books on the floor, one wall of the living room featured an arrangement of black–and–white photos.

After Helen brought her a glass of wine, Virginia went to look at the photos, a mix of landscapes, a grove of silvery birch trees in the snow, the town pond in summer, and portraits. One portrait drew her eye, a nude woman draped in a sheer scarf, one knee drawn up. The photo turned the woman's body into a kind of sculpture. "Beautiful photographs," Virginia said.

"Oh, Lily used to take a lot of pictures," Helen said. "She was a paid photographer at Smith, she took all the team and club photos, and candids for the yearbook. She thought she was going to be a photojournalist."

"Oh," Virginia said. "Why didn't she? What changed her mind?"

"Her father. No daughter of his was going to work for a newspaper." Helen's voice had turned gruff, approximating Lily's father, and then she patted at her hair, which she wore tonight in a low, old–fashioned bun that made Virginia think of Mrs. Dalloway. Or maybe it was Helen's long face and big eyes that reminded her of Virginia Woolf. "No, newspapers were too dirty, too crass for his daughter. And he didn't want her traipsing off to Korea or China or some such place where the men would— Well, anyway." Helen shrugged. "So she went to Columbia for English a year after I started, and her father still disapproved, but not quite as much. Now her father is long gone and here we are."

"Ah." Virginia considered how none of the Gang of Four wore pantyhose or plucked their eyebrows or colored their hair. And Louise most likely cut her own hair. Practical to a fault, Momma would say.

But no, that wasn't right, because Helen and Lily's apartment was beautifully furnished, not only those arresting photos, but with pale furniture and beautiful silvery-cobalt bowls that looked hand-thrown, and a warm Persian rug, all reds and golds and blues. It was a little like being back in Cambridge. Virginia told herself to stop thinking, stop judging; she cared far too much about appearances, about surfaces. She liked to think of herself as utterly different from her sisters—June and Marnie were shallow, materialistic beings, reveling in their traditional lives. But she was far more like her sisters than she wanted to be.

Louise had just arrived and was calling out hellos.

"I'm sorry," Virginia blurted out as Louise approached. "And thank you for helping me out, I don't know what came over me that night, and I meant to call, it's just that—" She sounded ridiculous.

"No need, you would have done the same for me," Louise said. "Everyone has those moments, and it's only been such a short time, since Oliver and all."

"Rebecca enjoyed talking to you."

Louise nodded. "Smart girl, like her parents."

"Thanks."

At the dining table, two fondue pots bubbled over blue Sterno flames, one with hot oil for the cubes of meat, the other with cheese sauce for bread. Virginia didn't like beef fondue, the way the meat was either tough and overcooked, or red and cold in the middle. But the intimacy of it, their arms and elbows knocking together as they set their spears of meat in the pot, was lovely and made them all laugh. Virginia remembered with sudden clarity another dinner party, maybe at Ronald and Betsy Garland's house, when Ronald had said something crude about the Gang of Four, some crass double-entendre about the four women's love lives, or lack thereof, and Oliver and Frank Randolph had roared with laughter, and Virginia hadn't been bothered enough to tell them to cut it out. Her cheeks and throat heated up in belated embarrassment.

Helen was talking about Kate Millet's book and the overwhelming masculine hostility in the literary canon, as the others nodded knowingly. Louise mentioned another book Virginia hadn't heard of, something about sisterhood. Virginia vowed to be better read, to catch up to the rest of them.

"So, the Bread and Roses meeting," Lily said. "How was it, Louise?"

"Well," Louise said. "I wish I could say it was terrific, but it was pretty chaotic." She turned Virginia's way. "I went to an organizing meeting of a women's collective in Boston last week," she said.

"Ah," Virginia said. If only she'd listened, or asked a question or two, instead of yammering on about herself last week, she would already know about Louise's trip to Boston.

"They don't believe in leadership roles—if you try to run a meeting, they call that star-hogging. And they don't believe in parliamentary procedure, either, so we spent three hours listening to one woman and then another talking about this and that, and nothing related to anything else, and hardly anything got done."

Now the others were talking about the marches for equality last August—Louise had gone to the big New York march and rally, while Lily and Helen had gone to the Boston march. "Even with all the hecklers and the cops being aggressive, the whole day felt organized," Helen said.

"Same in New York," Louise said. "Something like fifty thousand women marching in New York and listening to the speakers. This Bread and Roses meeting was nothing like that."

Virginia could have gone to the Boston rally last summer, or even the giant New York rally, and she could have linked arms with strangers, other women. She could have listened to Betty Friedan and Gloria Steinem and Bella Abzug. She could have brought Rebecca with her. Instead, she'd only read about those rallies and the thousands of women in *Time* magazine. Until now, it hadn't occurred to her that she too might take part.

"But there was one thing," Louise said. "A health collective. They're pushing for women-centered health care, and the woman whose idea it seemed to be was very persuasive. They've been running those consciousness-raising meetings around Boston too."

"Clarendon could use some consciousness-raising," Helen said.

"Maybe we should engineer another takeover of the president's office," Lily said. "Demand that more women be hired."

"Yes, since it worked out so well the first time," Louise said. "But why not. We could demand coeducation too."

"We should demand a normal-size women's bathroom in the library."

"A bathroom that's not in the basement."

"Demand that all fraternity members learn to sew their own clothes."

"And take care of a baby."

"And a toddler at the same time!" They were all laughing now as their demands got sillier.

"But Weissman," Corinna said. "He's a scientist. I'd hate to make him unhappy with another takeover."

"He'd understand, in the long run," Louise said. "He has to know that coeducation is an essential first step. If he doesn't, well, maybe his time has passed."

"I could host a meeting," Virginia heard herself saying. "One of those consciousness-raising meetings." She'd read about these meetings in *Time*, women filling up New York apartments, getting together to talk about their lives, to talk about political issues and the world. Without any men. She had friends now, and maybe she could make something happen.

"Yes, it's time," Lily said.

Corinna had left the table for more coffee, but she'd returned with her coat on, her empty plate in hand. "I left some brownies on the counter," she said to Helen.

"You're leaving?" Lily asked.

Corinna nodded. "I—uh—I just can't afford to rock the boat. I'm not even halfway through this study, and if I were to lose my funding for Woods Hole…" She held her free hand out in a half shrug.

"If we don't speak up for ourselves, no one will," Louise said. "This would be a small meeting, that's all. Surely that's well within our—"

"I'm not against people speaking up," Corinna interrupted, her forehead red. "But I need to put my head down and work. That's what I'm here for."

"That's what we're all here for, Corinna," Lily said.

"I know," Corinna said. "I'm not explaining myself well, I'm sorry." She thanked Lily and Helen, said goodbye to Louise and Virginia, and turned to go out the door.

They sat in silence, Corinna's footfalls as she went downstairs echoing in the apartment.

"Are the rest of us still in?" Lily said. "It's just one meeting."

In a basement practice room, Sam made notes for the other Granitetone singers while Stephen tapped out "In the Still of the Night" on the piano. Stephen was from Vermont and on ski patrol, and something about him reminded Sam of Tommy, although Tommy would be mortified by the falsetto solos that Stephen was willing to sing. Stephen moved on to "In the Mood"—he'd rewritten the lyrics to put the song into a guy's perspective. Despite the laughable lyrics, the song had a great structure and melody. The word *melody* reminded Sam of Elodie. Elodie, who'd talked to him, who'd held his hand, traced his veins with her finger, who said she'd be back soon, who might be willing to see him again. It wasn't just her beauty; it was all the experiences she'd had, like being in the middle of the Cambridge riots, and that calm certainty she carried. She knew what was important.

Two girls went clacking past the practice room, probably on their way to the ceramics studio. He wondered if they'd come from Wellesley for the term, and whether they knew Elodie. He was seized with the urge to run out and ask them. "Maybe things will get better if Clarendon goes coed," he said, trying for a nonchalant tone.

"Huh?" Stephen looked up from the piano as the girls turned a corner and disappeared. "I don't know, man. My older brother went to Middlebury, and he said it was like two completely different species. The girls are super smart, and the guys are either unmotivated or just plain dumb.

So the guys resent the girls and the girls look down on the guys. Not all, but most."

Probably Elodie looked down on all the Clarendon guys. The most basic, everyday insult at Clarendon was to tell a guy he was acting like a girl. *Don't be such a girl* got said more than *Don't be a dumbass* or *asswipe* or *moron*. And yet Clarendon guys obsessed over girls. "You think having more girls here would make the guys look dumb?"

Stephen shrugged. "Not necessarily. I just don't know how much better it would be."

The other Granitetones trickled in, and when Stephen started banging out the parts to "In the Mood," a couple guys groaned.

"Come on, man, we gotta be more relevant," Theo Burke said.

"Okay, how about Janis? Let's do Janis," Stephen said, and he plunked out the opening chords to "Piece of My Heart."

That song belonged to Erma Franklin, Sam wanted to say. Janis was only covering it, but no one would care.

"Tin soldiers and Nixon coming," someone else sang, mimicking Neil Young's wavery tenor.

"Okay, that's a little too obvious," Theo Burke said.

"All right, *you* pick something, Theo, and *you* arrange it," Sam said. "Then we'll sing it." He was sick of this in-between time of year, too late for skiing, too early for hanging out outside and playing Frisbee. And Elodie: Would he ever see her again? He'd missed his chance last fall when she was on campus all the time as an exchange girl. He let himself wallow in the painful pull of his crush.

In the snack bar after rehearsal, Sam grabbed a burger and fries, then stopped to say hi to Jerry, who sat alone with open books spread out around him, his ashtray full of butts.

"This Restoration drama class is completely useless," Jerry grumbled. "I put off this paper too long. Not that old Professor Parker will even notice, but I gotta work."

"Right," Sam said. "See ya."

"Later, Manhattan," Jerry said, and Sam went to sit with Stephen a few tables away.

"That guy," Stephen said, inclining his head in Jerry's direction. "What's his deal? He always looks mad enough to murder somebody."

"He's okay," Sam said. "He's—" but maybe better not to say anything about Topos, because Stephen wouldn't get it "—we're in the same math seminar."

But Stephen had already moved on, talking about the Granitetones doing a whole set of protest songs, how they could work on that after the tribute concert for Professor Desmarais. At the mention of Professor Desmarais—Oliver—Sam felt his face heat up. An image of Oliver popped into his head, Oliver playing his clarinet, looking left and right at his bandmates, all of them kind of laughing about something. He could see Oliver smiling in greeting, nodding at his solo, and he felt something dark and a little bitter. Oliver had been gone—dead—by the time Sam bailed out on that dinner. Sam would never learn what Oliver had meant by that invitation, and Oliver would never know that Sam had failed to show up. Whatever else Oliver might have wanted, Oliver had thought Sam was someone worth befriending. Oliver hadn't thought Sam was the kind of guy who bailed out, who disappeared.

He changed the subject, asking Stephen about his plans for next year. Stephen said he might go out West after graduation, maybe Sun Valley or somewhere in Colorado. "You know, spend a winter doing nothing but skiing and working a dumb job. Before med school and the rest of my fucking life."

Sam had dunked a fry in ketchup and was popping it into his mouth when something hit him on his cheekbone then skittered across the table. A balled-up straw wrapper.

"Bull's-eye," he heard. He looked up to see Teddy Burnham sitting with Charlie Biddle. Teddy, the biggest asshole on campus, thought he was God's gift to Clarendon. Freshman fall, Sam had had something like a crush on Teddy, those pale gold curls, and the memory of his own stupidity made him feel sick to his stomach.

"What was that?" Stephen said.

"I don't know." Another straw wrapper hit him on the neck.

"Let's go," Stephen said, pushing back his chair. "I need to get going anyway." He grabbed his tray.

"We just got here, I haven't finished my fries, and Teddy Burnham is an asshole," Sam said, a surprising flare of anger grounding him.

"I've got an orgo test tomorrow, so I should go." Stephen stood, grabbed his sheet music folder, his half-eaten burger in his other hand. "I'll see you at LC."

Sam nodded. He couldn't blame Stephen for wanting to avoid an asshole like Teddy Burnham. But he wanted to finish his fries, goddammit. And he wanted to put off the walk across campus in the cold rain. He wasn't in seventh grade, and neither was Teddy Burnham. Something hit his hand, a spitball this time. Fucking Teddy leaned back in his chair, clutching his belly, cracking up. Drunk, or high on something.

Sam stood up. He wavered, hands on the table, debating. He made himself walk across the snack bar to Teddy and Charlie's table.

"Hey, Sam," Charlie said, looking up in surprise. "What's up?"

Teddy smirked at him like an obnoxious ten-year-old.

"Hey, Charlie," Sam said, then turned to Teddy. "Will you quit it, please."

"Will you quit it, please," Teddy mimicked, in a high-pitched, irritating voice.

Sam felt too old for this tired crap. He hated that guys like Teddy got away with such asinine behavior, and that everyone else—Charlie Biddle in this case—would act all clueless, like nothing was going on. He was sick of it all, the teasing at Lambda Chi, the way he was always the butt of other guys' jokes. There was nothing more he could say, so he turned around and went to stack his tray, head down. As he dropped off his tray, he sensed a commotion behind him. Oh, fuck, it had to be Teddy coming after him. He didn't want to get walloped in a fight, and he turned around, cringing in expectation of whatever was coming at him next. But Teddy lay on the floor, still in his chair, legs waving in the air, gazing up at the ceiling, a stunned look on his face. Out of the corner of his eye, Sam took in Jerry, walking quickly in the other direction. Jerry never looked Sam's way; he just headed out the back door, and out of the student center.

Charlie stared down at Teddy, but didn't move to help him up. Teddy rolled over to all fours, cursing loudly. Neither of them even looked Jerry's way.

Sam turned and moved faster, past the college mailboxes. Shit. This wasn't going to help things. But on the other hand, those guys didn't have any idea that he was friends with Jerry now. Jerry had helped him out in a way that no guy in Lambda Chi would ever do, and he'd done so silently, expecting nothing for it. Sam wanted to be different, like Jerry, like Elodie. Not like Stephen, and definitely not like Teddy Burnham.

Chapter Ten

VIRGINIA HAD A JOB. *She had a job.* And not a secretarial job, either. Part-time, but with a possibility to advance. As she moved through the Clarendon library, she let her hand trail along the rows of card-catalog cabinets. She always felt the urge to open a few drawers and see if she knew the book or the author that her fingers had landed on, to feel like a student again.

She'd gotten the call two days ago from the college employment woman—an opening in the library. And this morning she'd run over to the library to meet with Cliff, the college's reference librarian. Cliff had gushed about Oliver's impeccable research skills and then cleared his throat repeatedly as he'd looked over her CV. "A library science degree would be helpful," he said, over his reading glasses.

"I have a master's degree, and all the coursework for a PhD," she said. "I can track down whatever needs tracking down, I know all the citation styles." Surely he didn't expect someone with a library science degree to magically appear in tiny Westfield to take this part-time, assistant-level job. She didn't want to beg for this job.

But it turned out that she didn't need to beg; Cliff had bent to scrawl a note on library letterhead, and now he reached across the desk to hand it to her. If she'd take this note to the employment office, she could fill out the paperwork and start next week. "Talk to Jeannette for a bit on your way out," he said. "And welcome aboard."

Jeannette, the other assistant, was stylish, in a short knit dress with Mondrian-like color blocks, chunky necklace and bracelets, her red hair in a layered pixie cut. "It's been a little lonely with Mariah gone," Jeannette said. "Her baby's fine, just six weeks early, in case you were wondering."

"That's good," Virginia said, not sure what to say about Mariah or the early baby.

"It'll be nice to have some company," Jeannette said.

She and Jeannette would work four mornings a week together and take turns with the afternoon and Saturday shifts. She'd meet with students who needed help getting started on research or who didn't know how to cite their sources, she'd order books and materials for students and faculty, and she'd manage the microfilm machines.

That night, Virginia and Rebecca went early to Mexican night at Mo's, their first time back since Oliver, though neither mentioned this milestone. Virginia told Rebecca about the library job.

"Okay." Rebecca poked at her enchiladas. "That sounds like fun." She told Virginia about the time when she was younger and had gone with Dad to the English department's cute little library and had tea and she'd wished that she could work or even live in that library. "So you won't be in there, but close enough."

"I might not always be home when you get home from school," Virginia said.

"Mom. It's no big deal."

"Right, no big deal," Virginia repeated.

In the front room of Topos, a guy and a girl, both of them in overalls, sat on the couch—the same couch where Sam had sat next to Elodie on that eventful night. They were studying, and they looked up from their books and regarded Sam, their faces blank. He had no idea what to say. "Hey, I, uh, I'm looking for Jerry?" he said. Plausible, sort of. Better than *Can you guys take me in?* or *Can you help me find Elodie?*

"Jerry's not around, he went to the tractor place with Cyril," the guy said.

"Oil and transmission fluid and a new hitch for the brush hog," the girl added.

"Right," Sam said, as if he knew what a brush hog was. "I'll just—"

"You can leave a note," the girl said, pointing at the doorway. "In the kitchen."

"Thanks." Sam retreated through the mudroom and then another door to the big kitchen. On the nearest wall hung two bulletin boards. On one, a sheet listed chore as-signments at Topos—daily, weekly, monthly chores. On another, scraps of paper described jobs around Westfield. Maybe he could take the pen hanging from the board and sign up: "Rebuild porch steps, Enfield" or "Assist in cow barn for three days, Thetford," although he'd probably fuck up those jobs, not that he wanted to milk cows at some

Thetford farm. He found more scrap paper in a basket and tried to think what to put in his note to Jerry, but there was nothing he could say without sounding like a putz. He should have thought this through before coming here.

The kitchen door swung open and two girls came through it, talking. One of them was Elodie. He was too surprised to say anything; it felt like a dream, when someone materialized next to you without warning.

"Hey, Sam," Elodie said, as if she ran into him every day. She wore a man's wool coat and a woolly hat. She shrugged out of both, then raked her fingers through her hair, twisting it up and into a knot.

"Hey, Elodie," Sam said, trying to stay cool, as if this weren't a momentous occasion. "What were you doing out there?"

"Pruning the apple trees, picking up the branches. This is Shelly," Elodie said about the other girl, who was taking off her coat.

"We're pruning the old trees so they'll give more fruit next fall," Shelly said instead of hello, as she passed through the kitchen.

"What are you—" Elodie began.

"Can I stay here?" Sam said, at the same time. "I mean, hang out for a while? I have to get the car back to someone, so not that long, but..."

"You can help me with the cooking, if you want," Elodie said. "Hey, Brennan," she shouted into the front room. "You're off kitchen duty. I got a volunteer here."

"Cool," Brennan called, from the front room.

"So give me a job and I'll do it," Sam said.

"Let me think for a second." She crossed the kitchen and poked her head into the fridge, then crossed the other way, out a side door to a shed. "Okay," she said, a minute later. "Carrots, parsnips, potatoes, onions. Beans." She pulled carrots and some other things out of the fridge and with her elbow she directed him to the shed for potatoes and onions. "Use the basket over there. Two onions and maybe fifteen potatoes."

Vegetables covered the counter when he returned; he'd never seen so many carrots at once. "How many people are part of this dinner?" he asked.

"Sixteen or seventeen," she said. He must have made a face, because she laughed and said that it wasn't hard, just a lot of peeling and chopping. He could hear Pete Seeger's banjo coming from the hi-fi in the front room now, and he suppressed a laugh—could you get any more cliché than peeling these grubby misshapen vegetables for a communal stew, with old protest music in the background? Elodie added vegetables to the pot in a mysterious order, and then spices from big jars on the counter. The kitchen started to smell warm and a little exotic with all the onions and mingled spices, as she talked about the Nearings' book *Living The Good Life*. Had he read it? He should read it. "Just think what the world would be like if we all went back to the land. Grew our own food, milked our own cows, a whole new society."

He didn't say that not everyone could go back to the land—like the millions of people crammed into New York City. Instead he made a joke about his mom, what she'd do if she couldn't get to Bergdorf's once a week.

"You might be surprised," she said. "Now for the bread. Martha makes the best bread." She directed him to two bowls covered with tea towels. Underneath the towels, mounds of bread dough lay shiny, puffed and warm to the touch.

★ ★ ★

At the long table, made of two picnic tables pushed together, they passed their plates to be filled, eating once everyone had been served.

"What are you doing here, Manhattan?" Jerry asked,
back from errands with Cyril and seated across from him
and Elodie.

"Oh, I uh, I had a question about math," Sam said. A
lame and unbelievable reason to come out here, and as Jerry
scratched his head, no doubt not buying his answer, Sam
quickly made up something about their program meshing,
using some computer jargon that he figured Jerry wouldn't
question.

"Okay," Jerry said.

Elodie wanted to know what Sam had meant about computer programs, and they took turns describing their project.

"Wow," Elodie said. "That's something I'd love to know
more about."

Sam wasn't the only nonmember at the table. Two vets
had come in late with Martha and Cyril, and Sam noticed
that one of the vets had just put a dollar into the basket
under the bulletin board. He swung a leg over the picnic
bench, and started for the basket.

"No, you cooked, Sam. You already contributed," Elodie said.

"Cheers to the cooks." Martha raised her water glass,
and the others saluted him and Elodie. Warmth and well-
being flooded through him. Something about this dinner
reminded him of Seders when he was little; they used to
go to Aunt Ella's house in Long Island City, with cousins
and grandparents and great uncles and random strays, and
he'd loved that sense of belonging to a big, noisy family.

"Okay, math time," Jerry said, once they'd cleared and scraped their plates into bins for compost and the chickens. Jerry believed Sam's stupid ruse. But he hadn't thought to bring his notebook out here, and now Jerry would know he'd invented a reason to come.

"Oh, right. So I think I figured it out while we were eating." Sam made up something inane about the fourth level and how they should just run the program a few more times, maybe tomorrow?

"That's cool, what you guys are doing," Elodie said. "I wish that I'd—can you teach me how it works?"

The three of them were back at the kitchen table, everyone else having dispersed, and Jerry lit a cigarette. "I guess," Jerry said. "Why do you want to know?" He squinted at Elodie.

"Love of learning, Jerry," Elodie said. "That's all." She held his gaze a little longer than necessary, and Sam wondered if Jerry was angry that Sam had showed up here, angry that Sam might be pursuing Elodie. But no girl would choose him over Jerry. Jerry's head was a little too big, and he had kind of a shambling way about him, but he also had all that wavy hair, and that too-cool-for-Clarendon thing. Jerry had charisma, which Sam sorely lacked.

"It's not rocket science," Jerry said to Elodie. Then, to Sam he added, "I can meet you at the computer center tomorrow after my two o'clock."

"Great," Sam said. But now he had no reason to stay, to get a little more time with Elodie, and he pushed back from the table. "Thanks for the dinner. I liked it a lot."

"Thanks for cooking, Sam," Elodie said.

Sam moved slowly through the house, lingered in the mudroom where he'd hung his jacket. He took his time making his way out to the porch, but he couldn't come up with a single reason to hang around without sounding desperate, like some kind of loser with no real friends.

As he picked his way across the driveway's ruts, he heard Elodie calling to him.

"Hey, can I grab a ride into town?" she yelled, from the porch.

"Sure, of course," he said. Like another scene from a miraculous dream: Elodie wanted a ride, she wanted to drive somewhere. With him.

Sam lurched into first gear and the car leaped forward out of the driveway. He wanted to know whether she had something going on with Jerry, whether she had a boyfriend elsewhere. "How do you keep up with classes when you're away from Wellesley?" he asked instead.

"I'm taking a break from school right now," she said. "I'm not sure about the meaning of a Wellesley degree these days anyway."

"Ah." He shifted up to third, pressing too hard on the clutch so the car roared and clanked. Focus. Focus on driving.

"You're a good guy, Sam." Elodie gave his hand, on the stick shift, a squeeze, and he had to give all his concentration to not crashing the car. He felt heat rising everywhere on his body, and dared to glance over at her. She was smiling out the windshield at the road as the farms on either side shrank to houses with small front yards, which in turn gave over to campus buildings. She was the kind of girl who was up for an adventure, he guessed. To calm himself, he took a long breath, let it out. As they drew closer to campus and passed the library, he dared to ask, "Do you want to stop in my room for a drink?"

She said nothing, which meant she was about to decline politely. "Okay, why not," she said at last.

He said a silent thank-you to God, to the Clarendon housing office and to Lambda Chi that he had his single in Fisher instead of a frat double this year. Elodie gazed up at the dorm as they rolled in to the back entrance. He slid the keys under the floor mat, where Dougie kept them, and hustled around the car to open her door.

In his room, Elodie sat cross-legged on the bed while he went to pick an album. Van Morrison, Marvin Gaye? No, too obvious. Maybe *Déjà Vu*—not make-out music, per se. As Crosby, Stills Nash & Young broke into their harmonies, he handed her a dining-hall mug of bourbon (thank God the bottle, a gift from Tommy, was still a quarter full) and then sat on the crummy easy chair that he'd covered with an ugly orange afghan.

"Tell me something you love, Sam."

He was dazzled with her ease, her beauty, her impossible presence in his dorm room. "You're always talking about love," he said, unable to think of a single witty comment.

She laughed. "Not always, just sometimes."

He was pretty sure he loved her, but he knew better than to say that. "Well, music." He mentioned jazz band and Granitetones. "And math."

"Math! You love math? Like that class you're taking with Jerry, the computer project and all that?"

"Yeah," he said.

"Tell me what you love about it." She patted the bed, inviting him to sit next to her, so he did, both of them sitting crosswise on the bed with a view out the window of Barrett dorm across the way and the library in the distance. He wondered what she thought about Clarendon—from this angle, the college looked solid, all brick and ivy, with the library's clapboard bell tower marking the time and the setting. It looked like a college that meant something.

He told her how ciphers, secret codes to encrypt messages, had been around forever, in every culture. He told her about the ciphers of the Great War, and of Germany's Enigma code that the Allies had cracked with the help of a computing machine. He told her about the eeriness of the Clarendon computer that never stopped working, and how new and modern the whole setup was. And how computer languages were getting better and better. "So last week we learned this new one, called BASIC. Beginner's all-purpose symbolic instruction code."

"Wait, say that again?"

"Beginner's all-purpose symbolic instruction code," he repeated. "It's this simple, plain language that anyone can learn, and then talk to a computer and tell it what to do."

"Beginner's all-purpose symbolic instruction code," she said. "I like it. It sounds like something that all humans could use. We're all beginners, right? And symbolic instruction code. Like, a code for love, a code for leadership, a code for peace that all us beginners should know."

"Yeah, I guess," he said. "It's just a way to use a computer without having to know higher math."

"Uh-huh." She laughed. "I see it as something else too. It's a beautiful phrase, Sam." She leaned closer, an invitation.

"Thank you." He leaned closer too, and kissed her, the briefest brush of lips.

"You're definitely not like the standard Clarendon assholes," she said.

"Thanks, I guess." He dared to kiss her again, letting

his hand rest on her shoulder, and she kissed him back. He could do this forever, sitting here with this strange girl kissing him. He could tell her anything because she was different. Everything in the world felt different now. He let his hand drift toward her breast—she wasn't wearing a bra underneath her sweater—but then pulled his hand back, in case that was standard-Clarendon-asshole behavior. He was too hard already and no doubt she'd be gone from his room in a minute.

"It's okay," she said. After a while his shirt and sweater came off, and miraculously hers. He got up to make sure his door was locked, then leaped back onto the bed, where they lay side by side, mostly just kissing. When she pulled off her jeans and underwear, he did the same. The feel of her belly and breasts and legs against him was too much, he had no idea what to do, he was going to fail, God he was going to fail—but after another minute, she was half on top of him and he was somehow inside her. He came way too soon, after only seconds, and tears spurted out of his eyes.

"I'm sorry," he said into her shoulder, humiliated. "I didn't mean to, I mean—"

"Shh." She took his hand in hers and held on to it. After another minute she moved it slowly across her breasts, one then the other. Down her belly, her smooth skin, her remarkable skin, and down to her tangle of hair. His hand skimmed her private parts, too delicate for him to touch. She led his hand, his fingers, into them, showing him what to do. He found a rhythm that she seemed okay with. After a few minutes she rose up to meet his hand, her pelvis rocking gently, as if the two of them were one creature. She lifted her chin, and she let out a long, soft "ahhh." He could feel her pulsing into him and he watched her face, her eyes as they closed and then opened, taking him in.

He hadn't had any idea he could do that. He wasn't a virgin anymore, and now this, more than he'd imagined. She liked him, and he liked her. He was a normal guy. She smiled over at him and he was hard again.

"Now you tell me something." He'd pulled his comforter over them; she was still here, she hadn't left him yet.

She turned away, smiling. "There's so much that needs to change. Desperately needs it," she said. "Do you want to help?"

"Help? You mean a protest march, against ROTC or something?"

"Maybe."

Planning a march sounded worse than planning the annual fraternity Spring Sing, which he always got roped into. "I haven't been so into that kind of thing. I mean, I want them to end the war as much as the next guy. The whole thing is a charade. The military-industrial—"

"Exactly," she said. "But it's bigger than that. We need more fundamental changes than just ending the war. American society is completely fucked up, you know? We need to get people to sit up and take notice. We need a new world."

There had to be something he could say about American society and a new world, but he was too addled with sex and stunned by her body, electric and warm, next to his.

"Are you with me?" she asked.

"Sure, I'm with you. I'm right here." He took her hand, let his thumb trace the veins and tendons under her skin.

"No, I mean are you with *us*. With the movement."

"Sure, although—"

"Although. There's always an although around here." She let out a tired sigh.

He tried again. "I didn't mean that I'm not interested, I just meant that Clarendon's, you know, it's *Clarendon*. Apathetic."

"Right. That's what I meant too, sort of." But she looked at him, taking him in, not saying anything. "The thing is, when you know something is wrong, when you feel something strongly, you have to act. You have to *make* something happen. You can't just take it and take it."

Elodie sounded so sure. Hardly any Clarendon guys cared about anything except the next beer, or maybe the Red Sox.

"But I can tell that you care." She tugged on his arm so that it went around her, and they were face-to-face. "Action is the thing," she said. "But first you have to be open. Awake and aware about the big problems in our society."

"I think I'm pretty aware—" he said, but her gaze stopped him. "I guess I just need to know a little more."

She sat up, reaching for her sweater. "It's been lovely, Sam, but it's time for me to go." She leaned back to shimmy into her jeans and sweater, then reached up to tug her hair into a ponytail.

He wasn't enough for her. "I could do something." He pulled his T-shirt over his head. "I want to help. I could— I could—"

"I have to go to New York, but we'll see. Drive me back?"

He nodded, praying that Dougie's car was still in the back parking lot.

He led Elodie down the stairs, his usual awkwardness descending over him like the lead blanket the dentist placed on you before X-rays. At least no one was hanging around in the hallway, so he didn't have to hear the catcalls and insults that the more obnoxious guys did whenever a guy brought a girl into the dorm. Out back, Dougie's car was right where he'd left it, thank God. He pulled the keys from under the floor mat and started the car, the Beatles' "Oh! Darling" blaring out of the radio and the heater blasting cold air on them. She leaned her head on the window, arms crossed over her chest. Yes, maybe he could join the movement, make a difference. If only he had some talent, or some charisma. If only he were someone else.

"Thank you, Elodie," he said. "I really—"

"Me too." She turned her radiant smile on him, then went back to her window leaning.

He did have something to offer, he realized, and wondered why he hadn't thought of it before. "A cipher, a code," he said.

"What?"

"If you want, I'll make an encryption code for you. You can use it, or someone else can use it, if they ever need a way to communicate without any..." But now he sounded so stupid, so fucking juvenile, he had to shut up. He turned onto Topos's long driveway.

"Huh," she said. "I mean, we do have telephones these days, you know—"

"Forget it, it was a dumb idea."

"No, it's a good idea, Sam. I think I know some people who could use it. It could be a help to them. Thank you."

She squeezed his hand and jumped out of the car without saying goodbye.

She hadn't gone into town after all. He thrummed with too much feeling; she'd wanted to be with him. And now

Stephen Stills was on the radio, telling him what to do, steel drums and backup harmonies advising him to love whoever he was with. Did he love Elodie? He didn't know. Anyway, by tomorrow morning, Elodie would have forgotten him, and she'd be off planning something brave and crazy with some other, better guy—but for now he felt all right.

Chapter Eleven

"IT'S A SPECIAL INVITATION," Mom said. They were both in the kitchen after school, Rebecca grabbing some Oreos and Mom opening the mail. Mom held out the card. "It's important for us to be there."

Rebecca read the invitation. She didn't want to go. She didn't know why, but she didn't. She'd rather stay home and watch TV, or even follow Molly and Todd, wherever they were going. Okay, that last part wasn't true. She just didn't want to go to the concert.

"I know," Mom said. "Believe me, I know. It's hard. Dad should be there. But the jazz band wants to give Dad a tribute, and we owe it to them and especially to Dad to be there."

Dad wouldn't be up onstage tapping his toe, his belly jiggling, and someone else would play the clarinet. She didn't even like that stupid old jazz music, music for old people. She felt tears threatening; she was so sick of herself lately.

"Let's go out and look for something nice for you to wear, how about that?"

She shrugged because if she said anything, she'd probably cry. She didn't want the rest of her Oreos, even though she'd thrown away half her ham sandwich at lunch.

Mom took her to Dixon's junior department the next afternoon, and she picked out a dress, dark blue velvet. Short. *I'll listen for you, Dad*, she thought, checking her appearance in the dressing room's three-way mirror. *I'll let you know how the concert goes.*

The night of the concert, she slipped on the dress, her tights and her short boots. She stood in front of her mirror swaying back and forth the way Molly's sisters Kath and Lacey and the other high school girls did, so her hair swung out behind her. She felt tall and grown-up, even a little bit pretty. She tucked her hair behind her ears and took the stairs two at a time.

As the auditorium filled up, some women Rebecca didn't know sat down with them, and Mom introduced her. One who taught biology, another who taught English, and then Louise, who she did know. Louise leaned over and asked her how school was going, and which class was her *least* favorite, which surprised her.

"Earth science, it's so boring," Rebecca said.

"It'll get better," Louise said. "School, that is. And maybe you'll go to Clarendon." Louise began to tell Rebecca about coeducation, that Clarendon might go coed before long. Rebecca had so many questions about that, but the houselights blinked and dimmed, and the stage filled with a group of boys, one of the choral groups. They launched into "Just My Imagination," and they made it sound even nicer than the radio version. The one boy who sang the lead sounded so full of longing that she felt like running up there and taking his hand to console him. Could only boys sing this kind of music? Because she wanted to sing like that when she was in college.

When the jazz band took the stage, a man with a mustache announced that they were dedicating their performance tonight to Oliver Desmarais, a stellar clarinet player and a wonderful history teacher. The band stomped and yelled, while the audience clapped loud and long. Louise and Corinna both let out whoops as if they were at a football game. Rebecca saw Mom wipe a tear and then put a hand to her face, as if she couldn't believe what she was hearing.

"Five-six-seven-eight," Rebecca heard from down in front, and the band's horns played a staccato introduction to "Take the 'A' Train." Those horns sounded so festive. The song flowed into another familiar song, one of the albums Dad used to play on the stereo. *Dave Brubeck*, she read in the program. All around her, Mom and the other women snapped and swayed, kind of dancing in their seats to the jazzy music. Thank God no one from school was here to see her with these weird older women.

She looked around at the theater, at its concrete walls, its long mesh curtains. Kind of modern and bare, the opposite of the little English library. She'd never looked closely at this place. *So what*, Molly would say. *What is there even to look at?*

I don't know, she'd answer. *It's just that my dad spent a lot of time here, and I've spent a lot of time here too, and that makes it special.*

Then came another old song that she recognized, and after that "A Taste of Honey." And last of all, Ray Charles's

"Hallelujah," with a young black student singing. The audience stood to applaud after that, and now she felt like there was this bigger thing embracing her, only she couldn't give a name to whatever this thing was. It was mostly a good feeling, but kind of itchy and uncomfortable too. At this moment she wanted to be older, and she wanted to be younger. Just something other than what she was right now.

From the car, Virginia spotted Sam outside the Westfield Inn, hunched against the late-March morning. She was about to give him a ride to Boston, a little unorthodox, but somehow related to getting her own act together.

After the concert, the jazz band's version of Ray Charles's "Hallelujah" still swirling in her head, Virginia had steered Rebecca upstairs to the meeting room. She'd gotten a glass of wine for herself and a ginger ale for Rebecca, and stood with Lily and Helen. Lily said that Louise had gotten the health educator from Boston to agree to speak at their meeting.

Rebecca wandered off to the snack table, where she filled a plate with cookies. Virginia watched as Rebecca sat carefully with her plate, and crossed her legs at the knee, and as Corinna seated herself next to Rebecca a minute later. Rebecca chatted with Corinna as if she were a college student. From this distance, Rebecca looked older, taller; Virginia could see Oliver's lips and Momma's cheekbones in her face.

Virginia sighed at the passage of time and at her mess of feelings. But she felt a pulse of gratitude too. She had these friends now, and she had a job. She'd do her part, host that consciousness-raising meeting. And she had Friday off— it felt good to use that phrase, *a day off from work*. She'd take herself to Boston on Friday, get herself back into the mindset of a researcher. She felt a surge of energy: she was moving forward.

Sam Waxman, her student from last fall, passed by, and she turned to compliment him on the performances.

"Thanks," he said. "We worked hard on our set, had double rehearsals these last two weeks."

"Ah," she said. "Well, you sounded wonderful. Professional, honestly."

At the snack table, she overheard Sam talking to one of his bandmates about needing to get the fuck out of Westfield.

"I'm going to Boston on Friday," she blurted out, instead of chiding him for his cursing. "If anyone needs a ride."

"I could use a ride," Sam said. He introduced the other boy, Stephen.

"What would you do in Boston?" Stephen asked.

Sam shrugged. "Take the train to New York. See some old friends."

"You should go to jazz clubs downtown, you moron," Stephen said. He turned to her. "You know his dad runs Red Wagon Records?"

"No kidding," Virginia said. "Oliver would have been excited to hear about that. Did he, did you ever—"

"Yeah, I mean, we talked about it a little, at rehearsals sometimes." Sam was blushing. "Not that there's all that much to tell." He shrugged again.

She tried to give him an encouraging smile. "Well, give me a call if you want a ride," she said. "We're in the book, the only Desmarais in Westfield."

They got on the highway in Lebanon, Sam quiet in the passenger seat. Virginia considered telling him how when they'd first moved up here, the highway hadn't been finished. There was that scenic stretch of Route 4, the river on one side, Mount Kearsarge on the other, but so curvy and narrow that it had made little Rebecca carsick. Now they had the interstate and could whoosh along at seventy miles an hour all the way into Massachusetts. But she didn't say that; he'd only look at her blankly the way Rebecca did, unable to imagine how things used to be.

On the radio, a jazzy horn sequence opened the next song. "A-a-a-nd up next, we've got 'What's Going On,'" the DJ announced, in an unnecessarily dramatic voice. "By Ma-ar-ar-vi-in Ga-a-aye!" Sam asked if he could turn it up a little, and she nodded an okay.

He drummed on his corduroys, and after a minute he sang along. Marvin Gaye had the loveliest voice, a voice full of grief about the war, the riots, everything wrong with today. Sam too. "You have a nice voice, Sam," she said, as the song wound down.

"Thank you," he said. "I've been trying to work out an arrangement for the Granitetones, but I haven't figured it out yet."

"You should," she said. "It's a great song." She thought of those mothers of sons in high school and college, having to listen to Nixon saying that the war was ending, but first they needed to finish invading yet another country in order to push back the creep of Communism.

She asked about his classes and he said something about computers and running equations on the mainframe computer. "There's this new language you can use to run it, and also these smaller computers they have there. It means that now anyone can use a computer."

"A new language, wow." She couldn't make much sense of his description, but his enthusiasm was wonderful to hear.

"President Weissman says that pretty soon there are going to be little computers everywhere. Someday everyone can have one in their school or their office."

"Wow." She tried to picture a grown-up Rebecca sitting in an office, feeding punch cards into a computer, all while talking to someone else at the next desk, as if that was no big deal.

On the radio, a Carpenters song faded away and the CBS Radio News minute began. "As reported earlier, the US Capitol Building was bombed early this morning. We have reports of a demolished men's lavatory, and possible damage to the structure under the Senate side. No reports of injuries or fatalities thus far." A sound of papers rustling, then the newsreader starting again. "The Weather Underground has claimed responsibility for the bombing, which they say is in protest of the United States' invasion of Cambodia."

"Ohhh," Sam said. He covered his eyes with his hand, as if he couldn't take this kind of news anymore.

"Are you okay, Sam?"

He shook his head and blinked. "Uh, fine. Sorry. It's just that, I mean, when is this war ever going to be finished?"

She started to say that bombing federal buildings wasn't the way to force an ending to the war. But what was the way? The protests hadn't done it, Congress hadn't done it, Nixon certainly wasn't doing it. Instead, she asked Sam whether he knew any of the vets on campus.

Only one, he said. "Jerry. He's a good guy, and he—" Sam stopped. "Most of the vets think we're pampered morons. Which I guess we are. But this guy Jerry is okay, we've gotten to be friends, I guess."

The bombing news and talk of vets and the war seemed to have upset him, so she looked for safer conversational territory. She mentioned Copley, the reason for her trip to Boston today, and Copley's time in London, how he'd turned into a major portrait painter in England, like Gainsborough or Reynolds, even though he'd come from the colonies.

"An American," Sam said.

"Right, although there wasn't such a thing yet. He left Boston in 1775, and he stayed in England during all the years of the Revolution."

"Ha. Smart guy."

"Yes, he was. Very canny."

"I liked your class," Sam said. "I didn't know anything about that stuff, and now I do. I impressed my mom talking about Caravaggio and chiaroscuro." He pulled a notebook out of his backpack. "Math," he said, and bent to his work, still nodding along to the radio.

In Boston, she parked on Huntington, and she pointed out the T stop and told him how to get to South Station, where he could catch the New York train. "Are you going to be okay?"

"Sure. I take trains all the time," he said. "I'm from New York, remember?" He grinned; he'd straightened up and he looked more confident standing on this city sidewalk. A bit of lightness bubbled up inside her—it was good to feel useful—and she laughed and waved goodbye.

Inside the museum, the American gallery was quiet. Only two other women here, who stood in front of Sargent's picture of the Boit daughters, the girls in their corners staring out at the viewer, except for the one half-shadowed girl, who faced away. Sargent's early portraits, especially of children, were appealingly creepy.

She girded herself and strolled past the Copleys, taking them in as a group. *Watson and the Shark*, Sam Adams, Mercy Otis Warren. The early Boston portraits had more verve. *Paul Revere*, 1768: his gaze was direct, and here he sat in his shirtsleeves, engraving tools before him—Revere didn't pretend to be a gentleman. Maybe she could draw comparisons between Copley and Sargent, how their years in London changed them, forced them into a stylistic corner.

Midday, Virginia went downstairs to the basement cafeteria, ate a sandwich and a cookie, eavesdropped on a table of old ladies in cardigans. She thought about Copley and Sargent, Copley's precision and Sargent's loose brushwork, the way they handled fabrics and other surfaces.

After lunch she wandered into an exhibit of American portraits, and found herself standing before two pendant portraits, a Philadelphia husband and wife. She considered the wife's lace collar and cuffs, indicated with only dots and dashes of white over black, the blue and yellow brushwork making the nap of the black velvet dress gleam softly. "Sarah Miriam Peale, b. Philadelphia 1800; died Philadelphia, 1885." One of the Peales, perhaps a daughter of Charles Willson Peale, who'd had all those children, all of them artists. Virginia studied the two portraits. *You must take me seriously, for I am a man of means and ambition*, the husband's gaze said. *Perhaps, but you whimper in your sleep*, the wife's calm eyes answered. As a grad student, Virginia had dismissed the Peale brothers as boring, as mere disciples of Copley who'd never achieved the aliveness of Copley's portraits. But now she wondered about this Sarah Miriam Peale, how she'd gained these skills as a teenager and made these portraits at age twenty-one, so long ago. She wondered what else this Miss Peale had done, what other pictures she'd made. Maybe Virginia could focus on Miss Peale's portrait work instead of Copley. But already she could hear Professor Kimball at Harvard: *Come now, Virginia, the quality just isn't there. I'm sorry to say it, for the Peales are such an interesting family. But you must spend your time on artists worth studying. Go back to the Ashcan School, you wrote good papers on them.* Professor Kimball wouldn't mention Miss Peale's femaleness and how studying a female artist would put Virginia at a disadvantage; he wouldn't need to.

Outside, the afternoon had grown mild, too warm for March. The grass on the museum's little curve of lawn was already greening up. She paused on the top step to take in the springlike day and the people below who were using the museum steps as lounge chairs, enjoying the sun and the mild weather. Halfway down, a young man sat writing in a notebook and eating potato chips from the bag. Dark hair, duffel coat, backpack; she felt a surge inside, felt herself smiling. Sam hadn't gone to New York. She'd have someone to ride back to New Hampshire with. Maybe he could have dinner with her and Rebecca, or they could go out to Mo's. She could ask him if he—

But it wasn't Sam. It was just another dark-haired college student, awkward long legs thrown out in front of him. Her chest and neck prickled with heat—she'd wanted his company too much. She'd been too happy to see him.

She wondered what Oliver would think. She was only trying to help—Oliver would have done the same thing, wouldn't he? He *had* done the same thing. He'd taken plenty of students out for a coffee or a beer over the years, had called her to say he and a couple others had to stay late, an emergency meeting about this student or that student. Still, her cheeks burned with the realization that she'd been thinking about a college boy.

She took two wrong turns getting back to Storrow Drive, where the Friday-afternoon traffic crept along. To her left, across the filthy but glinting Charles River, the outer buildings of Harvard asserted their quiet brick majesty: Cambridge, where she'd been a whole other person. She imagined an alternate self, still dressed in her grad-school black turtleneck, black skirt, black tights, even now striding from point to point in Cambridge, unencumbered by a failed dissertation, by pregnancy, birth, miscarriages, an unhappy untenured husband, a dead husband.

On the radio, a single muted trumpet coaxed Dionne Warwick to sing about love. *"What the world needs now,"* Dionne sang, her voice lifting with the melody. Oliver had made fun of Burt Bacharach; he thought Bacharach's tunes were treacly, but Virginia loved this song.

When she'd first met Oliver—Houghton Library, they'd first encountered one another there—and they'd gone on a few dates, she'd made a list of the things that weren't right about Oliver, to talk herself out of him.

—He didn't like dogs. Okay, he sort of liked dogs, but he didn't love them.

—Or cats.

—He lectured—he got going on something, started discoursing on the Wars of the Roses, the Spanish Civil War—and he couldn't stop himself.

—He had way too many opinions about music. Like her,

he was the youngest in his family, and he had three older brothers who'd taught him about early jazz and the big-band greats. Chick Webb, *Stompin' at the Savoy*. Louis Prima. Benny Goodman. Ella Fitzgerald singing with Dizzy Gillsepie. She liked all that stuff too, she just didn't want to talk about it, or listen to Oliver go on and on about it.

On the other hand:

—He was smart. Sharp. And funny.
—He was optimistic and idealistic. He believed in progress. He'd believed in Stevenson, had campaigned for him, even though it drove his brothers and his mother crazy. *Oliver, you used to work in* banking, they'd said, accusingly, as if that meant everything. *Not anymore*, he'd answered.
—He was cute. Blue eyes and freckles and red-gold hair. He would always look young, or at least youthful.
—He loved her. He thought she was the most beautiful thing.

As she crossed the border into New Hampshire, the traffic thinned to nothing. On the radio, the hourly news report led with the Capitol bombing, noting that a guard had gone to the hospital suffering from smoke inhalation. An expert speculated that the Weather Underground would strike again, since that was the way these organizations worked. "Terrorizing people in waves of attacks," he said.

She snapped the radio off. Insulated in the museum, she hadn't given a thought to this bombing; it was remote, nothing to do with her. But she felt herself standing again in the MFA, imagined a bomb going off in the Rotunda, the old Copleys and Sargents, Miss Peale's portraits of the young husband and wife, ruined by fire and smoke, the building crumbling around her. She pressed hard on the accelerator, to get home faster.

Pushing open the door of the apartment, Sam yelled that he was home. He'd asked the doorman to call up to his mom before he got into the elevator, to give her a little warning.

"What's wrong, Sam?" Mom asked. He hadn't come home to New York for a random weekend since freshman spring, had he, so why now, she wanted to know. Her eyes were big and fearful, ready to exclaim about whatever his reason for coming home might be.

"Nothing. Nothing's wrong, I just wanted a weekend away."

"Okay. That's fine," she said. "I'm glad to see you, just surprised. I'll make spaghetti for dinner, won't that be nice?"

"Sure, Mom." Should he tell her he was probably going to meet Elodie? But he didn't know when or where, or even if it would happen. He'd brought Elodie's letter home in his jacket pocket, touching the thin paper, ragged where she'd torn it out of a notebook, every time he slid a hand into the pocket.

"Umm, there's this girl—" But he realized as the words popped out that he should have said nothing. His mom's eyes grew even bigger, and she hugged him and said how wonderful, and that she was so happy for him, as if he'd just said he was going to graduate Phi Beta Kappa.

He'd given too much thought to Elodie's secret code. A simple shift cipher, he'd decided, but maybe he could add another level to it, complicate it. Elodie herself was a cipher, he thought. He might not be able to understand her, but he'd enchant her with his cipher, he'd show her how to use it to encrypt and decode messages, and they'd send secret messages to one another. He'd worked on it in a corner of the library's basement study room, scratching away in his notebook. He stayed up late after house meeting, copying the encryption keys onto clean paper in neat block letters and numbers, and at last, he held the papers up, pressed his lips to them. His first gift to her. He slid the cipher into an envelope, wrote her name on the front and his name on the back, and kissed the envelope too.

He'd borrowed Dougie's car the next morning to take his code to Topos, where he found Cyril, the commune's dad, at the long kitchen table, inscribing numbers into two big ledgers. "She's on her way to New York," Cyril said about Elodie, pulling off his reading glasses and gazing up at him.

"Right," Sam said.

"With Hank and Shelly," Cyril said. "Elodie's got an aunt down there, a town house or something that they think I don't know about."

Sam nodded as if he already knew that.

"Anything else?" Cyril didn't say, *Join us, Sam, you belong here with us*, or *Why don't you come along with me to the tractor place?* He slipped his reading glasses back on—he just wanted to finish his bookkeeping, the gesture said; all these young people were getting on his nerves.

"Nope," Sam said. "I better get back, I have class."

Elodie's letter had arrived the day of the jazz band concert. Sorry, she'd been back to Topos for only a day and a half, and now she was planning to stay in New York for another week or two. Thanks for the cipher, and was he heading to New York anytime soon? Let her know, okay? Maybe she could help him get involved in the Movement. *Movement* with a capital *M*, she'd written. She'd scrawled a New York phone number at the bottom of the letter.

On Saturday morning, he sat in the coffee shop on Waverly Place where he and Tommy always went. Except now Elodie sat across from him as they waited for their food. Last night, when he'd called the number Elodie had given him, he'd had to leave a message. And then it wasn't Elodie who'd called him back but some other guy, who said that Elodie had to go out but she would meet him in the morning, that he should just name a place downtown. He tried not to think about these other guys and what Elodie might feel about them.

Elodie was dressed wrongly for the blustery weather, a T-shirt and jeans, and a sweater that didn't look all that warm. She'd wound her long hair up into a topknot. He wanted to say something about her hair, how it was subtly beautiful, even when it was tucked away into a knot, but he was afraid he'd accidentally insult her, and she'd say beauty was a capitalist construct, or something.

She was talking about some new project for the Movement. "I can't tell you all the details, not yet, but it'll definitely make a difference. So are you with us? Do you want to help?"

"Uh—I—"

"We've got to act big, to make people notice."

"In New York?" he asked.

She did that head-tilt thing, yes, no, maybe.

"Is it—is this anything like the Capitol bombing?" He didn't know why he'd just said that. She wasn't in the Weather Underground. She was just an activist, and also a person who liked to cook. A person who liked to talk about love.

She gazed at him. "There are people who need your help, Sam."

"Someone could get hurt, or killed," he said, testing. She didn't contradict him; she waited, hands folded under her chin, elbows resting on the table. If only they could talk about her remarkable eyes. If only they could walk around the Village holding hands—he'd put his arm around her to keep her warm, and she'd lean into him.

"What kind of help?" he finally asked.

She pressed her knuckles against her lips, thinking. "Just some technical things, things you're probably an expert at."

She was about to ask him to do something dangerous, something dumb or criminal. He didn't know how to answer her.

"You're not with us, are you?"

"We're college students, Elodie. And I don't know who 'us' is."

She laughed. "'Us' is all of us, if you think about it. I just want things to be better. I want people to stop getting killed. People are dying every minute. The world is more fucked up than it's ever been."

He wanted to laugh at her hypocrisy—whatever group she was involved with was planning something violent. Was it Weatherman? Their food arrived, and he took a quick bite of eggs. This morning he'd passed a vet who sat on the sidewalk outside the West Fourth Street station, silently panhandling, and he wondered for a second if the guy had ever encountered Jerry. It had been a stupid thought, and he'd dismissed it. The image of the panhandling vet returned to him now, and he wondered what the guy would say to Elodie.

She picked up a triangle of toast and used it to gesture at him. "There isn't a lot of time, you know."

"Maybe I could, I mean, there's tons of stuff to do at Clarendon, maybe I could organize something—" But the guys at Lambda Chi would only laugh and say, *Yeah, right, Sam. No can do. Go back to being chaplain, that's what you're good at.* And the ROTC guys would beat him up. Elodie didn't understand Clarendon at all. Still, he wanted her passion, her certainty. He wanted her to love him, or at least to admire him a little. He took a breath, let it out. "Yeah, I could do something at Clarendon," he said.

She smiled. "Shake up that patriarchal, military-industrial-trainee cocoon. It needs some shaking up, doesn't it?"

He nodded, arranging his face into a smile too, trying to imagine what she meant by shaking up, and an electric thrill of desire and fear ran through him.

"Something symbolic," she said. "Something that stands for tradition, for Clarendon's role in the military-industrial complex." She'd ordered only toast and coffee, and she ate another toast triangle as she mused on what Sam could do at Clarendon.

A bizarre image of Clarendon's computer on fire settled in his head. Computers were a force for good, just think of all the things you could do with them, all the things Weissman wanted them to learn about programs and languages. But Weissman had gone to Los Alamos with Feynman during the war and had worked on the bomb. Although that was just the lore around campus, maybe it wasn't even true. The atom bomb had ended the war; it was justifiable use of a terrible weapon against a nation that refused to quit fighting. But now the bomb was part of the Cold War. And by extension the war in Vietnam. His head hurt with this spiral of competing thoughts, and his bacon was undercooked and flabby. He'd just wanted to see Elodie, to touch her, to sleep with her. That wasn't going to happen. She was different down here.

He wanted to tell her all that was good about Clarendon. There had to be plenty of other guys like him, wandering around on their college campuses and not quite fitting in. They just wanted to find their place. They wanted to figure themselves out, as they waited out the draft. As much as he didn't fit in, as much as he got teased and made fun of, he kind of loved Clarendon. If only Elodie were a plain old Clarendon student—if Clarendon had magically turned coed—maybe she'd have more normal-size goals. Maybe she'd be as apathetic as the rest of them. And Sam wouldn't have to go to such extremes to sit across a table from her and lay eyes on her.

"I can see you've got some doubts, Sam." Elodie rested her head on her hand. There was her beautiful smile again. "But I'm glad you're thinking about it. We'll give it some thought too. Something a little different."

Who was this "we" she kept talking about? But he only nodded, as if he thought it was a good idea too.

She slid out of the booth, pulling two dollar bills out of her pocket and pushing them across the table. "I've gotta run." She stood up, then leaned down to hug him. As she did so, he moved a little to the left so he could kiss her. His mouth connected with hers, but she was businesslike, pulling away and straightening up too quickly. She slipped away, back through the narrow coffee shop, and she didn't turn and wave as she went out the door. She'd never answered him about the Capitol bombing, hadn't said that whatever she was working on, it was nothing like that.

At the pay phone in back, he called his dad's apartment and said he wanted to come by.

Chapter Twelve

DAD HAD MOVED TO the West Side after the divorce, to the Apthorp, one of those rambling old buildings on upper Broadway. Sam needed to bring them something, but what did you bring a baby? Baby Adam. He didn't know if Adam had had a bris; if he had, Sam should have been there. He had no idea what baby Adam might want. A blanket? One of those red-and-blue shape-sorter toys, like he'd had when he was little? He should have thought to ask Elodie for some ideas. But she'd probably say that baby toys should be banned, since they were part of the military-industrial complex. He climbed out of the subway at Seventy-Second Street, the West Side smelling of garlic and bagels. He spotted a bookstore across the street— a book. No one could argue with that.

The children's section was upstairs. He circled the little room, all bright colors and posters, with colorful rugs on the floor, not sure where to begin. Two girls sat cross-legged against a wall, reading, and a plump older woman asked if he needed help. After he managed to say that he was looking for a book for a baby, she steered him to the babies and little-kid section. He let his eyes adjust to the colors and shapes of all these books for tiny children, and then he spied the pink-and-pale-blue *Pat the Bunny*—he remembered this one, how he'd loved the soft powdery smell of this book. He lifted it to his face, and the smell took him right back to childhood. Yes, he'd get *Pat the Bunny* for baby Adam. Adam would have the exact same experience Sam had had as a little kid looking at this book, doing all the little activities, smelling it over and over. At the register, the woman slid the book into a shopping bag. "Boy or girl?" she said, and when he answered "boy," she cut long strands of blue ribbon, curled them with the blade of a scissor and tied the curls onto the bag's handle. She smiled as she handed the bag to him. "What a thoughtful young man you are," she said. "Have a wonderful day."

Yes. Yes, he would. He still felt off-balance from the morning, from his weird breakfast with Elodie, as if he were walking sideways, but maybe the rest of today would be wonderful.

By the time he got to Dad's building, he'd lost that feeling. His gift was stupid, it was just a little papery book. Dad clearly didn't want him to visit, or he'd have invited Sam sooner—the baby was more than three weeks old. He started to turn away, to head back across the park to his own apartment. No, he wouldn't chicken out. He'd just drop off the book and say he couldn't stay. He owed at least that to Adam, his little brother.

Dad's apartment building had one of those interior court-yards; you went through a gate and under an arch, and there you stood in this spacious garden, big patch of grass in the middle, trees and flowerpots and benches along the edges. God, he would have loved this courtyard if he'd lived here when he was a kid. Little signs marked the edges, Keep off the Grass, Stay on the Sidewalk. He imagined his child-hood self running and jumping on the grass, and the door-men yelling at him, *Hey, kid, get off the grass.*

Patty, Dad's new wife, was the opposite of Mom, super smiley and okay with whatever Dad said. When Sam had called Mom from outside the subway to say he'd be home in a little while, but was going to make a quick stop at Dad's, she'd been quiet for a minute.

Of course, Mom had said. *I don't want you to get too—* She'd paused. *Never mind, just give them my best, okay?*

In the elevator, unhappiness jabbed at him. He didn't want to see Dad with a baby, the whole idea was preposter-ous, but he forced himself to trudge down the hall, which smelled of other people's cooking because so many people lived here. Dad's door was propped open; Sam knocked and went through.

In the tiny kitchen, Dad was setting bagels on a platter, cream cheese and lox on another plate, and he came for-ward, platter in hand, hugging Sam with his free hand. Dad wasn't a big hugger, so that was a surprise. Dad smelled like always, but a little sweaty too, like he hadn't had a shower.

The apartment had only modern furniture—plasticky translucent chairs and a small glass dining table, and a weird couch with no arms—but it was cluttered, a basket of di-apers on the floor, laundry in another basket, tiny soft pajamas draped over one of the translucent chairs. The apartment was a one-bedroom, and Sam wondered where they kept the baby.

From the couch under the window, Patty called a hello. The baby lay on Patty's lap sleeping, his tiny hands clasped under his tiny chin. Patty wore a baggy blue top, and she looked awful, her skin too shiny, dark circles under her eyes. She turned her face up for a kiss.

"Hi, Patty." Sam handed her the bookstore bag. "That's for the baby. I'm sorry it's so small."

"Oh," Patty said. "I'm sure it's lovely. Thank you, Sam." She leaned forward to call to Dad. "Sam brought a gift, Harry."

"Great!" Dad's voice was so hearty and fake that Sam had to hold in a laugh.

"Go wash your hands and you can hold the baby," Patty said.

He did so, then scooted in next to her on the couch. It was an uncomfortable couch, kind of stiff, the seat part too wide, and he leaned back a little, trying to get himself situated. Baby Adam had a head full of black hair, which seemed a little weird, and he asked about it.

"It's falling out already, see?" Patty said. "Pretty soon he won't have any left."

"Is that okay?" Sam asked. "Is he okay?"

"Sure, it's fine."

"That's like you, Sam, remember?" Dad said, taking a seat across from him. He bit into a sesame bagel.

"How would I remember that?" Sam said.

"From photos, dumbass—"

"Harry," Patty said. "Is that necessary?"

"Sorry, Sam, I'm a little tired."

"That's okay," Sam said, surprised at Dad's quick apology.

Patty handed him a clean diaper. "Put that on your shoulder." She lifted the sleeping baby up, her arms cradled underneath. "Here you go." The baby rested against his chest now, soft head leaning on his shoulder. His own big hand covered the baby's entire back. Baby Adam made a sighing sound, but he didn't wake up.

"Just like that," Patty said. "See, you're a natural."

Sam's eyes teared up, shit, he was going to cry. Patty's eyes were shiny too. "Isn't he a sweet little thing?" she said. "He's just got his days and nights mixed up, that's all. He wants to be awake all night."

"Tell me about it," Dad said. "We're all exhausted. I don't remember it being like this."

"That's because Adele probably had a baby nurse." Sam heard the edge in Patty's voice.

"You're right, sweetheart, there was a baby nurse. Irish woman. Man, she was something. Very bossy, kept sending me away, barely let me see the baby—barely let me see you, Sam. Then Adele's mom came for a month. Yeah, they kept sending me away, sending me back to the office."

Baby Adam snuffled, moving his little head from side to side, as if he needed to wipe his tiny nose on Sam's shoulder, then let out a bleat of a sob. Sam turned Patty's way, not sure what to do. Patty reached over, gently lifting the baby up and back into the crook of her arm.

"Just going to feed him now." Patty and the baby disappeared into the bedroom, which left him alone with Dad. Sam got up to get a bagel.

"How're you doing, Sam?" Dad said, after Sam sat back down. "I'm sorry it's been a while. This has been—" he threw an arm out to indicate the messy apartment "—a lot. And there's just a whole lot of crap at work right now."

Dad did look pretty tired, the lines from mouth to nose deeper than usual.

"Yeah," Sam said. "Everything's fine, school's fine." He wanted to tell about Elodie, and he even wanted to tell about the jazz band's tribute concert last week, how together they'd sounded, for once. Too many things to tell. "The baby seems good," he said. "Healthy, right?"

"Right," Dad said. "He's a good baby. Like you were. Except you didn't have your days and nights mixed up like Adam." He leaned close, lowered his voice. "Patty's a little emotional, but that's to be expected, I guess. I'm too old for this."

Dad asked him how his classes were going, so he talked about Weissman's class, how he'd gotten a lot more proficient with the mainframe and had been part of a group that sent a message from one computer to another, from Clarendon down to IBM headquarters in Armonk. He didn't mention the project with Jerry or the cipher he'd made for Elodie.

"Huh," Dad said. "IBM, huh? So it's a class about the computer?"

"It's a math class, but with a computing component. For my major."

"Huh," Dad said again.

Sam waited for Dad to make one of his usual cracks about worthwhile majors and crap majors, and striking out and doing things on your own, the way Zayde Waxman had done.

"I always knew you were really smart," Dad said, and he swatted Sam on the knee, which caused Sam's half-eaten bagel to slide off the plate and onto the floor.

"I always wanted to go to college," Patty said, from the

bedroom doorway. Baby Adam was on her shoulder, asleep again, conked out as if he'd been kept awake for days. She smiled down at Sam. Now she'd probably tell him to make the most of college, that these were the best years of his life, the way grown-ups always did.

"I don't even know what to say to that," Dad said.

"You don't need to say anything, it's not a comment about you," Patty said. "Make the world a better place, Sam. I know you can do it."

Virginia took her time cleaning up after dinner. As she scrubbed the casserole pan and stacked the clean dinner dishes, she considered her coworker Jeannette, her ease and lightness as she moved around the reference room. In her pantsuits and color-block dresses and short layered hair, Jeannette was youthful, but she showed the same authoritative yet cheerful manner with everyone. Jeannette wasn't cowed by the sharp demands of endowed professors like Frank Randolph (at the reference desk, Virginia had hidden behind a stack of books when he'd come in looking for an antique book of maps, not wanting to face him). And Jeannette wasn't irritated by the silliness of the boys' questions, or the way some of them draped themselves across the desk, trying to flirt with this nice young librarian, hoping she might offer to do their research for them.

"I love finding out new things, don't you?" Jeannette had said. "Any time someone asks me how to find something, I learn something too. Yesterday it was Darwin and barnacles, a little while ago banknotes and coinage in colonial America. Now tell me more about Miss Peale, what you've got so far."

Virginia had told Jeannette about writing to Professor

Kimball at Harvard, how she'd described this new research thread, Sarah Miriam Peale's portraits. But she didn't have the confidence to declare that this, *this*, was worth her while and everyone else's. To study Miss Peale's influences—Copley, obviously, and the old masters, Rembrandt, though the old master pictures would have been copies—and her place as a working artist in a prosperous young America. But what had allowed Sarah Peale her own confidence? Sarah Peale had said, *Here I am, hire me, I know what I'm doing as well as my male cousins, as well as my father and my famous uncle.* Sarah Peale's sister was also a portraitist. Maybe Sarah and her sister hadn't known any better, had just gone charging ahead.

She rinsed the percolator, filling it with coffee grounds for tomorrow, then crossed the hall into the den to draw the curtains. Rebecca slouched on the couch, watching *The Brady Bunch* just as she used to do every Friday night. It made Virginia feel tender for her daughter, but to say anything would wreck the moment, so she just sank down to watch TV too.

Carol Brady was supposed to be a widow, Mike Brady a widower, though you'd never know it. The two were flat and undamaged, twinkly with wry humor. Maybe that was because they'd each found their perfect counterpart. *Or maybe that's because they're made of cardboard*, Oliver would say. On the screen, Mike, Carol, and daughter Jan were in Mike's home office, Jan crying about a disastrous day at school.

The Partridge Family, which came right after *The Brady Bunch*, was more of the same. Until now, Virginia hadn't noticed that Shirley Partridge was alone, widowed or divorced. Shirley Partridge too was wry, eye rolling, full of witty quips, and all her kids bouncy and cheerful. No one was drunk. No one was angry. Whatever the problem of the week was, it was cute and solvable.

During the ads, Virginia reminded Rebecca about the women's meeting. Rebecca half listened, eyes on the screen, watching the cheerful, singing McDonald's workers. Those goddamn women's libbers, Virginia's dad would have said, if he'd lived long enough to read about the marches, the movement.

Was she a women's libber? Long ago, at Smith, she'd felt she belonged. The girls came from all over, from New England, but also California, Texas, Wisconsin, and Virginia. "Virginia from Virginia" or "V from V," her freshman hall mates called her.

Senior year, other girls had lined up teaching jobs, and two were going home to work in their families' businesses, a newspaper in Pennsylvania, a bank in Ohio. Two were headed to grad school in education. And one brilliant girl, their valedictorian, to medical school. Virginia was none of these things. She'd thought about art history, had sent away for information about graduate programs, but she wasn't sure, the way everyone else was. At last she went forward with grad school; she'd just keep doing what she'd been doing these four years. If she'd had the certainty and confidence of a Sarah Miriam Peale back then, where would she be now?

Maybe when Rebecca got to college everything would be different. No more white gloves at dinner and on dates. Coed colleges everywhere, coed dorms, coed bathrooms. No grouchy, suspicious housemothers looking to keep all the boys out, out, out.

"Why are you looking at me like that," Rebecca said, eyes on the TV.

"Oh, nothing. Just thinking about college, how different it will be for you from how it was for me."

"Well, duh, Mom, of course it will be different. You went to college a long time ago."

"In the olden days, right?"

"Uh-huh. When everything was black-and-white."

The evening of the meeting, Virginia waited with Helen and Lily. They'd decided—well, Louise had decreed—that it would be best to run an informational meeting with expert speakers, the woman who'd started the health collective in Boston, and later branch out into smaller discussion groups. Virginia had been relieved and irritated in equal measure—relieved because the idea of hosting such a meeting felt a little embarrassing, and irritated because Louise sometimes acted imperiously, like the Louise that Oliver used to complain about.

After Louise had reserved the largest Clarendon classroom, they'd all worried that no one would show up. Helen had spoken with one of the exchange girls, who'd said she and a couple of others wanted five minutes to talk about their own project, something about coeducation. And Virginia had told Jeannette, who'd suggested making a flyer—that was what the college kids did, didn't they?—so Virginia had typed up two notices, pinning one on the bulletin board outside the library's stacks, and one at the town library.

Tonight the room felt too big and echoing, more auditorium than classroom. Virginia checked the snack table, where they'd set out oatmeal cookies, popcorn, chips, punch. She pushed the napkins around, restacked the cups, as if a good-looking snack table would guarantee a successful meeting. Louise was still outside waiting for the speakers, who were driving up together from Boston, one from the Boston chapter of NOW, the other from the Boston Women's Health Collective.

At last two women came through the door, women Virginia had never seen before. Helen steered them to the sign-up sheet. Then Jeannette! Virginia had to give her a hug, she was so glad that someone she knew had shown up. Next, four exchange girls. They must have called on friends at other schools, because a minute later there was a whole clump of them, twenty-five or thirty.

And then Eileen and Gerda. Virginia went to greet them. Eileen let out a high-pitched giggle, and said Paul didn't have any idea that she was here tonight, and that she couldn't stay long.

"Does it matter?" Gerda asked.

Virginia imagined Oliver's reaction. He'd be peeved, disapproving. Or maybe, like Eileen, she wouldn't have told him where she was going tonight. She pointed out the snack table to her neighbors, and when she looked again at the rows of chairs, she saw that the classroom was nearly three-quarters full. And still a few more women came through the door.

Virginia made her way to the front row. Louise was seating the speakers at a table at the front of the room, and she nodded at the four of them.

Louise stood next to the speakers' table, waiting for the room to quiet down. She thanked everyone for coming out on a rainy night. "We're at the start of something big here, and we're happy to introduce some wonderful speakers."

She read the National Organization for Women's mission statement, and asked the group to welcome NOW's Boston representative.

The NOW woman wore a maxiskirt with a blouse tucked into it, her long hair pulled back in a low ponytail and granny glasses that slipped down her nose, an old-fashioned look. Virginia chided herself; appearance wasn't what mattered, yet it was still the thing she noticed first.

"Let's have a show of hands," the NOW woman said, smiling out at the group. "How many of you have applied for a mortgage? Not you young college women, but the householders among us." Hands went up here and there, and the NOW woman waited a beat. "How many applied without a husband?" The hands disappeared.

"How often do we talk about how difficult, sometimes impossible, the banks make it for a woman to get a mortgage, a loan, even a department-store credit card, without a husband's signature and approval? That's right, we don't talk about it. Yet we all know it."

The NOW woman began to talk about the differences in men's and women's salaries, how a woman with a graduate degree earned only as much as a man with an eighth-grade education. The audience groaned. "We're nearly three-quarters of the way through the twentieth century, but women are trapped in a nineteenth-century world."

As she described NOW's platform and the rights the group were calling for, the woman's voice took on the cadence of a chant. Virginia sensed the exchange students in the rows behind her getting to their feet, as the rest of the audience clapped with enthusiasm. She felt the zing and spirit of all the energy in the room; her hands burned from clapping and she began to feel like she was part of something.

The second speaker, older, plump, with short curly hair, stood up and waited for her handouts to be passed from one person to the next. Stapled-together pages, Boston Women's Health Collective: A Guide. There weren't enough handouts, so people had to share, leaning in together to look.

"We think it's time for a new movement of woman-centered care," the speaker said. "The patriarchy has done women terribly wrong, teaching us all the wrong lessons and giving us the wrong kind of care. From an early age, we're taught *not* to value our own bodies and our own capabilities." Virginia peered at the Health Collective's booklet on Helen's lap, and got a glimpse of hand-drawn illustrations, female and male reproductive systems.

"One of our goals is to help women stop feeling shame about their bodies," the speaker was saying. "Here's a simple exercise. You can try it here, in the restroom, or in your own bedroom at home. Learn what your own genitalia look like—*yes*, you can do it," she said, as gasps and giggles rippled around the classroom. "You simply take a hand mirror or even a compact, and examine yourself. Taste your own secretions." Another series of drawn-in breaths and suppressed laughs.

Virginia felt her temples and chest warming, felt the urge to laugh out loud. She stared up at the wall clock so as not to burst out laughing.

"If anyone wants to see herself, I've set some hand mirrors on the table over there." The speaker pointed to her left.

A young woman squeezed past her friends and made her way to the table, smiling back at the other young women as if she were accepting their dare. She picked up a mirror and left the classroom, using the mirror to wave at her friends. The girls buzzed and whispered, and a few more followed the first one out of the classroom.

Helen elbowed her. "Oh, good Lord, they're going to do it right in here," she whispered. Virginia followed Helen's gaze to the far side of the room, where three or four of the girls had gone to sit on the floor, and were now pulling jeans down and skirts up. They sat cross-legged or with knees up, bending over and gazing at their own private parts with compact mirrors. They were laughing, enjoying themselves, comfortable in their self-imposed nakedness. Near the back, someone had left the room, the door banging shut.

"Is that legal?" Virginia asked. "Should we—"

"I'll block the door," Louise said. "We don't want any men wandering in." She sprinted to the door and stood against it, covering the door's narrow window.

The speaker was still talking, oblivious to the undressed girls in the back. "Because after all, you are your body and *you* are *not* obscene."

Obscene. Those girls were baring their private parts in front of each other. What if a campus policeman wandered into the room? Would they all be arrested? Virginia wasn't brave—God, she'd never be as brave as those girls sitting in the corner, who now calmly tucked blouses back into skirts and jeans as if they hadn't been essentially naked in a room full of strangers.

Louise signaled to Virginia to take her place guarding the door, and once Virginia got to the door, Louise hurried to the podium. "Wonderful, thank you," Louise said. "We're so pleased to have you here and to learn more, and we're eager to help the Women's Health Collective in whatever way we can." She shook the speaker's hand. "Let's all get ourselves organized." She cleared her throat, looked at the paper in her hand. "We have one more item on the agenda, so Coeducation Now, would you come forward?"

The young woman who'd been the first to take a hand mirror, but who at least had done her examining in private, marched to the table, with two others close behind her, a general with her lieutenants.

"We *demand* coeducation at Clarendon," the young woman said. "We don't ask anymore, because politeness doesn't work. We *demand* it." Her voice grew louder, higher-pitched. "We demand our fair share of what the men in this nation have always had. The best educations, the best jobs, the best memberships. We demand a decent share of that."

"Coeducation now, equal rights now! Coeducation now! Equal rights now!" The young women, these brave, foolhardy girls, led the chant, standing up and clapping. One girl climbed up onto her chair, and the others followed. Virginia slowly stood too, clapping and chanting like the others. But she felt prickly and hot, uncomfortable with their noisy, shrill demands.

But what if this kind of chanting had taken place twenty years ago and the men's schools had gone coed back then? She could have gone to one of the men's schools for college, and they wouldn't have been *men's schools*, they would have just been *schools*. She clapped her hands together until they stung, to make up for her own discomfort.

A flashbulb popped; a Clarendon boy was in the room. He stood just inside the door, camera lifted to his eye, taking pictures of the girls standing on chairs with their arms overhead. He took shot after shot, angling himself to take in different views of the classroom. Virginia hustled back up the aisle and grabbed the boy's arm, to try to steer him out of the room. "This isn't a campus meeting," she said. "This is a—"

"Let go of me, lady!" He shook off her arm, lifting his camera again.

"I'm sorry, but you'll have to leave now." Virginia had to yell to make herself heard over the noisy chanting and clapping. She stepped in front of the boy and his camera, waving her arms, so he couldn't take another picture.

"Let's go, buddy," Louise said, next to her now.

"Your flyer didn't say anything about no photos," the boy said. "Your flyer made it sound like you *wanted* people to come. You can't kick me out!" Still, he'd lowered his camera and now he backed out of the room, making exasperated sounds.

At the door, Louise watched to be sure that the young photographer had left, then closed it behind her, blocking it with her body as she'd done before. The exchange girls' chanting grew raggedy. Soon the room rustled and buzzed as women bent to gather coats and umbrellas or stood to leave, talking to one another. Louise was a still point in the noisy room, her eyes on the floor, fist pressed against her mouth, thinking.

"With any luck, he didn't get any incriminating photos," Virginia said.

"Who even knows what's incriminating these days," Louise said. "And he's right. It was a meeting on campus, he had the right to know what was going on, and maybe we should be glad of the publicity." She nodded, as if to agree with herself, but she didn't look glad.

As the other women filtered out of the classroom, Virginia caught only fragments of their chatter, but it sounded lively, the way people sounded when filing out of a theater after a funny movie. Still, as she watched Louise move to the front of the room, back to the two presenters, Virginia thought of Corinna, who wasn't here, who'd made it known that she thought this kind of meeting was a bad idea. *I can't afford to rock the boat*, Corinna had said during that dinner when they'd first talked about such a meeting.

At the snack table, Virginia emptied the pretzel bowl into the trash and picked up stray cups. "It was an inspiring night," she said as she passed Helen, who stood eating a leftover cookie.

"Yes, it was," Helen said. "I'd like to think we're making a difference, but…" She trailed off. "Well, what's done is done. Thanks for your help, Virginia," she said, brisk again.

Virginia had been dismissed, but she didn't take it personally. Helen was worried, just as Louise was. And they hadn't even ended the meeting properly, hadn't asked the women to set up discussion groups of their own.

Chapter Thirteen

REBECCA TRIED NOT TO keep count, but Molly had ignored her for at least three days. She told herself that it was only because they weren't in the same homeroom this year. She had Mrs. Dorfman, her favorite, *favorite* teacher in the world, and Molly had boring old Mr. Beasley, and kids always hung out more with the other kids in their homeroom. At midmorning break, she tried not to notice that Molly leaned against the wall between Jenny Sorenson and Sydney, whispering.

At the soda machine, Rebecca worked to strike up a conversation with Beth Karpas, who was a so-so friend, but Beth was only interested in Ben, who stood nearby in his group of goofball followers, talking about the grossest things they would eat or drink. Beth paid too much attention to that clump of stupid boys, laughing at whatever they were saying. Ben wasn't even cute, not like Todd, Molly's

190 • SARAH McCRAW CROW

boyfriend. But maybe Todd wasn't Molly's boyfriend any-more. She didn't know what was up with Molly these days.

At the end of seventh period she hurried out of the school building and then hung around by the bike rack, examining her fingernails and watching for Molly.

"Hey," she said, when Molly came through the door by herself, thank God. Rebecca started to walk, hoping it looked like she'd been doing something, not just hanging around like a fool, waiting for Molly.

"Hey." Molly looked straight ahead toward the Claren-don football stadium in the distance, as if she had to think about where they were headed.

"So how was Todd's—"

"My mom says your mom is a bad influence and I might need to find some new friends."

"*What?*" Bad influence? Mom? What the hell.

"Your mom had this meeting that she invited my mom to, and it turned out to be a bunch of radicals. Communists, my mom says."

"Communists? My mom's not a Communist. She's just a mom." This made no sense. Mom had gone to a meeting the other night, but it was something at the college, something academic. Mom had gone to it with Louise and her other new professor friends.

"It's all this women's lib stuff, you know?" Molly looked at her sidewise for a second, then looked away. "They don't want anyone to have a *family*. They want to make it harder for families to survive."

Rebecca had only a rough idea of what women's lib was, or what it had to do with families, but she knew better than to ask why Molly cared. "Maybe your mom got the wrong idea."

Molly closed her eyes, probably exasperated at Rebecca's obtuseness. "My mom was *there*. At the meeting. It was a bunch of radicals, and your mom is one of them."

Such a hot, stinging mess of feelings and questions. If it was such a radical meeting, why was Mrs. Koslowski there? None of this made any sense. Still, Rebecca had been mad at Mom for so long, had felt deeply that so many things were Mom's fault, that Mom had been doing just about everything badly since Dad died, embarrassing Rebecca over and over. But now she got an image of herself next to Mom during the jazz band's concert, how she'd felt that night in her velvet dress, as if she'd already moved on to high school. And then that surprisingly interesting conversation she'd had with Corinna, who'd asked her about her hopes and dreams as if she were a college student, not some eighth-grade kid. Also, Mom was just Mom, someone who made Brunswick stew and pudding cake, and Corinna was an interesting person and a professor, who thought Rebecca was someone worth listening to.

Molly shrugged. "Anyway, we have to stick to good Catholic values."

Rebecca stopped, but Molly kept walking. "I don't even know what that means," Rebecca said to Molly's back. "I'm not Catholic. My mom isn't, either, but she's not a radical. She's a—she's a good person. See you later." She started walking again, angling away from Molly. It wasn't like Molly was an angel. She knew that Molly had drunk beers with Kathleen and Lacey one weekend when their parents were away and Kath and Lacey had had a bunch of friends over, and that Molly had puked. Rebecca turned left at the corner, as if she'd been meaning all this time to go downtown after school, instead of back to their neighborhood. All she wanted was to go home, but she didn't want Molly to see that she was upset.

A few minutes later, she found herself on Main Street, the wind blowing hard down the street so her hair went flying up around her head. To get out of the wind she turned into the stationery store where she and Molly used to go because the front section had bins full of funny cute things, wind-up toys and tiny stuffed animals, weird dice with too many sides, pencils that wrote in four colors at once. She had a dollar, maybe she'd buy something. But the grouchy owner watched her, frowning as if she were about to steal from him. She wished he'd go back to the register, or go sort the birthday cards. How could someone so grouchy have such a great supply of toys? She bought a mini yo-yo for thirty cents, even though she didn't need a yo-yo and it probably wouldn't work because it was too small, but she was a good person and she would never steal anything, not even a stupid thirty-cent yo-yo.

Helen called to tell Virginia about the front-page article in the college newspaper, with the headline Girls Go Berserk! The article had gotten a lot of the details wrong, Helen said. The reporter had called their meeting "a strident, shrieky push for coeducation," and it made no mention of NOW, the Boston Women's Health Collective or the self-examinations (thank God). But the second paragraph noted Louise's presence, calling Louise the leader of the meeting. "Not even correctly reported," Helen said. "But I have a feeling there are going to be some repercussions."

"You mean Louise? But she has tenure."

"We're all *women*, Virginia. It doesn't take much. And to be seen running an unsanctioned meeting with so-called berserk exchange students who aren't welcome here in the first place, that's more than enough."

Maybe Corinna had been right, Virginia thought now. Better to keep one's head down and work, work harder than the men, but keep quiet. Still, no one had gone berserk, and the idea of repercussions for a mere meeting seemed terribly out of balance. She wanted to act, to do something, but she didn't know how. "What are we going to do?"

"I don't know," Helen said. "For now, wait and see, I guess."

A day later, the *Westfield News-Ledger* had it too: At College Meeting, Speakers Advocate for Women's Rights, Demand Coeducation at Clarendon, the big headline on the front of the paper's local section blared.

"Ugh, they made us sound like a coven of witches," Virginia said, and Rebecca leaned across the table to see.

"Molly said that you're a radical, and you've gotten mixed up with the wrong kind of people," Rebecca said. "I told her she didn't know what she was talking about. Her mom is all upset about families or something."

"Eileen? She was at the meeting too." Virginia tried to recall whether Eileen had left the meeting early, before the shock of the girls viewing their own private parts in public. She hoped so, but the sound of the exchange girls' noisy demands and the flash of the student's camera, and his rudeness, had taken over her memory. She'd been a little brave in jumping up to stop the student photographer, she thought. Or maybe she'd been too careful, merely fearful that the meeting, and her own small efforts, would be made public, and ridiculed or shamed. All that energy she and Louise and Helen and Lily had felt at the start of the meeting, when the room had filled up with so many women, and when the NOW woman spoke so persuasively—all that wonderful energy had dissipated once they'd shooed the Clarendon boy out. She'd seen the resignation and worry on her new friends' faces.

"None of this would have happened if Daddy were still alive." Rebecca slapped the paper down.

"What does that have to do with it?" Virginia let out a breath as she waited for Rebecca to plunge into another hormone-fueled tirade. But Rebecca said nothing more, just took her dishes to the sink, where she rinsed them quietly, then left the kitchen to finish getting ready for school.

Virginia stayed at the table, the offending article staring up at her. None of this would have happened if Oliver were still alive. She felt her breath catch in her throat, at the surprise that she could hold this thought and not break into sobs. She was moving on, a little, and this new knowledge made her feel strangely despondent.

After Rebecca left for school, Virginia read the article again. The only women quoted were a student, who was identified as one of the Coeducation Now leaders, and the representative from the National Organization for Women; the article said that female faculty at Clarendon had organized the meeting, but it gave no names. No mention of the exchange girls taking off their clothes to examine themselves.

Maybe it was strange that Virginia hadn't thought to examine her own self, that the idea of it had sounded silly to her. *You are not obscene*, the speaker had said.

In the downstairs bathroom, she found an old powder compact in the medicine cabinet. She sat on the closed lid of the toilet, slipped off her underwear and opened her robe. She angled the tiny mirror, but could only see a sliver at a time: her pubic hair, coarse, dark and vaguely shameful; a slice of her vulva, pink and glistening. She touched herself experimentally, leaning back against the hard, cold top of the toilet. She tried to tune in to what felt good, as the booklet from the Women's Health Collective had advised, and felt her breath moving in and out faster. The phone rang, and she leaped to her feet, pulling her robe tight around her, and she ran to pick it up, face burning as if the caller had seen what she'd been doing.

"Professor Desmarais?" a familiar voice said. "This is Sam Waxman." She managed to greet him normally, her underarms prickling with sweat. "I'm sorry to call so early," Sam said. "I have kind of a weird request, and feel free to say no." He was talking about a campus musical competition, asking her to help out. "Anyway, it would take about an hour, hour and a half," he was saying. "For some of the guys it's a big deal. It's one of those dumb Greek traditions and every year I end up getting—"

"Sure." She'd been holding her breath; she let it out. "I'd be happy to do that. It sounds like fun. I'm surprised Oliver never judged this competition."

"Oh, *God* no," he said. "I never would have asked Ol—Professor Desmarais—sorry, that came out all wrong. It's just not the world's greatest competition, that's all. It can be a little dumb. Do you want some time to think about it?"

"No, I'd be happy to help judge. Thanks, Sam."

The thanks were all on his side, he said. He told her the time and place, and said he had to run to history class.

Chapter Fourteen

SAM NEVER SHOULD HAVE agreed to help Dougie Perkins recruit judges for Spring Sing—that was his first mistake. He owed Dougie for borrowing his car, and he figured he'd want to borrow Dougie's car again, to get to Topos and to find Elodie whenever she came back. If she ever came back. But as usual Dougie demanded more, asking Sam to emcee the competition.

"No," Sam said. "Ask Stephen. Ask one of the deans."

"Come on, Sam, all the old traditions are dying, no one wants to emcee, I'm out of ideas here. We can't just let Spring Sing die, can we?"

"We can," Sam said. "It's always terrible. It should be put out of its misery."

"But you know what to do on the stage, you can keep things moving and it's hardly any work. Come on, man!"

And now here Sam was on the Sunday afternoon of Spring Sing, running the whole damn competition, and doing the stupid master of ceremonies thing. Even after he'd said no. He was the worst kind of pushover.

Professor Desmarais and her daughter stood in the aisle, Professor Desmarais smiling up at him, and her daughter with her arms crossed, hugging herself, probably wishing she was somewhere else. He hopped down from the stage to show them to the judges' seats, front row, marked with Reserved signs, as if anyone cared about getting a front-row seat to this stupid event. Professor Desmarais introduced her daughter, Rebecca, and they all talked for a second about skiing.

"This is such an honor, Sam," she said. "I'll do my best." Rebecca rolled her eyes at this, Sam noticed.

"Thanks, but don't get your hopes up," he said. "The singing can be kind of horrendous." Rebecca laughed, and Mrs. Desmarais shushed her, and said she was sure the singing would be fine.

"I mean, it's a nice tradition, it's been going on for a long time, and everybody does their best, it's just—"

She stopped him with a hand to his arm. "I get it. I'm still happy to be here."

Behind her were two more judges: Professor Jernigan from the math department, his hair every which way like a ten-year-old's; and Mrs. Martin, the provost's wife, who could have been a friend of Sam's mother, with her poufy blond hair, frosty lipstick and pink knit pantsuit.

And last, Jerry. "Thanks, man," Sam said.

"You owe me big-time, man," Jerry said. "Giving up my Sunday afternoon for this. Do not tell *anyone* at Topos about this."

"No, man, I'd never do that." He did owe Jerry big-time, and not just for Spring Sing. He handed the judges their clipboards, mimeographed papers and pens attached. Dougie had made a grid on the paper: frats and honor societies listed down the left, with spaces for notes and numbers. Each group would sing two or three songs, Sam told the judges, who all gazed at him, listening, even Jerry. "You decide the points for songwriting, musicianship and showmanship, so to speak. I appreciate your willingness to do this," he said. The four judges laughed and said reassuring things, that they'd do their best, and Jerry patted him on the back, as if Jerry were one of the grown-ups too.

Now Sam stood at the side of the stage, watching as people trickled in to Frazier Hall. The exchange girls were seating themselves in the front row. There were a lot more girls here this year; maybe the others were girlfriends cheering on their boyfriends.

Dougie poked his head out from behind the curtain. "Five minutes, man."

Sam nodded, and went to tap the microphone to test it once more. Most of the sound in Frazier Hall came from backstage, where two-thirds of the school population was right now. He heard shouts and bursts of laughter, as guys shuffled and stomped around on the back stairs.

Dougie flashed the houselights. "Two minutes," he called.

That nauseated feeling Sam always got before going onstage rose up in him, along with a heavier sense of resignation. He'd get harassed and be the butt of a new round of jokes at the next house meeting, all for agreeing to stand up here like a jackass. He hated stupid Frazier Hall with its uncomfortable folding seats and its narrow balcony in back. He hated this whole fucking place. He didn't belong here. He started to turn around, to say, *Sorry, man, I quit, I can't do it this year,* when a flash of something, a movement at the door, caught his eye.

Elodie.

She stood near the back of the hall, taking in the scene. She walked up the aisle, cool and contained, her long silvery -brown hair loose over her shoulders. She didn't sit with the other exchange girls, but alone.

Elodie was back at Clarendon. For whatever reason, Elodie was here and he was caught, paralyzed, stuck onstage. But Dougie, behind him, had just called out an okay for Sam to get started. As he pulled his notes out of his blazer and walked to the center of the stage, Sam wished like hell that he could beam his thoughts to her—*You know I'm not one of them,* he'd say, *I don't belong here.* But all she'd see on the stage was another fraternity jackass. Unless she'd come to see him. He felt a prick of hope.

"Welcome," Sam called, his too-loud voice bouncing back at him. "Welcome to the sixty-first annual Clarendon Spring Sing Competition," he said. "We have some stellar groups competing today. But first, let's give a round of applause for our excellent judges!" He named them, pausing to let the audience clap as each judge gamely stood and waved to the crowd.

"The groups will perform in random order, as selected by the head of the Interfraternity Council, Dougie Perkins. And now! I give you—" he paused again, as if to build up suspense "—the Phi Rhos!" He faked a smile and stepped off the stage.

The curtain rose on the Phi Rhos. In their coats and ties, hair slicked to the side, the Phi Rhos stared out at the audience. Sam felt a moment of pity: these guys were scared. One of them stepped forward and started snapping, and the group launched into "Under the Boardwalk." Their voices wobbled and went off key, but they weren't terrible. The next song was a version of "All Shook Up," the lyrics changed but indecipherable. The Spring Sing tradition was to take current hits or old standards, rewriting the lyrics to mock other fraternities or teachers, or Clarendon itself.

Theta Chi followed, with a decent performance. The boys whooped and elbowed each other as they exited, pleased with their bawdy lyrics about road trips to find girls who were willing, about the Dekes who went looking for sheep and cows to screw, and lonely Saturday nights in the observatory.

Then Robe and Mortarboard, a senior honor society. They harmonized well, probably because they had two Granitetones and two glee club members. Then Sig Ep, who sang bland old Clarendon songs, but at least they sang on key. This was going okay. When Lambda Chi's turn came around, he'd slip over and sing with them.

Kappa Alpha took the stage. Assorted preppy assholes and burly guys who played hockey or lacrosse. Each of them held a piece of paper. Most groups didn't use props, and KA didn't usually take part in Spring Sing. They started a song, to the tune of "Farmer in the Dell" and lifted their little signs so the sparse audience could see. NO CO-HOGS, the signs said. The song was about co-hogs, they didn't want any fat, ugly co-hogs at Clarendon.

Sam took in the judges' reactions. Mrs.—Professor—Desmarais's eyes were wide, her cheeks red. The provost's wife frowned and raised herself out of her chair to look around the auditorium for help, and Jerry had a hand to his forehead, shielding his eyes. Then, from the audience, a ripple of movement. The exchange girls were bending down to reach under their seats. They stood as a group, lifting their own posters over their heads, to face the stage and the KAs, then slowly pivoted toward the small audience. "Coeducation Now" and "Join the 20th Century, Clarendon," their posters said. It seemed everyone had a plan for today, except Sam.

The KAs began another song, shouting instead of singing about college girls trying to be boys, and how no Clarendon guy would ever want to get it on with them.

Dougie raced up the side stairs onto the stage, pulling Sam back to the center. "Say something," Dougie hissed. "Before we get completely screwed and the whole school gets put on probation."

Sam flipped the microphone switch. "We're going to have a brief intermission," he said, as the second stupid KA song wound down. Guys from other frats emerged from backstage; some shook the KAs' hands, while others grabbed at the signs.

"What do we do now?" Dougie rasped, then leaned into the microphone. "Guys! Only one group on the stage. Give the others their turn! Come ON!" But no one was listening, and the exchange girls began to shout in unison about coeducation, running a kind of protest march down the aisle to loop around the front and back up again.

"We've gotta stop them, we gotta get everyone off the stage." Dougie moved into the fray, but Sam hesitated. Why was it up to them to corral all those assholes? And now he took in Elodie marching up the aisle with the other girls. He didn't know if this was her gig, or if she was just helping out, but he had to do something to show his solidarity with her. If he had to get violent to bring these guys under control, then he'd do it. He stepped into the fray, and as forcefully as he could, he grabbed at the nearest navy blazer. The guy spun around: Teddy Burnham. Of course. Teddy Burnham, number-one asshole.

"Don't touch me, you fucking pansy-ass," Teddy Burnham yelled, and before Sam could duck, Teddy had punched him in the nose. Sam reeled back, bending over in pain that sparked outward from his nose to his eyes and head. He put his hands to his face, wet with blood and snot now. He had to clobber Teddy, that was all. He straightened up and started to swing. But Teddy had moved away to wrestle with someone else, leaving Sam alone. His vision wavered and shimmered, the floor tilting up at him—and then he was horizontal, down on the hard floor, dizzy and cold. He let himself lie there, eyes closed.

He heard someone shouting, mouth too close to the microphones. It was one of the class deans, who must have been in the audience all along. "That's enough, *that is enough,*" the dean shouted into the microphone, but the brawl kept going behind him, loud and stupid. The auditorium was a roar of noise, the boys onstage yelling, as the exchange girls chanted, *"Coeducation's time has come! Coeducation's time has come!"* Elodie. Where was Elodie?

From the floor, he opened an eye, squinted out at the exchange girls. Elodie watched him from the aisle as she chanted and marched with the protesters. She moved away from the protesters, took a step toward him, then another. She was going to come to him. Yes, and she might even be proud of him. At last, they would be together.

His field of vision was blocked by someone leaning over him. Professor Desmarais. And behind her, Professor Jernigan.

"Sam?" Professor Desmarais yelled. "Are you okay? Looks like you fainted."

"I'm fine." His voice sounded thin and lame.

"Let's just get you upright here," she said. Professor Jernigan lifted him by his armpits so that he was half sitting against the wall just beyond the stage. Professor Desmarais pulled a pack of tissues from her purse and dabbed at his face, as if she were his mom. "Henry's going to get ice, he'll be right back."

It wasn't as noisy onstage as it had been a minute before; some of the guys must have left. Sam could see Jerry and another guy standing like rock-concert roadies at the front of the stage, arms crossed. The girls moved in a slow line back down the aisle and out of the auditorium. Elodie hadn't climbed onto the stage to check on him; that had been too much to hope for.

He scanned the auditorium, his vision blurry in his right eye. Elodie was gone.

"Mom, what are you *doing*?" he heard someone say. "You're not even—" It was Professor Desmarais's daughter, peering at him. "Eww, that looks bad."

"I don't know where Henry's gotten to. Maybe you'd better go on to the infirmary," Professor Desmarais said.

She didn't need to fuss over him like this. He just wanted to find Elodie. "I'm fine, I'll just go to the gym and get some ice from the trainer. It's no big deal." He started to stand, getting to one knee and then lifting himself up. He felt like shit, his nose throbbing, right eye blurred, head ringing.

"I can at least give you a ride," Professor Desmarais said.

A dean and a campus policeman ran up the aisle toward the stage, where only two other students remained, Clarendon guys not being as stupid as they looked. Sticking around would mean they'd get written up for ungentle-manly behavior, and their frats put on probation.

"Sorry, son, I'm going to have to write you up," the po-liceman called to him.

"Don't you dare—" Professor Desmarais got to her feet, propped her hands on her hips. "This boy did his best to keep the peace and got beaten to a pulp for trying. I don't know where you've been all this time but you're definitely talking to the wrong person. Go talk to the Kappa What-evers, they started this whole mess. Honestly. For good-ness' sake." She bent down again. "Come on, Sam, we'll give you a lift."

Sam didn't want a lift, he wanted to find Elodie. But he didn't want to talk to the police or the deans, either, to answer their questions because they were too moronic to figure things out on their own. "Okay," he said. "Thanks."

Professor Desmarais walked on one side of him, Rebecca on the other, both of them seeming to think that he might pass out again. She'd parked close by, along the college green, and it started to rain as he slid into the back seat. A minute later, as they turned the corner, his eye caught Jerry on the green in the rain, talking to someone and using a newspaper as an umbrella. Elodie: Jerry was talking to El-odie. He had to get out of the car.

"Um, would you mind letting me—" he began, but then Jerry leaned in to say something to Elodie, holding the newspaper over both their heads. No, Jerry was lean-ing close to kiss her. Not a you-take-care-of-yourself-old-friend kind of kiss, either. The kind of kiss that was real and long, a deeper connection with her than what he'd ever had.

"Yes, Sam?" Professor Desmarais met his eyes through

the rearview mirror, and Rebecca, next to him, looked at
him too.

Sam needed to jump out and run across the green, to
belt Jerry and grab Elodie. But he reached too fast for the
door handle and the movement made his eyes swim, his
head and nose throbbing at the sudden movement. Jerry
and Elodie. Elodie and Jerry. Of course. It had been that
way since before he'd met either of them. And she wouldn't
have been proud of him for being part of such a stupid,
establishment kind of thing; that was a joke. He slumped
back against the seat. Everything he did turned out wrong.
"Uh, nothing. Never mind."

At home, Mom steered Sam to the couch in the den,
saying, "There now, sweetie," just as she did whenever
Rebecca was sick, then hurried off to get a bag of frozen
peas for his nose and eyes, calling over her shoulder for Rebecca to turn on the TV, an unnecessary reminder. Rebecca found the Red Sox—a college boy would like the
Red Sox, she figured. She asked him if he wanted a soda,
and he nodded, looking at her through his uncovered eye.
She went and grabbed two from the fridge, and now Mom
had returned to the den, telling Sam to take these aspirin
and put these cotton balls in his nostrils. Yuck.

"You just rest for a bit, Sam, and we'll get some supper
ready," Mom said.

This was so weird. Rebecca wanted to call up Molly
and say, *So there's a college boy in my house! Right now! The
singing competition went completely nuts today and he got beaten
up. He was in the jazz band with Dad, and Mom was worried
about him, so...* No, it sounded too weird. Anyway, she had

to show Molly that she got it, she understood that Molly didn't want to be friends anymore.

Over spaghetti, Mom peppered Sam with questions. Sam held the ice pack against his nose, answering politely. Rebecca could see that he didn't want to be here, that he just wanted to go home, and Mom was being her usual clueless self talking too much.

Mom was getting ready to drive Sam back to his dorm when the phone rang. "He's fine, just needs to keep some ice on the eye, maybe visit the infirmary in the morning," Mom said into the phone. "Yes, if you don't mind." Mom covered the mouthpiece and told Rebecca and Sam to hang on, go watch TV in the den for a few minutes, as if she and Sam were both eight years old. They both obediently left the room.

The Red Sox were over, and *Wonderful World of Disney* had started. Tonight it was a mystery about a teenage girl. Sam wouldn't want to watch that, so Rebecca got up to change the channel.

"You can leave it there," Sam said. "It doesn't matter."

"I don't watch that kind of—"

"Your dad was a good guy," he said.

"Oh," she said, surprised. "He was—" She heard her voice start to waver. "I always cry a little when I start to talk about him but then I'm fine. My dad was weird, but he was the best."

"I'm sorry for your loss," Sam said.

"Thank you."

"Your mom is nice too," he said.

She felt herself shrugging, not quite willing to agree. "She's not doing so well. I mean, she doesn't have many friends." Neither did Rebecca, but she didn't want to admit that.

"Ha, I don't, either, these days," Sam said.

Rebecca laughed. "I was just thinking the same thing. My best friend isn't talking to me."

"My best friend was kissing the girl I like," he said. "Maybe *best friend* is a stretch, but still, he's a friend and it was a blow."

"That's terrible," she said. "He's not a very good friend, then. Maybe he's just a jerk."

"Maybe." Sam smiled at the TV, where the teenage girl was arguing with her dad, who wore a policeman's uniform.

Rebecca considered whether she'd kiss him if she were his age, and decided no. But maybe that was because of his scary black eye and his gross swollen nose. Still, he seemed like someone she might be friends with if she were in college. "So why do you like this girl?"

"I don't know, it's a little hard to put into words," he said. "She has nice eyes, she's smart. She always has a cause. You know, things she cares about. She wants to make a difference."

"Like today?"

"Yeah, kind of. So how about you?"

"Me? Oh, no, nothing. Well there's this one kid, Josh. He seems kind of nice, but I…" She stopped. She wanted to explain how she sometimes wished she were a different person, in a different family. Maybe like Molly's family, with big sisters to advise her on clothing and makeup, and a strict dad, well, maybe not like Molly's dad. But a dad.

Sam nodded. "Yeah, I know what you mean, it's hard to know sometimes."

Mom was still on the kitchen phone, talking too loudly. Why did Mom always have to be so embarrassing? Rebecca apologized for Mom, then heard herself starting to tell him about Mom's meeting that was in the newspaper, as if he was a friend and not some strange guy. She blurted out that her friend Molly had stopped talking to her because Molly thought Mom was a radical.

"Ah, so your friend isn't very open-minded, is she?" Sam said. "Let's make a pact. We'll hold out for friends that aren't jerks."

"Ha," Rebecca said. He had his hand out, and she slapped him five. She felt herself blink at the strangeness of sitting here, talking to this guy as if they were the same age. She was glad Mom rescued Sam today, she realized, not that she could ever in a million years say that out loud to him.

Mom called that it was time to go. "Professor Jernigan thought you were very brave, Sam," Mom said, and Sam lifted his uninjured eyebrow at Rebecca, making her laugh.

In math class, Professor Jernigan, not President Weissman, stood waiting at the board. "Emergency meeting," Professor Jernigan said, when they were all seated. "President Weissman was called away. You got me instead today."

"What's the big emergency?" Jerry asked.

Sam rolled his eyes at Jerry's comment, which made his nose hurt. The skin around his eye had gone through a rainbow of colors, blue-gray to green, and now greenish yellow. His nose was still red and painful, but less swollen today. Jerry didn't notice Sam's eye-rolling; Sam hadn't had much of a chance to give Jerry the silent treatment, since Tuesday's class had been canceled.

"Meeting with some of the trustees. If I had to guess, I'd say the singing competition last week captured their attention, and the trustees want to know what's up. But since I've got you fellows this morning, have you talked about time-sharing language already? No? Okay, then. You'll need this when we get the network up and going." He turned back to the board.

Out on the sidewalk after class, Sam took in the May morning, bright and clear, more summer than spring, guys around him talking about a beach trip and Frisbee on the green. He sped up to break away from the cheerful summer-weather talk. Jerry caught up to him a minute later, as they passed the library.

"Hey, Manhattan," Jerry said. Sam scowled at him. "Bad night, huh?" Jerry asked.

"I saw you together," Sam said. "On the green. After Spring Sing." He didn't say Elodie's name or mention the kiss in the rain.

Jerry looked away, gave a little nod to the air. "So we had a thing, a while back. I was, I was trying to get her to see reason."

"You never told me you had a thing with her," Sam said, and he felt the flimsiness of his retort. Elodie didn't like him enough to see him for more than that too-brief meeting at the Waverly Place coffee shop.

"Listen, I got no claim on her," Jerry said. "But you should stay away from her."

That didn't add up. "Why?"

"She has too much money, she's too sheltered. She doesn't get it," Jerry said, not answering his question. "She's either in way over her head, or about to be."

"She's not a stupid girl," Sam said. "She's one of the most—"

"I didn't say she was stupid," Jerry said.

Sam didn't want to hear any more. "I gotta go." He started to run.

"She's at Topos. There's some meeting late tonight," Jerry called.

Sam didn't turn around to ask what the meeting was about.

When he considered whether to go to Topos later, that vision flew up at him, Elodie and Jerry together, kissing in the rain on the Clarendon green, as if they were reenacting *Love Story*. And he was just a loser. His right eye gave a little throb, as if to say, *Yep, that's right, buddy, you are a loser.*

No, he wasn't a loser. He was a guy who cared. He would go talk to her, that's what he'd do. Dougie's car wasn't in the dorm lot, and he didn't want to go over to Lambda Chi to start asking around. He started walking north with his thumb out.

At the Tavern's entrance, Virginia scanned the tables, spotting Louise and Corinna in one of the far booths. Corinna waved across the room, and Louise lifted her glass in greeting. The bad news had arrived, Helen had said earlier, on the phone. "Louise got the notice, her tenure status is officially being questioned," she'd said. "We're meeting at the Tavern, if you want to join us."

Virginia wove around the tables, the Tavern half-full, and slid in next to Corinna. When she saw Helen and Lily coming down the stairs into the basement restaurant, she signaled to them. She wanted to thank them for including her, but that would be silly; they'd gathered for Louise, that was all.

"Another round," Louise said, marking a circle with her glass. The booth was a little too small for five, Virginia between Corinna and Lily as if they were high school girls, squeezed together because that was the way they always did it.

"To moral turpitude," Louise said, after the waiter set their drinks on the table.

"To moral turpitude," they answered, clinking glasses.

"And personal misconduct," Louise said.

"I just don't see how—" Virginia said.

"There are a few things that can lead to your tenure getting questioned or taken away," Helen said. "Personal misconduct and moral turpitude. But no one knows what moral turpitude even means."

Louise finished her drink too quickly, swirling the left-over ice so a piece shot out and skittered across the table. "It means you're a woman, that's what it means. If you're a man you can get away with countless bad behaviors, you can hit on students without any consequence, and you can be a bad teacher, a terrible researcher, never bother to publish again. But if you're a woman—"

Helen put a hand on Louise's arm. "What did they say?" she asked gently.

"They said that because I've been encouraging radical behavior in young women, who as everyone knows are more impressionable and potentially less morally fit than young men, they're going to hold a hearing to determine my status. I'm officially on probation. And apparently the exchange program for the girls is under review. If they cancel it, it's all on my head." She raised a hand to get the waiter's attention.

That strident pushy woman, Virginia heard Oliver's complaint from the past, echoing in her head, and *Louise shouldn't be grandstanding like that...the Clarendon boys only gave her the faculty award because they don't know any better...* At last she understood what Oliver had been saying, and worse, what the other men had meant when they'd nicknamed these women the Gang of Four, as if one woman's tiniest achievement or advancement meant they'd all be clamoring to take over the place. What a clever and insidious nickname. "This is wrong," she said.

"Thank you," Louise said. "Although easy for you to say, since your job isn't on the line."

"Maybe there's no place here for a woman," Corinna said. "I'm sorry I wasn't at the meeting. I should have been there."

"That meeting." Louise smiled around the table and started to cry.

"Louise didn't do anything wrong." Virginia looked from Corinna to Helen to Lily. "It's bullshit," she heard herself saying—the first time she'd ever cursed. "It's absurd to pretend that young women are less morally fit than young men. All we have to do is walk two hundred yards into one of the frats if we want to see the opposite of moral fitness. And Louise has *tenure*."

"Let's get some dinner," Helen said.

They drank two carafes of wine with dinner, and Virginia listened as the others told stories of bad behavior by men on the faculty, and the weaselly administrators who couldn't cope when there was a controversy, who made excuses, or created committees to study issues, instead of making a decision.

It was late, after ten o'clock when they left the restaurant and as they walked in a clump toward their cars, music floated over them from one of the outlying frats at the edge of campus. The thump of a bass, twangy harmonies, *"Down on the corner, out in the street..."*

"A party," Louise said. "Let's go." She swayed, an unstable giant half dancing, half stumbling.

"It's a frat party, Louise. That's not for us," Corinna said.

"Let's go find some moral unfitness, like you said, Virginia," Louise said.

"Oh, well, I—" The music was coming from Delta Mu, Oliver's old frat. "Oliver used to go there sometimes, to have a beer."

The others turned her way, staring openmouthed. "*Oliver?* He did?"

Virginia took in their horror. She'd never thought it wrong, only a little strange, and yet also endearing, that Oliver went to his old fraternity on homecoming and other alumni weekends. "I mean, it was his fraternity back when he was an undergrad, and he went over there now and then." The music sounded enticing now. "We could go in for just a minute, see what it's like," she said. "I've never been inside a frat."

"Yes, let's." Louise strode off in the direction of Delta Mu. "Moral unfitness for all."

"Come on," Virginia said, following Louise.

"No, that's a hideous idea!" Helen said. "The frats, they're the worst of everything. They stand for—hell, they *are*—the patriarchy. Louise, listen to me! What in the world are you thinking?"

"I'm thinking that I played by the rules my whole life, and look where it got me," Louise called over her shoulder.

"All right, Virginia, *you* said it's fine," Lily said. "So go on. Go keep an eye on Louise."

It wasn't fine. She needed to think before she spoke. She swallowed and nodded. "Okay, I'll make sure nothing happens."

"I'll go with you, Virginia," Corinna said. "Safety in numbers."

"Good luck, then. We're going to call it a night," Lily said, and she and Helen set off for home.

A knot of young men clustered outside the frat's front door, laughing about something. Louise swerved around them to the side of the house, where another door was propped open. The three of them followed a student through, entering a short, unlit hallway where a couple clutched at one another, and then a large wood-paneled common room filled with Clarendon boys and their dates, most of them dancing; the whole room had been turned into a dance floor. The lights were low, but Virginia could see that rugs had been rolled up, furniture pushed back against the walls. The room smelled of beer, sweat and cigarette smoke. They followed Louise as she wove around the party, a few students whispering and pointing at Louise, and one boy offering them beers from the rack he carried. The beer was flat, yet not unpleasant.

A song started. It was that Nancy Sinatra song, the one about the boots. "Woo! Woo!" a girl yelled. The whole room danced and sang as one organism.

"Right on! Professor Walsh is here!" Virginia heard a boy say. "Let's dance, Professor Walsh!" Louise wiggled and stomped, trying to match her partner's moves.

"We should go," Corinna said, the two of them at the edge of the dance floor, watching Louise doing her awkward dance.

"I'll get her," Virginia said. As she moved into the fray a boy took her hand. The music had changed, one of those Jackson 5 songs that Rebecca used to sing along with. The boy lifted her hand to twirl her, and she let herself twirl away, then back again, holding his hand. The drinks had hit her, and that moment of twirling had made her feel years younger; she felt like she'd just learned something new and magical. She was having fun.

The music changed again. "What the fuck, Chip?" someone yelled into the momentary quiet. "Who's your old lady?" The boy dropped her hand and slid away, and Virginia felt her body heat up in shame.

"Lady, what is your *problem*?" a girl yelled at Louise. "You stepped on my foot and almost broke it!" Some of the couples were clutching at each other now in a slow dance, while others trailed away from the dance floor.

"What is *my* problem? What is my *problem*?" Louise yelled. "*This*—" she threw her arms out wide "—is my problem, all of it!"

Virginia grabbed Louise's arm, pulling her away, and Corinna took Louise's other arm. "Let's go, Louise," Corinna said. Young people, pretty, handsome, drunk, sweaty young people, stared at them, backing away to make room as the three of them passed. One on each side, she and Corinna steered Louise back out the side door.

"It's my fault, I'm sorry," Virginia said, once they were back on Main Street. Louise charged ahead, muttering about young fascists and the old-boy network.

"Nothing to be sorry for," Corinna said briskly. "We're all a little—well, things aren't as they should be right now. I'll drive Louise home." She moved ahead too, leaving Virginia alone on the sidewalk. In pretending to be one of them, trying to join them, Virginia had only made things worse. She'd led Louise into making a drunken scene in a frat, and it would probably get back to the history department. Whatever they'd been doing tonight probably counted as moral turpitude.

★ ★ ★

Sam stood in the muddy, unlit driveway, debating. For a few moments tonight, he'd turned into one of those guys he used to wonder about: a guy hitching back to Topos with a farmer. A pickup truck had stopped for him, and without asking where Sam needed a ride to, the driver, a middle-aged man in a canvas coat and driving cap, started talking. He was on his way home after visiting his brother's youngest son in Vermont, back from Vietnam, he said. The nephew had gotten his bell rung pretty bad from an explosion and had also broken a leg, but he was home. Anyway, the man needed a little help rebuilding trellises for his raspberries, which would free him up to finish liming and manuring his last field, all right?

"I'll post a note on the board," Sam said, and asked for a pen to write down the information.

"You fellows and gals did good work on the fence repair and the apple picking last year," the man said. "I have to give you that."

"Thanks," Sam said, on behalf of the fellows and gals at Topos.

"I don't approve of the free love and this knee-jerk anti-Nixon business. How do you think it makes my nephew feel?"

Nixon was a crook, and Sam didn't know what to say about the injured nephew home from the war. "I haven't seen any free love," he said. "Only the usual non-free kind." He'd made the farmer laugh.

But Sam hadn't asked Jerry when the meeting was tonight. Maybe he'd missed it entirely. This time he couldn't make up some lame excuse for being out here. No, he should just say it out loud: he'd come here to find Elodie.

He forced himself to charge across the driveway and up the house's side steps. Inside the house, he could hear voices in the front room, and from upstairs, the plucking of a guitar—Dylan, of course. He wished he had a joint or a few glasses of Topos cider to give him a boost.

"You're patronizing me." Elodie's voice carried from the front room. "And maybe you don't understand how fucked-up everything is."

Sam stood waiting at the edge of the front room. Six people sat on the floor, some with their backs against the couch. *What do you people have against chairs*, he wanted to ask, but he'd only sound like someone's square dad. Elodie took in his presence and waved him over as if she'd been expecting him.

"Actually, I have a pretty good idea," Jerry was saying, as Sam approached. Jerry nodded up at Sam, then turned back to Hank.

"Let's not get heated," Hank the senior said. Hank had a beard now, which had come in darker and bushier than his pale hair. With the beard and those frameless glasses Hank looked a lot older than even a couple months ago. "It's a small operation. It's not that big a deal." Hank noted Sam's presence, frowning up at him. "Is he okay to be here?"

"He's fine," Elodie said. "Sit down, Sam." She scooted to the side, and he squeezed between her and Shelly, the girl who'd been pruning apple trees that night he'd cooked with Elodie. Shelly nodded at him blankly—she didn't remember him.

"Maybe it's not a big deal, but I thought we were here to talk about ecology," Jerry said.

"Some of us have gotten to a better understanding of things," Hank said. "We've all tried peaceful protest, we've seen what happens. Do I need to remind you about the May Day protests?" Jerry made a grunting sound, not agreeing or disagreeing. Hank turned to Sam. "You know what happened right? The Feds came down hard on a completely peaceful demonstration in DC, they brought in the fucking marines, fucking paratroopers and tear gas—"

"We all know," Jerry said.

Sam nodded with the others. The phrase *May Day* rang a bell, but the protests blurred together, one front-page photo after another: a hundred thousand in DC, ten thousand at Kent State, thirty at Clarendon—the protests would get put down, the battering rams would come out, the protesters put in jail or worse.

Hank lifted some papers from his lap and began to read. "The time is *now*." His voice had grown deeper, as if he were giving a speech. "Political power grows out of a gun, a Molotov, a riot, a commune...and *from the soul of the people*..."

"You're the one getting heated, man," Jerry said. "No more manifesto crap, that stuff never works."

"First of all, it's not crap," Hank said. "Second, Elodie said this was an ecology meeting to get you to sit and listen for a minute. We can't help Mother Earth if we don't get the humans to see reason. So therefore, if we can raise a little money to fund the—"

"Who's going to give money for something like that?" Jerry said.

"We wouldn't have to go into specifics," Hank said. "We have fundraisers all the time. Or often enough."

Next to Sam, Elodie took his hand, squeezed it, and let go. "Hey, Hank, Sam is the one who made the code for us."

"Ah," Hank said. "Thanks, man. We appreciate the work, you dig?"

"Uh, yeah," Sam said.

"What did you *do*, Manhattan?" Jerry said.

"See, other people want to help us out, Jerry," Elodie said. "Sam's code was super helpful."

"Oh, Jesus," Jerry said.

Sam hadn't been thinking when he made that cipher for Elodie, and now he saw himself kissing the two pieces of paper. He was such an ass. Only he could be so dense that he'd consider an encryption code, a stupid little project he'd borrowed from some long-dead British spy, to be something other than what it was. If he said anything now, that he'd only *kind of* meant it for the Movement, that mainly he'd been showing off for Elodie, they'd know his idiocy. His face was aflame, but he stayed quiet and tried to listen, slowly taking in that Shelly was talking about the prongs of some operation somewhere else, a response to the fascist pigs. They could support these actions with their own actions. Hank mentioned something about Elodie's aunt's empty town house in the Village, and Elodie nodded.

"And I'm just saying that we all gotta do our part, and make it bigger, more pervasive, so everyone will get it, you dig?" Hank said.

"No, man, I don't," Jerry said. "But if you want to look at it that way, I did my part. I didn't have much choice about it. But now I do, and I'm out of here." He pushed up to standing and stomped upstairs without another word.

"*You* of all people know this has gone on too long," Elodie called up to Jerry, but Jerry was gone.

Sam argued with himself. If he said he was in, for real this time, he'd have access to Elodie. They'd drive to New York together, she'd need him, she'd admire his dedication to the cause, and maybe she'd finally fall for him. But

Hank sounded too heated, as Jerry had said, and there was something sinister in that word, *operation*. He felt himself standing up, even as he was still deciding. "I need to get back," he said, and the others turned to stare up at him.

"Now? You just got here." Hank shook his head. "I knew we shouldn't have let this guy——"

"You don't need to worry about me." Sam didn't want to know any more, and he didn't want the others to know what a fool he'd been.

"Have a little faith, Hank," Elodie said.

"Hey, but we appreciate your work, you dig?" Hank said.

"Sure, man." Sam put a hand up to wave goodbye, then turned to go. He heard Elodie following him out of the room.

"Hey. I miss seeing you," Elodie said, in the mudroom. "Can we get together sometime?"

"I don't understand," Sam said. Anger and confusion welled up, and he tried to figure out how to express himself without yelling or starting to cry. "We had something, at least I thought we did," he managed to say. "And then I see you kissing Jerry on the green, and now——"

"That was just a goodbye kiss. That was——" She stopped, crossed her arms over her chest, like any girl hearing what she didn't want to hear. "You and I had something. But I've got to stay focused right now because things are happening. That's what I came to tell you, Sam. I think you want to be part of it too."

He wrestled with the flurry of conflicting feelings that leaped up, one after the other, into his throat, circling through his heart and gut. He wanted to be brave; he wanted to be normal. He remembered the farmer's job request, and he took the paper out of his shirt pocket and handed it to her. He went out the door, shutting it quietly behind him.

He crossed the driveway to the road, as quiet now as if it were the middle of the night. The silence and emptiness made this edge of Westfield feel vast and strange and far away. He started to walk, sticking to the edge of the road, listening for cars. The day's summery weather had fled, leaving behind a cold, clear New Hampshire spring night, and from time to time he looked up at the pricks of stars all around him. Eventually he took in a blurry band of light that must be the Milky Way, a cloud of stars, a galaxy's worth of endless stars. Westfield was good for stargazing, you had to give it that.

Midday, Virginia opened the front door to a policeman. No, not a policeman, but the stretchy gray uniform of campus security. A moment of fear flitted through her gut—something with Rebecca? But Rebecca was upstairs in the shower—Virginia had slept poorly last night after all that alcohol, and this morning had woken up as late as Rebecca. She shook her head to clear it.

The security officer gave his name, and she gave hers. Oliver would have known the man's name, would have shaken the man's hand and known some key detail about him, his love for fishing, maybe. The officer looked to be near retirement age, his belly pushing at the gray knit shirt. Did she mind if he came in for a minute, just a few routine questions, he said.

She offered him coffee as she showed him into the living room. He sat, his cap propped next to him on the couch.

"I'm sorry for your loss, Mrs. Desmarais. Always enjoyed talking to Professor D."

She thanked him, as she tried to imagine what had brought him here.

"And I'm sorry to barge in like this, but we've got to follow up. It's a national thing, really. Nothing to take personally."

"What should I not take personally?" She felt something go plunging inside her. The frat they'd danced in last night, that was why he was here. She'd held hands with that kid, she'd twirled and swooped, acted like a complete idiot.

"We have word that some women, er, faculty, were trying to start a protest in one of the frats. Just following up on that tip."

Thank God Oliver wasn't here. But if he were here, he'd be the one to talk, to defend her honor. Of course, if Oliver were here, she wouldn't have gone to the frat last night, and it had been Oliver's frat after all. And she wouldn't be friends with Corinna or Lily or Helen. Or Louise.

"Oh, no, there's been a misunderstanding," she said. "We happened to walk by after dinner and went in for a minute to dance. That's all. You see, they were playing…" she trailed off. She sounded like a silly, thoughtless girl, and he wouldn't care about the music.

"Nothing to worry over. I got your name from Miss Beacon." Corinna. He bent to write something in a steno notebook with a stubby pencil, but he didn't seem particularly interested in her answers.

"Right, of course." She decided to tell him that they were inside the frat for ten or fifteen minutes, maybe less, until one of the young men, who was quite inebriated—she heard herself sounding like Momma—got rather belligerent, and so they all left the fraternity right then.

"Okay then." He folded the notebook closed. "We're trying to help out the Westfield police. Everyone's a little on edge these days. Things can get out of hand, like at that radical women's meeting, and then that college performance where the protesters interrupted and we had to be called in. Trying to stay on top of every lead."

Virginia felt herself blushing, as if he'd been talking about her in particular. She should smile and nod, say nothing more and steer him out of the house. But he was wrong, and she needed to tell him that. "The women at that meeting weren't radical," she said. "They were talking about women's health care and women's work. That sort of discussion is hardly unusual for a college campus."

He smiled at her as if she really were that silly, thoughtless girl. "From what I heard, the common denominator for both those events was the protesters. They may not mean to stir things up, but they do." He leaned forward, lowered his voice. "The thing is, there are groups out there that want to take advantage, wreak havoc. We have to keep an eye out, in case they're active in Westfield. Trying our best to watch out, to prevent the violence before it happens."

"What kind of groups?"

He shrugged. "All kinds. Commies, radicals, SDS, you name it."

"In Westfield? At Clarendon?" Westfield was nothing like Chicago, or Kent State, but she'd said too much already.

"You never know. But I thank you for seeing things clearly." He hoisted himself up to standing, and so did she.

"Thank you too." She walked him to the door, playing the role of calm, concerned matron, her insides churning. With that frat visit, she'd screwed everything up for Louise. And maybe Corinna and Helen and Lily too.

"I miss seeing him around campus," the officer said at the door. "I'm sorry for your loss, Mrs. Desmarais."

Chapter Fifteen

LATELY REBECCA FELT LIKE a part of her had cracked open, and if she tipped even a little, all the hideousness inside would come spilling out. She was tired of being lonely, tired of being someone who couldn't make a new friend. She was tired of the way Molly acted nice one day, distant the next. Somehow she wasn't cool enough for Molly yet also not correct enough. Molly had given her a bottle of Jean Naté for her fourteenth birthday, but had never asked what Rebecca was planning, even though Rebecca had her answer all worked out, *Oh, you know, just dinner with Mom, no party. You know, since Mom's still kind of sad and all.* Which was false. Busy with her new job, Mom still would have said "Yes, let's do it," if Rebecca had uttered the word "party." But Molly had never asked, only left the gift in Rebecca's locker.

At midmorning break she decided to talk to Josh, who happened to be standing alone by the soda and snack machines. Josh was finishing a pack of peanut butter Nabs. Not her favorite flavor, but none of those Nab crackers were very good.

"Hey, Josh," she said.

"Hey, yourself." Orangey peanut butter coated one of his top teeth. "Do you want to study for the world history test together?" he asked. "I have seventh period free, no practice today."

"Yeah, okay," she said, surprised at his invitation. "Uh, library?" She felt a blush coming on; when kids sat together in the library during seventh period, it meant they were going together. "Or how about Mrs. Dorfman's classroom?" Mrs. Dorfman, Rebecca's homeroom teacher, was the coolest eighth-grade teacher. Mrs. Dorfman taught English, and she had the usual Robert Frost and Emily Dickinson posters with poems on them, plus photos of Robert Frost's farm in Derry and Emily Dickinson's house that she'd taken herself. And a photo of some bearded guy reading a poem in a bookstore. City Lights, 1957, it said under the photo. Mrs. Dorfman's room had a reading corner with beanbags and a rainbow-colored braided rug, as if they were all back in first grade. But Mrs. Dorfman wanted kids to feel free to come in and rap with her, do their homework, whatever.

"Okay," he said. "See you then."

She got to Mrs. Dorfman's classroom before Josh. Maybe no other kids would show up, so she and Josh could just study and talk. She didn't want anyone making kissing noises as if she and Josh were in love, or looking at her like she was a freak.

"Hello there, Rebecca," Mrs. Dorfman called from her desk, and for a minute Rebecca wished it was just her and

Mrs. Dorfman, sitting in the beanbag chairs. She loved the way Mrs. Dorfman enthused about stories and poetry without being fake. She loved Mrs. Dorfman's boots and her short knit dresses and her long hair, which she didn't bother to straighten. Some days Mrs. Dorfman's curls looked a little crazy. Maybe Rebecca would have long curly hair like that when she was older.

"Hi, Mrs. Dorfman." She felt her face warm up—she couldn't say that she was about to meet Josh so no one in the library would see them. "Okay if I study in here? Josh asked for help with world history."

"Of course." Mrs. Dorfman smiled, but not a smirky I-know-what-you-kids-are-up-to smile.

Rebecca plopped herself down in a beanbag chair, and decided to get her diagramming homework out of the way. She didn't hate diagramming sentences the way everyone else did. It was like a puzzle, and you got to make a little drawing, which was fun. She finished the last sentence; good, that was done. But no Josh. She looked up at the clock: seventh period was more than half over. Maybe he'd signed out and left school early, since he didn't have practice today. Maybe he'd only been making fun of her. Or maybe—

"Sorry I'm late," Josh said, in front of her now. "Mr. Beasley wanted some of us to help clean up the dugouts." He was a little sweaty around the temples and he shook his head sharply to get his hair off his face, the way a wet dog would do.

"No problem." Another blush crept from her chest to her neck and ears. She grabbed her notebook and history book from her stack of stuff on the rug, while he sank onto another beanbag and looked at her expectantly. His eyes were green, not brown, she noticed.

"Okay," she said. "Start at the beginning of chapter fourteen?"

He nodded, tugged his textbook out of his backpack. His smile looked a little bit scared. "I didn't do so great on the last test. I hate this class."

"Yeah," she said, not wanting to admit that she loved this class. She was such a dork. But maybe she could help him.

After fifteen or so minutes of quizzing each other, the bell clanged its shrill end-of-day sound. "You want to walk around Westfield on Saturday?" Josh said. "Maybe with Todd and Molly?"

She felt her face heat up again. "Uh, sure, I guess." God, she sounded so wishy-washy. "Molly and I are—" But she wasn't going to get into any of that. "Sure. I'll talk to Molly."

"I'll talk to Todd. Thanks for the studying," he said, even though they'd only studied for fifteen minutes and she couldn't imagine it would be much help for the next test.

Turning onto Flintlock Street, she and Molly started the long downhill walk toward the campus. It felt almost like a summer Saturday, the sky pink and blue and gray, like it might rain later. *"Holy Moses,"* Molly sang, the way they used to do, one of them singing a line of a song. Everything felt cool as they walked and sang Elton John, as if she and Molly were back to the way they used to be. Except for the four cigarettes she had in her jacket pocket, which she'd taken out of Dad's desk this morning. She stopped singing. "So is this a date?"

Molly shrugged. "I don't know. Dates are for Kath and Lacey. You know, like a movie date or prom night."

"Right." She'd thought about Josh too much, imagining going to a movie, where they'd have to sit close together in the dark, and he might do that dumb thing that boys did, faking a casual yawn and stretch, then draping an arm around the unsuspecting girl. She wouldn't mind that; Josh was a nice guy, and he was cute, with dimples. He'd acted polite and normal when they studied together.

They approached the Clarendon green, where Josh and Todd sat on a bench waiting. Molly picked up her pace, and Rebecca did too, flipping her hair from side to side as if she were a high school girl.

"Hey." The boys hopped up to standing, and they all stood there looking at each other, no one saying anything.

"What do you guys want to do?" Molly finally asked.

"I don't know," Todd said. "Get a doughnut at Mo's?"

They headed toward Main Street and Mo's. But even from up the street they could see people waiting outside—Mo's was always packed on Saturdays.

"Let's just walk around the campus," Rebecca said.

"Okay," Josh said.

As they crossed the green two by two, Rebecca took in the gleaming windows of the little English library, where she'd sat studying one afternoon a year or two ago. Imagined her younger self looking out at this older, sadder self. A sigh escaped her.

Josh leaned closer. "Bored already? Westfield is pretty boring, isn't it?"

She laughed. "Oh, no, I was just remembering something. It's nothing." She didn't say she'd been thinking about a time when Dad was still alive, a time when she could never have predicted what was ahead. She spotted the gate for the old college cemetery. "We could go check out the cemetery," she said to change the subject, but she could see from Josh's scrunched-up expression that this wasn't a great idea. "I mean, if you think that's too weird, it's just old and historical, my parents used to bring me here…" She trailed off.

"Okay, sure." Josh opened the gate. "Let's check it out."

When Rebecca was little, she'd come here with Mom and Dad. Mom had given her paper and pencils to make rubbings of old headstones, the cherubs and twining vines carved along the tops of the stones, while Dad told stories about the old names. She followed Josh in between the worn slate headstones and the larger boxy granite and marble memorials, the dates so old that it didn't seem like dead people were all around them. She climbed onto one of the big memorials, as if it were a big granite couch, and Molly joined her. They sat next to one another with their arms around their knees, and the boys plopped down in the grass.

Music floated over them, streaming out of a dorm near the college green. Beatles. *"Get back, Loretta…"* Paul Mc-Cartney said, his voice sounding like he had a cold. The music changed abruptly, to something she didn't recognize.

"Grateful Dead," Molly said. "Kath has this album. She's going to California to see them this summer. At least that's what she says."

"Cool," Todd and Josh said at the same time. Todd elbowed Josh, Josh elbowed back, and Todd pushed Josh so he tipped over.

"Hey," Molly said, "Rebecca has cigarettes."

Josh sat up. "You smoke?" She could hear the surprise in his voice.

Rebecca shook her head, embarrassed.

"Rebecca is full of surprises." Molly threw an arm around her as if nothing had changed. "You never know with her." Molly held out her free hand for a cigarette and Rebecca retrieved them from her jacket.

"I, uh, I don't have any matches," Rebecca said. God, why hadn't she thought of that?

"I'll go ask around." Josh pushed up to standing and ran in a loping way out of the cemetery.

When he returned with a mostly empty matchbook, he and Todd lit their cigarettes and then lit the other two for Rebecca and Molly. She could see that none of them knew what they were doing, which made her feel a little better. First came the familiar smell of cigarette smoke, but it stung her throat and tasted awful. She squeezed her eyes shut, coughing. "Blech," she said, and the others laughed.

Molly's eyes watered too, and she squinted and rubbed at them.

"When I go to Clarendon I'm going to blast rock music in my dorm room every day," Todd said. "It'll be so cool."

"You know there are only boys at Clarendon, right? No girls." Molly sounded irritated. Maybe she was insulted that Todd wanted to go to college where she couldn't.

"They may get girls," Rebecca said. "My mom's friend says they're working on it right now." She waited to see if Molly was going to say something about the women's meeting and the radicals and Commies, but Molly only nodded through her cigarette smoke.

"Cool." Josh smiled up at Rebecca.

She wished that she and Josh were sitting next to each

other, but this was okay. She took in the mild day, the chickadees chirping in the tall pines around them. A few minutes later she felt headachy and nauseated, and she lay back on the cold granite, put a hand to her forehead.

"You okay?" Molly asked.

She nodded. "Just a little sick to my stomach."

Josh got to his feet, and stood peering down at her.

"I'm fine," she said.

"Is it—are you feeling—because, you know, we're in the cemetery and everything—" Molly didn't finish.

This moment always cropped up sooner or later. She'd catch a look as it went between two classmates or two teachers: *We feel sorry for this girl, don't we?* Or else someone would look at her for a second, then quickly turn away. She knew what that meant: *I know about you. You're different, tainted now.* She just wanted to be normal, but normal kept slipping away. She was always going to be sad. She was always going to be weird.

"What do you think it's like inside the frats?" she said instead of answering Molly.

"Kath and Lacey have gone to one," Molly said. "They went to KA and told the guys they were from Gilman Junior College. Lacey's friends buy pot from a guy there."

"What was it like?" Rebecca asked.

Molly shrugged. "Kath said it smelled bad. They didn't stay long, just had a beer and checked things out and then left. It's no big deal, everyone from the high school goes to the frats all the time. Kath says the trick is to go when it's not a party weekend. If it's just a regular night, a weeknight or a Sunday night, you can walk right in and hang out, and no one cares."

"What if we did that?" Todd asked.

"They'd never let us in, dumbass," Josh said. "No one would mistake us for college guys."

"What are you, chicken or something?" Todd said.

"No, man. I just don't want to get beat up by some big college guy, some hockey player, you know?"

Rebecca laughed at the thought of some giant college hockey player pounding Josh into the ground, but they all turned to look at her like she was crazy. "Sorry, it just sounded funny. I don't want you to get beat up, either."

Late morning on Monday, the reference room at its quietest, Virginia ticked through another Peale biography, this one from the '40s. Half her brain reviewed Friday night, replaying her absurd stop in the frat—she kept hearing her own stupid voice, *We could go in for a minute, see what it's like.* Virginia had encouraged Louise's drunken outburst because of her own momentary wish to see what the young people were doing in there. She had to think of something, some way, to help Louise.

She turned her focus back to the Peale brothers' biography. Despite the mentions in the index, Sarah Miriam Peale was peripheral—only a niece, only a daughter—to the brothers' story. Virginia felt a sudden strong desire to get away from Westfield. If she could hole up in the archives of the fine arts academy in Philadelphia, she might track down a few more of Sarah's portraits, most of which had disappeared into homes and attics, never exhibited. But she needed money, time, someone to stay with Rebecca—she couldn't do this. She was still doing everything wrong. She closed the book, releasing its dusty-mold smell, and rested her head on her forearms.

"Coffee? I'm going to the stacks," Jeannette said—there

was a coffeepot in the staff room outside the stacks. Virginia lifted her head to nod.

Jeannette returned with the coffee, which was cooked down and stale, and she asked about Virginia's research. Virginia told her about the rough list she'd made of the known portraits and still lifes. It felt like a mountain range stood between her and the rest of the portraits. And she wanted to tell Jeannette about how she might have wrecked things for Louise. But the less said, the better.

"You'll get there," Jeannette said, her confidence unwarranted. "One thing we know how to do is research, so we'll research grant money to cover your travel. I'm sure it's out there."

Grant money. She was so lucky to have Jeannette as a coworker. "Thank you, Jeannette. Where would I be without you?"

Jeannette laughed. "Hey, did I tell you my chapters came?" After the women's meeting, Jeannette had called one of the Boston women, wanting to volunteer. The women's collective was revising their health booklet, and Jeannette had signed up to help edit the new version. The one good thing to come out of that meeting, Virginia thought.

She was still musing over the hidden portraits and Jeannette's confidence about grant money for travel when Henry Jernigan passed by the reference-room doorway. She hadn't seen him since the Spring Sing. At the doorway, Henry stopped, then waved vigorously, as if he were ashore and she at the rail of an ocean liner. At the desk a minute later, he exclaimed over her presence in the library—he hadn't known she worked here. His springy hair was cut short so it wasn't as flyaway as before.

"I'm sorry I left you hanging at that Spring Sing mess," he said, once she'd explained about her new job. He'd already apologized on the phone, had told her how he'd gone home to pack ice into a plastic bag, and when he'd returned only the janitor remained. "I meant what I said about getting dinner," he said. "To thank you." She said she'd call him when she got home, and they'd make a plan.

In the afternoon, June called five minutes after Virginia had hung up the phone with Henry Jernigan, and she told June about this upcoming dinner date, Westfield Inn coffee shop, nothing fancy. But as soon as the words left her mouth she knew she should have said nothing. "It's not *that* kind of a date, it's just that he's new in town, new to Clarendon," she amended.

"Oh, no, Ginny," June said. "No, no, *no*! It's way too soon. And hey, you never sent a thank-you note to Mr. Burgess for the interview, and it's been three months."

"How—how do you even know that? And why do you call him Mr. Burgess?"

"Force of habit, from the boys," June said. "You're missing the point. Any dolt knows to send a thank-you note after a job interview. I can't think how they'll ever want to hire you now."

It had been all Virginia could do to put that interview behind her. Now she told June about her new job, which she should have done weeks ago.

But even now, June was stuck on the idea of Virginia moving back to Norfolk. "Anyway, it's too soon for you to go on a date. Wait a year, at least."

"It's not a date. He just wanted to thank me for—" she

didn't want to get into the strange Spring Sing breakdown "—some volunteer work I did for the college."

"I just mean that you need to stay quiet after such a big— after any big loss. Not make any big decisions and all that."

"It's just dinner. It's not a big decision." Virginia changed the subject, asking about June's two boys, both at UVA.

June pinged between her usual brags and laments about her sons, and then returned like a terrier to her usual refrain, "Marnie thinks you'd be happier down here. Momma too."

"I don't want to talk about any of that, Junie," she said. "At least, not until after my dinner date." At least tweaking her big sister still felt okay.

June let out a growl. "You never, ever listen to me."

"I listen. I just don't agree." She said goodbye, and went to put in a load of laundry. Talking with June had perked her up, had distracted her from her own foolish behavior. She called Marnie to complain about June, and she let herself listen to Marnie's gossip about Norfolk, soothing and inane.

Chapter Sixteen

THREE DAYS LATER, VIRGINIA and Henry Jernigan made their way through the lobby of the Westfield Inn, silent. She couldn't think of a single thing to say; they'd used up all their conversation on the five-minute car ride here. To her left, in the inn's parlor, some older alums and their wives had gathered for drinks, and she could hear one of the men talking and then a noisy spasm of laughter. All those old couples together for fifty years—she'd never get to have that. Oliver wouldn't, either. The familiar pangs of loss and sorrow struck her. *See, you're doing it all wrong, Ginny,* June would say. She probed those pangs, felt again the lack of Oliver, the dull ache of him being gone. She'd made yet another mistake, walking into the inn with a strange man. She should be home with Rebecca; she should make a nice meal for Louise, who was in limbo, waiting for her hearing.

"Hellooo…" Henry called, as if from a distance. "I do

that too sometimes, just get lost in whatever I'm thinking about. Used to drive my wife crazy."

"Oh, sorry," she said.

"My ex-wife, I should say," he said. "We got married right after college. She left me four years later when I was just about finished with grad school. She got sick of waiting."

Not what she'd expected. "I'm sorry about that."

He smiled, his eyebrows furrowing so he looked sheepish. "It was a long time ago. She's happily remarried, three kids now."

"Well," she said. "That's good, I guess." She sounded insipid. She turned and led the way to the coffee shop, where the lights had been dimmed in an attempt at atmosphere, but better to eat in the coffee shop than the inn's hushed dining room with its acres of carpet, its white tablecloths and silver domes covering the dinner plates.

At the table—he hadn't pulled out her chair for her, the way Oliver used to do—they stared at each other, and then at the menus. A waiter appeared and said that martinis were on special tonight. "Okay," she said to the waiter. "Why not."

"Me too," Henry said. "Two martinis." When the waiter disappeared, Henry leaned forward. "So, about that time I ran into you at the A&P," he said. "I—uh—I'd realized that I'd never said anything to you about Oliver, about your loss, and then I went and did the same thing at the singing competition. That was inexcusable. I'm very sorry for your loss."

"Thank you." She considered whether to offer some platitude, but instead asked about his work. He began to talk about how he'd wanted to do physics undergrad, that math had been a fallback. He'd done a little work with computers at Cornell, and now he spent a lot of time working with the mainframe. "It's pretty exciting stuff, at least for me." Their drinks arrived and they ordered their food, and once the waiter had left them, Henry returned to his computer talk. She listened, with a dizzying sense of being back in college, of following the old mantras—find out what *he's* interested in, let *him* take the lead in conversation, because men are interested in women who are interested in them!

"...and of course even more useful in broader economic studies, let's say, studies of employment patterns or voting patterns or hospital usage. Honestly, it's going to be transformative." He took a breath—he'd been talking too fast, like an excited kid. She smiled and nodded, pretending to be fascinated.

He pushed at his glasses. "I'm sorry, I know I tend to go on and on about things. It's something I've always done."

She laughed, then covered her mouth to hide the laugh, so as not to seem insane. "I—I—you see, I was thinking just now about the rules for dates that we learned when we were young." He looked at her with alarm. "Ah, that is, the main rule was to always ask the guy about whatever it was he liked, you know, car-engine repair or football, or whatever he was interested in. To keep the conversation going."

"And you were doing that with me just now," he said. "Were you?"

"Sort of, but I didn't need to—I mean..." But she sounded cruel, as if she were admitting that he'd bored her, and she'd only pretended interest. They were interrupted by the arrival of her codfish cake and his chopped steak, and they ate for a few moments without talking. She'd hurt his feelings. But this wasn't a date, it was only an outing, to give two lonely neighbors something to do on a Saturday night.

"Okay." He set his fork down. "So what if the rules went both ways? Why do they only go one way?"

"Pardon?"

"You said, the main rule was to ask the guy about his interests, right?"

"Right."

"And the assumption is that the girl, the woman, has no interests, at least none worth talking about. Why is that?"

All those magazine articles she'd read as a teen, all the things she'd heard from June and Marnie and *Seventeen* were about the boy: what *he* liked, what *he* wanted, what *he* was interested in. She felt herself blush at the obviousness of that belated realization. Had her own interests been so inferior? "You're right, of course, but—"

"So! Let's hear them." He leaned back in his chair—they were waiting for their maple sundaes now—and smiled. "You've got interests. Car-engine repair, am I right?"

She laughed and told him about her abandoned dissertation, about Copley, and how she hoped to begin again with Sarah Miriam Peale.

He asked her to tell him more, and she tried to describe what she'd learned about Sarah Miriam Peale. "The thing is, it all feels new, like I'm uncovering something that hasn't been studied to death," she said. "I want to know how she did it, how she got all those commissions as a young woman so long ago. People actually hired her."

"Because she knew what she was doing." He made it sound like a given.

"Well, yes, and the family business was portrait making, so she had that. Still, she was a working artist a very long time ago." Now she found herself talking, speculating about Sarah Miriam Peale's influences, the materials she might have worked with, how she might have handled portrait sittings, bossing Philadelphia gentlemen about—*stand please, no, sit down, sir.* She'd been talking for ten minutes without a break, and she stopped.

"Think what I would have lost if we only went by those rules you talked about before," Henry said. "I wouldn't have learned anything about those artists, or your work, or the thinking you've done about it."

"You're kind to say so."

"Is that a rule too?" he asked. "To tell someone he's kind?"

She laughed and shook her head no. "I talk too much," she said.

"Me too," he said. "Generally at the wrong times."

"Do you like Westfield?" she asked. "It's such a small town, and isolated. And the winters, you know. They're long."

He took a bite of his maple sundae, tilted his head to one side. "Still getting used to it," he said. "But I don't mind the winter, I like the snow."

"Me too," she said. "Do you ski?"

"A little cross-country," he said. "Maybe one of these days I'll try downhill skiing."

She told him about her ski accident, how the football had hit her head, her fall. The ankle that remained puffy, aching in the middle of the night.

"You're braver than I am," he said. "Maybe I won't try downhill skiing after all."

Maybe she could tell him about Louise's strange situation, her tenure getting questioned, even the women's meeting that had caused all the trouble, and he would have something to say about all that. It might be nothing like what Oliver would say. Would have said.

But instead they were talking about the movie *Downhill Racer.* That was the last movie she'd seen with Oliver, and they'd had a fight when they'd gotten home. Oliver had enthused about going skiing in Switzerland, and she'd replied that it would be too expensive, and the high altitude could be tough and maybe he should lose some weight first, because what if— And he'd said, Oh, come on, it was only a pipe dream, Virginia, and could she at least let him have that, and did she need to criticize him at every single turn? And she'd stomped upstairs because he was so sensitive and angry lately. Oliver had been troubled for months before he died, and she'd barely noticed.

"I guess you didn't like the movie very much, huh?" Henry said.

"Oh, right. No, it wasn't my favorite." A thought struck her, and she spoke before her more careful other thoughts could drive the first thought away. "Do you want to see a movie some time?"

"Is that one of those rules?" he asked. "Just kidding. Sure, a movie would be great. I haven't seen a movie in months."

On the short drive home, they talked about the Spring Sing and the nonsensical brawl. "You'll think me a fool, but it never occurred to me that anyone would be against coeducation, least of all the students," he said. "There were only a few girls in my classes at Cornell, but they never had any trouble, at least not academically." Her looked her way, caught her eye.

"It seems obvious, doesn't it?"

"I heard that Weissman had to meet with the trustees a

couple of times to reassure them that our boys aren't complete dopes," he said. "Makes me wonder if Weissman's job is on the line."

Virginia felt another prick of loss; Oliver would have shared such inside information with her, and she'd have speculated with him on Weissman's motives and whether he was about to be fired. "It's funny how the least bit of protesting turns the campus on its ear. The girls have a legitimate cause. They're so much braver than I would have been."

"Maybe the protest and the boys fighting, and that women's meeting have gotten the trustees' attention."

"I was at that meeting," she said. "I was one of the—I helped to plan that meeting. And Louise Walsh has gotten into trouble over it, which seems terribly unfair."

"She's in history, right? Friend of yours?"

"Good friend." She hoped Louise would say the same of her, although that would be expecting too much. "She's one of the people who's gotten me through."

"Ah," Henry said. "Sometimes I think it was a mistake for me to come to Clarendon. The college seems to be in the middle of some sort of transition, figuring out what kind of place it wants to be in the future. I think it may get worse before it gets better."

In her driveway now, he turned the car off, his hand still on the stick shift. His forearm and wrist, ropy with tendons, poked out of his cuff, and she swallowed, feeling something she shouldn't. *You were right, June,* she thought. It was too soon for a date. "I'm glad you came to Clarendon."

"And I'm glad you're here," he said. The car's engine made a ticking sound as it cooled. He leaned close, and she did the same, drawn by the nearness of his body, and they kissed, briefly but electrically. Startled, she pulled away from him and opened the car door.

"Thank you, Henry. I had a lovely time." She slid out of his car and shut the door as quick as she could, walking away before she could do something even more foolish.

Saturday night, Sam came home early from Lambda Chi's spring beach party. He hadn't found a date, and it was painful to hang around a party where everyone else and their dates had concocted creative half-naked costumes. The whole thing was another stupid Clarendon tradition. Plus everyone still thought it was hilarious that Teddy Burnham had knocked him out with one punch. Even now, he and his nose were fodder for more jokes than usual. Worse than that, he felt bad vibes coming from the KA guys whenever he passed one of them on the green or in Commons. Teddy Burnham and a handful of KA guys had gotten suspended for a week, and KA was on indefinite probation, and Sam felt the KA guys' dirty looks, as if he were responsible for their caveman-like behavior. He couldn't wait for the term to be over. Except for Elodie. Even after everything, he dropped into daydreams about the two of them on campus, or better yet, New York, walking through Central Park on a hot summer afternoon, entwining themselves on a blanket in the Sheep's Meadow. Or taking the train out to Long Island for the day, swimming and lying in the sun, skin to skin.

Someone rapped softly on his door. "Sam? Hey." It was Hank the senior.

"Can I sit down?" Hank pulled out Sam's desk chair and sank onto it. He took in Sam's room, the wood trim, the lack of posters. "I lived here freshman year," Hank said.

"In one of the corner triples. Sometimes I miss those days, living in a dorm, being a clueless freshman and all that."

"I should have lived off campus this year," Sam said.

Hank wasn't listening. He'd bent over, forearms on thighs, staring at the floor—a coach about to tell his team to get their shit together in the second half. He straightened up. "We're going to change the world, you dig? Even if it's only a little at a time."

"Yeah, sure." Sam couldn't bring himself to say, *Yeah, man, I dig.*

"We're refining our thinking. Small is beautiful, too. We've got a little money, and I'm heading down to Hooksett to get supplies. Can I get a commitment from you? Elodie hopes—"

Elodie hoped they could still be friends, or something like that. "Why doesn't Elodie come tell me what she hopes herself?"

"She's—away," Hank said.

Sam said nothing.

"We need your help, Sam. You know how badly a lot of us were treated, when we were only trying to make the administration see reason. They responded with force, and we lost everything. Or have you forgotten that?"

"Of course I haven't forgotten it," Sam said. "I agree, they shouldn't have called in the National Guard—"

"They used force on us, and then they made us sit in jail for a month. *Then* they kicked us out."

Hank hadn't been kicked out, but Sam didn't quibble. "I know, man. I know. It's a bad time and the administration guys are all assholes." Dean Gilbert was an asshole, but was President Weissman? *Now then, men, here's where it gets really interesting,* he could hear Weissman saying, deep into the reasoning that underlay one of the ancient ciphers their class had studied. *Wasn't it amazing what they were able to do with their limited understanding of math*, he'd say.

"Meanwhile, the fact remains that you're already involved, Sam."

"'Political power grows out of a gun, a Molotov,' and what was the last thing?" Sam said, remembering. "Isn't that what you said? At the meeting?"

"Elodie's counting on you. Thursday night, behind the chapel. Elodie will be there. You can make a difference." Hank's voice had gone strangely flat, as if he didn't believe what he was saying.

"Are you okay?"

Hank nodded. "Thursday, 11 pm. Chapel. Be there." He stood, pushed the chair back under the desk and flashed a peace sign at Sam, but said nothing else. A minute later, Sam heard the dorm's heavy front door banging shut two floors below.

Hank's words rang in Sam's head: *We're going to change the world, you dig?* Hank sounded like the cartoon version of a radical. You dig, man?

The memory of a bad summer night came to him, a night at the Village Vanguard the summer before he started college. Dad had asked if Sam wanted to go downtown to hear some new guys playing old stuff, had even ordered him a vodka martini, and at first Sam thought this was just Dad deciding to be nice, to treat Sam like an adult. During the set break two musicians came to their table to talk to Dad, one old and fat and white, with a goatee and cap, and the other even older, black, with aviator sunglasses. Sam wasn't listening to the two old guys because he was trying to make sense of what Dad had told him a few minutes before, that he'd be moving out tomorrow, that this was Mom's decision, that it was for the best that they separate. Except now he recalled something he'd forgotten: how the old white jazz guy ended every sentence with *you dig, man?* And Dad kept saying, *I dig, man.* And how wrong it had sounded, kind of the way Hank had sounded just now.

It was funny how the littlest things made the Paretsky twins happy. The last time Rebecca babysat for them, she'd brought her old plastic bucket of crayons and some notebook paper, and they'd all colored at the Paretskys' kitchen table. Tonight she'd dragged her old box of Barbies out of the back of her closet, hauling it down the street to the Paretskys' house. She'd turned the TV to *Bewitched* and then *Mary Tyler Moore*, but the girls barely looked at the TV, preferring to make up stories with these old Barbies, introducing their own dolls to these weird older dolls that had even messier hair than their own Barbies. She let each girl pick out a tiny dress and matching plastic heels to keep.

The night was mild, and on the walk home she thought about summer, and Josh. She'd probably run into him this summer at the town pool, and maybe he'd ask her to hang out, and they'd sit on their towels and talk about whatever high school kids talked about. Mrs. Paretsky had asked if Rebecca wanted to help them out during the summer, be a mother's helper, and she'd said sure because she liked the twins and they liked her. But she didn't want to spend her whole entire summer with seven-year-olds. Her thoughts drifted back to Josh. They'd lie on their beach towels next to each other, maybe at an actual beach, Lake Sunapee or Hampton Beach, and he'd turn toward her, putting an arm around her shoulders, and she'd let him kiss her. It would magically be sort of private, and she'd be tan and beautiful. Molly could be somewhere nearby, but not necessary on the scene.

As she neared home, a strange car idled in the driveway, probably one of Mom's new friends, Louise or Corinna. Rebecca liked thinking of them by their first names, and the way they talked to her, seriously, but not in the usual annoying way of moms and teachers.

From the edge of the driveway, she saw that there were people in the car; the light over the garage lit up the car's interior, outlining Mom in the passenger seat and a man in the driver's seat. Mom was saying something, her words indistinct, and then she leaned over to kiss the man. Mom was kissing some strange guy. Mom. In the strange guy's little car. In their driveway.

Rebecca needed to do something, but she'd grown paralyzed. The car door opened with a click, and the tiny sound freed her up to move. She dropped the old Barbie box in the grass and ran through the yard, but Mom was in a big hurry and had already gone through the side door. She followed Mom through the mudroom and into the kitchen as the unfamiliar car backed out of the driveway and pulled away.

"Hi, honey, how were the Paretsky girls?" Mom said, draping her cardigan over a kitchen chair, as if she hadn't just been *kissing* some random man.

All the strangeness that had sloshed around inside for so long spilled out into one giant mess of bad feeling. Missing Dad, missing having a real family, missing the way things used to be. The general yuck of too many things, the friends who weren't quite friends, of maybe going together with Josh but maybe not. Why did Dad have to die, and not Mom? She hated how full of hatefulness she'd gotten. "What is *wrong* with you?"

Mom whirled around. "Excuse me? *What* did you say?" Mom's voice had a tone that Rebecca had never heard before.

"I said 'what is wrong with you?'" Rebecca had lowered her voice; she knew better than to keep yelling, but she was so angry that her eyes hurt and her face felt like it was on fire. "You're married to Dad, or have you forgotten him already?"

"I—oh, no, of course not, Bec, now just hold on there—" Mom stepped forward, getting ready to fold her into a hug.

No hugs. No more talking. Rebecca took a step backward toward the mudroom, then another. "You're the *worst*, you know that?" She ran to the side door, pulled it open and slipped through it, slamming it behind her. She ran back down their driveway and onto the street. But she didn't know where to go. Molly's house? Molly's room in the upstairs back left corner was dark, and she couldn't face Molly or her parents right now. She had no place to go, so she just let herself run.

A minute later, a car engine rumbled to life, reversed and lumbered down the street. Mom, coming after her, getting ready to apologize again. She'd lost all respect for Mom, and tears streamed out of her eyes as she ran, blurring her vision and haloing the streetlight ahead.

She slowed to a jog, debating whether to keep moving along the street or dart off into someone's yard, cut through backyards to get from one street to another, the way she and Molly used to do. She'd scare Mom more if she just disappeared, but she also wanted to let Mom have it. To yell some more, to let more of that river of bad feeling out, so it wouldn't be inside anymore.

The slow-moving car's headlights illuminated the wet pavement, the pale rhododendron blossoms at the edges of yards, the maples' branches overhead. A minute later, the car rolled along next to her—this wasn't their car, it was Mrs. Koslowski's station wagon. Molly's sister Kath leaned over and rolled down the window. "Hey, girl, where you running to at this hour?" Kath asked cheerfully. And then she added, "Get in, Bec."

Rebecca got in without a word, and as she slid into the seat, a hiccup of a sob escaped. She wasn't sad, she was furious, so why was she crying?

"You can keep me company," Kath said. "I gotta pick up Frankie, that little pest. Senior spring and I'm grounded, can you believe it." Kath and Lacey were always getting grounded, according to Molly.

Rebecca wondered if the grounding was because Kath had been hanging out at that frat. "I'm sorry."

"It's okay, it's only for this weekend and next weekend, and I still have a paper to write and one final exam. Not that they care that I passed out of my other four exams. *Nooo*," Kath said, her voice rising and falling over the stretched-out word, "that's not good enough for them. I'm sure your mom would be a lot nicer about it if you got all A's and A-minuses, huh?"

Rebecca got all A's, and Mom never said anything one way or the other. Maybe that was a little better than Molly's strict parents.

Kath was talking about next year, how she'd wanted to go to Boston College—"I mean, come on, it's Jesuit, for God's sake"—but they were making her go to Gilman Junior College for at least a year. If she got good grades then maybe, *maybe*, BC after that. "It's because they think I'll get knocked up or something if I go to school with guys."

"Ah," Rebecca said. She wished like hell she had something witty to say, a knowing joke about guys, or getting pregnant by holding hands, but everything that flew through her head was far too stupid. "I'm sorry. I'd like to go to BC. It sounds like fun."

"It's not even that fun, to be honest. You have to take theology classes with old priests, for one thing. But it's basically in Boston and they have amazing football and hockey games. I'm going to get there one way or another."

She vowed to have a goal like Kath's, to care about something like a college so much that she'd talk to a younger neighbor that way. *I'm going to get to Clarendon, one way or another*, she'd say, as she drove a tearful Paretsky twin through the dark. *I'm going to study European history, because that's what my dad taught.* She swallowed another sob, took a breath. "Tell me about KA," she said. "The frat. What it was like in there. What the guys were like."

Virginia wiped off her Saturday-night eye makeup with a tissue, and set out for next door: the Koslowskis first, then the neighborhood by car. Surely Rebecca hadn't gone far; she was probably watching TV right now with Molly. The humid, still night air felt safe and almost welcoming, the way it promised summer. Surely there was nothing to worry about. She knocked on the Koslowskis' sliding-glass back door, and from the kitchen, Eileen, already in her bathrobe, waved her in. The kitchen held the earthy, garlicky smells of Eileen's stuffed cabbage, but it was clean, pots and bowls and cutlery put away, counters wiped, and Eileen was ready for bed, her skin shiny with night cream.

"Hi!" Virginia said, trying for an ordinary tone. "Is Rebecca here? I—uh—" But now she'd have to explain about the date. "We miscommunicated, and I thought she might have come over?"

"I don't think so." Eileen turned to call for Molly. "Molly's just been home watching TV tonight."

Molly entered the kitchen sleepy eyed, messy haired, and dressed as Rebecca had been, in bell-bottoms and a sweatshirt. Molly was taller and more developed than Rebecca, taller than Eileen. The Koslowski girls all had Eileen's fair coloring, her open face with Paul's green eyes. *Mature-looking girls*, Momma would say, judgment in her voice. *Oh, Momma*, Virginia would answer.

"Haven't seen Bec since school yesterday," Molly said.

Virginia wasn't going to cry again. She had to pull herself together.

"Oh, sweetheart," Eileen said, folding Virginia into a hug. "We're fine, Molly. You can go back to the TV."

In spurts, Virginia told what had happened, this fiasco of a night, her sort-of date with Henry, and Rebecca blowing up at the idea, and how she'd run out the door. She tried to make the date sound like more of an obligation than a pleasure, and she didn't mention the kiss. "You know what, I think I'll just head out and go look for her for a little while." Her eye-makeup tissue was still in her hand, and she wiped her eyes. "Drive around town a little."

"I'll send Paul out," Eileen said. "It'll be *fine*, don't worry. And I understand, I do. A woman needs a man, and a man needs a woman. It's clear that you've been off-balance all year. Once you find someone, you'll get your balance back."

Virginia was too surprised to reply. Eileen had just said the most ridiculous thing. And yet, she *was* off-balance; she was lost. At least Eileen didn't think worse of Virginia for going on a date, even though she thought Virginia was a women's libber, a radical, and she'd been quietly judging Virginia's erratic year from next door.

"Why don't we call the police, let them know," Eileen said, brisk now. "If one of them sees her, they'll bring her right home." She crossed the kitchen to the phone and picked it up.

Virginia recalled the security officer at her door and in her living room. "No, I don't think we need to do that just yet."

A door slammed at the front of the house, and the oldest Koslowski daughter entered the kitchen, followed by little Frankie and Rebecca. Rebecca's nose was red and one of her eyelids had swollen—she'd been crying too. Virginia started toward Rebecca, feeling a huge sigh escape, but Rebecca crossed her arms over her chest and lowered her head, glowering at the floor. Molly returned to the kitchen, sprinting to hug Rebecca, and Virginia tried not to mind.

"You're always welcome here, sweetie," Eileen said to Rebecca, declaring her superior mothering.

"Thank you, Eileen," Virginia said, suppressing her irritation, and waiting while Molly whispered something to Rebecca and Rebecca whispered something back. "Let's go home, Bec." She half expected Rebecca to refuse, but Rebecca nodded, thanked Kathleen for the ride and went out the door ahead of Virginia.

"I *don't* want to talk to you," Rebecca said, when they were back in their own kitchen, the two of them leaning against opposite counters. "I don't understand how you could do something like that."

Virginia took a breath. "I can see how you might feel that way, but it's not how you think."

"How is it? How is it not how I think?"

"You just need to be older to understand marriage, and—and—life." Virginia heard herself. She sounded false, offering some bland, obfuscating truism the way she used to when Rebecca was little, when Rebecca asked question after question about everything and everyone she encountered.

"Maybe *you* don't understand marriage."

Virginia let out a breath. "Maybe you're right." At this, Rebecca's face crumpled and she started to cry. At last Virginia was able to put an arm around her daughter and walk her upstairs and hug her good-night at her bedroom door, telling Rebecca that she loved her more than anything and was so happy she was home and safe.

Awake as usual in the middle of the night, Virginia replayed Rebecca's accusations. "Marriage is a great mystery," she'd stood up to read at June's wedding, twenty-some years ago. Ephesians. And "he who loves his wife loves himself… the two shall become one flesh." Anyone who'd read the New Testament would know what came right before those: "Wives, submit to your husbands." It made her laugh in the middle of the night; June had never once submitted to Jim, her husband, in any matter—their house, Jim's wardrobe, the boys' schooling, the azalea varieties in the yard.

She could only grasp at bits and pieces, things about Oliver that she'd loved and hated, maybe in equal measure. Like his wild enthusiasm for jazz, the tiny smoky clubs he'd found in Boston. Oliver had claimed the title of musician in their marriage as well as academic. Why had his jazz band rehearsals taken precedence? And always a meeting, an extra set of office hours, that he had to go to. She got up and ran a glass of water, to slow her stream of thoughts.

Oliver must have known he was a cliché, a European history prof who played jazz and smoked a pipe. Virginia would grouse about the pipe, its smoke, the mess he made with it, and Rebecca would squeeze Oliver in a hug. *I like the pipe*, Rebecca would say, *it smells nice*. And Oliver would shrug and smile at her over Rebecca's head.

How she'd envied his work, even all those meetings, the way his students hailed him when the three of them were out on Main Street. She recalled a moment from last summer. After supper, a perfect late-summer meal of roast chicken, sliced tomatoes and corn, Oliver had said he was going to quit the jazz band. That he needed to focus on work.

Oh, she'd said, surprised. Was this because she'd agreed to fill in for Dan Mason while he was on sabbatical, teaching the one class in the fall and another in the spring? It wasn't fair that he didn't want her to work, and she said so.

"How did you—that's not what I said." Oliver sounded exasperated. "I said I was thinking about quitting the jazz band. How did you get to that other conclusion?" They were at the table, Rebecca upstairs with her math homework. She'd started eighth grade, and she was slipping away.

Virginia pressed her fingers to her eyes. "Sorry."

"What's wrong?" he asked, his voice softer.

"I guess I'm afraid I'm not up to it. I haven't taught in such a long time, and I feel like a fraud. They're all going to know—"

Everyone felt that way, he'd said, and he felt like a fraud all the time. "Well, not *all* the time, but some of the time. Anyway, you'll be fine, you know those Italian and Dutch artists like the back of your hand, Virginia."

"And Flemish," she said. She wiped her nose with a paper towel.

"And Flemish. And if you have to bluff a little, they'll never know."

She looked at him, hoping for something, tricks, tips, something.

"I only mean, to expand, share your own theories, and so on. It's all there."

"Wait, we were talking about the jazz band," she said. "I didn't mean to—let me start again. You love the jazz band, don't quit the one thing that gives you joy."

"You give me joy, Rebecca gives me joy."

The word *joy* echoed in her head, round and elastic, a strange, old-fashioned word. There wasn't much joy between them. "You'll make time for it, like you always do," she said. "Everything will be fine, Oliver."

She'd wasted days, months, years, refusing the joy between them, and now he was gone.

Chapter Seventeen

THE BRIEF NEW HAMPSHIRE spring had given over to a heat wave, and Commons was noisy and hot this morning, the industrial fans blowing bacon-scented air over the long tables. Sam's friend Stephen was the only one at the Lambda Chi table, his sheet music and chemistry notes spread out around him. Sam wished there were some way to get Stephen's take on things, whether it could be worth it to help Elodie out, to meet her and Hank on Thursday night. He'd tried to persuade himself that he'd find a way to help Elodie while not supporting anything violent. Still, a part of him wanted to break something. He was sick of feeling like a loser.

"Dougie's looking for you," Stephen said, gazing at him for a second before returning to his chemistry notes.

"Me? What does he want now?"

"His car got stolen."

"Stolen? I doubt it. Probably a couple Lambda Chi guys took it and forgot where they parked it." Sam saw himself slipping Dougie's keys under the floor mat, and as the memories of that shining night with Elodie rushed back at him, something clicked into place, like when he used to solve the Jumble puzzle in Bubbe's *Daily News*, the mess of letters resolving into a word. He drank half his coffee and ate three bites of Cheerios. "I gotta go." He grabbed up his tray with a clatter, the cereal sloshing out of the bowl.

In Lambda Chi's common room, Sam found Dougie pacing and muttering. "I heard about the car," Sam said. "When did you last see it?"

"Yesterday morning," Dougie said. "I think. But I've had all that stupid-ass IFC stuff and I had an econ test and an Eastern Religions paper, and I wasn't thinking about the car, I mean, I shouldn't have to watch it every second, you know?"

"Right, you shouldn't."

"Fuck, I hate this place," Dougie said. "It could be anybody. The guys can be such assholes, nobody gives a shit about anything."

Sam considered whether to contradict Dougie, who had more Clarendon Bobcats sweatshirts than anyone, who ran cross-country and played JV tennis, who served in perpetuity on the IFC. Dougie had been awarded a Silver C junior year for being the kind of rah-rah guy he was. "Did you check out the other lots?"

Dougie nodded.

"All of them?"

Dougie shrugged.

"I have class at ten, but we can go around to the lots and look if you want," Sam said.

"My dad's going to kill me." Dougie followed Sam out the back door to the alley behind Frat Row, where the frats' tiny backyards and dirt parking lots formed similar eyesores. Beer bottles, plastic cups and cigarette butts lay scattered in the patchy grass and dirt, with other assorted dropped items, bikes on their sides, an open notebook, a windbreaker, one high-top sneaker, an apple core. Along the back of one house all the first-floor shutters hung loose, probably because some guys had tried to pull them off the building for fun. On another a window screen showed a giant football-shaped hole. One car at KA had a bashed-in headlight, and Charlie Biddle's MG was striated with scratches from a recent sideswipe. Dougie's car wasn't in any of the frat lots.

"I don't want to graduate," Dougie said, as they turned around to march back up Frat Row. "I don't want to lose my deferment. I don't even have a job."

"You'll find something, Dougie. Don't worry."

"Don't call me Dougie." Dougie straightened up, then deflated. "It's Douglas. Also you still owe me, Waxman. I mean, it could have been you, for all I know."

"Jesus, Dougie. Douglas, I mean." He didn't call Dougie an asshole even though Dougie was behaving like one. He had to get to class. "I'm sure the car will turn up. This is Westfield. Nothing ever happens here." He didn't share the other thought that had asserted itself; he pushed that thought back down.

Maybe Sam could ask Jerry, casually mention Dougie's missing car. But Jerry wasn't in math class. *Leave it alone,* the reasonable part of his brain chanted, *go do your own thing.* But he wanted to know what Elodie and Hank and the others were planning, and he wanted to see Elodie. It hurt to admit that he wanted to see her.

Inside the Topos farmhouse, Sam found only Cyril, alone in the kitchen with his ledgers, like last time. Jerry was gone; he'd left for Queens late last night, Cyril said. "His dad had a heart attack. Don't know when he'll be back."

"Ah," Sam said. "I'm sorry."

Cyril nodded. "Anything else?"

"Is—uh—Elodie around?"

Cyril shook his head slowly. No. No, Elodie was definitely not around, and Sam felt at once relieved and deflated. "She's not coming back," Cyril said. "They're going to get us all thrown in jail. If people find out they've been based here, Topos will go away. All our work for nothing."

"Do you know where she went?"

"New York, I imagine." Cyril regarded Sam over his reading glasses, another appraising look. "Do you have something to do with this nonsense? If you do, you'd better get going."

"No, no. No, I was just looking for Jerry."

Cyril's wife, Martha, came through the kitchen door carrying a clutch of eggs in a basket. "Something's eating the strawberry plants, Cyril. Chipmunks or voles." She nodded a hello to Sam. "It's always something."

Why had Cyril and Martha gotten involved with these younger people, Sam wondered. Martha stood at the counter, settling each egg carefully into a hanging basket. A vein stood out on her forehead; she was upset.

"This is like your family, isn't it," Sam said, before realizing he'd spoken his private thought aloud.

"What we have here is something good," Cyril said. "We made something good."

"I know," Sam said. "Thanks."

In Clara's hair salon, upstairs on Main Street, Virginia poured herself a coffee. The salon always smelled a little exotic; Clara ordered her coffee from Vienna, where she'd grown up, and she sprinkled cinnamon in the coffee grounds.

"Time for something new?" Clara led Virginia to the sink, where she washed Virginia's hair, more gently than usual, then massaged Virginia's temples with the pads of her fingers. She wrapped Virginia's head in a towel, put a hand to her back to help her sit up.

From the styling chair Virginia took in her own reflection as Clara combed out her hair. It spilled over her shoulders onto the blue plastic cape. "Um, maybe just a trim."

Clara stopped combing, and they looked together at her reflection. "A little something that frames your face? And maybe a little frosting? The longer hair can be a bit heavy. Wait just a moment." She turned to pull a magazine from a stack: *Mod Hair*, a magazine devoted to nothing but hairstyles. "There, you see? Something like that." The model wore a short, pixie-ish style, rather like Jeannette's. Jeannette was too good-natured to be irritated at Virginia copying her hairstyle.

"Sure." Why not.

"It's only hair," Clara said. "It will grow. We can count on that."

Virginia emerged onto Main Street smelling of the frosting chemicals. She felt lighter. New. At the first window she passed, she tried to catch a quick glimpse of her reflection, to see what someone else might see. Her hair was layered and shaggy now, and half-blond, and with the frosty lipstick that Clara had given her, she looked like a different person. It was too much; Rebecca would be offended. Virginia kept doing the wrong things.

She spotted Louise half a block away, and she waved as Louise approached, but Louise didn't see her. "Louise!" she called.

Louise took in that someone had called her name, staring at Virginia. "Oh! Virginia? Wow, I didn't recognize you for a second there."

She patted her new short hair. "What do you think?"

"It's—uh—it's—"

"You think it looks bad."

"No, not at all," Louise said "It's nice, but you look a little like a stewardess, or something."

"A stewardess!" She'd gone too far.

"Don't take it the wrong way, don't listen to me," Louise said. "It looks nice. I don't know anything about fashion. You want to get some lunch? I'm done for the day."

"Sure." The Tavern's basement door was directly across the street. "The Tavern?"

Louise shuddered. "God, no. Never going there again."

Settled in a booth at Mo's a few minutes later, they both ordered the diet hamburger special and ice teas.

"So what have you heard?" Virginia asked.

Louise shook her head. "Still waiting for the hearing. I've got an interview at Wellesley next week. They have a couple of openings in history they haven't filled yet, and it's one place where it's not a crime to be a woman." She held her hands out, palms up: *What can you do?*

"If you could hold on a little longer, things are changing, I've heard that there've been extra trustee and committee meetings, and Weissman's pushing a new—"

"I've heard that too, but that's not going to change how my situation goes. If there's a plausible way for them take away my tenure, they will," Louise said. "I've always known that my tenure was different from all the others'. I don't belong here anyway."

Virginia laughed with recognition, then saw that Louise was offended. "No, no, that's it. That's how I've felt since we moved to New Hampshire. That I don't belong here. It's just funny to hear you say that."

"Hysterical."

"I'm sorry, I'm not making light of your situation."

Louise nodded. "Let me tell you about not belonging. My father said I'd never get a husband because I was ugly and I read too much. He said I thought I was too good for our family. He died before I finished my doctorate, but even my mom didn't come to the ceremony. I was the only one there without family. The only woman, and the only one there alone. I stood out then, just like I always do." Louise slumped to the side, letting her head rest against the wall.

"Oh," Virginia said. "I'm sorry. My father wasn't that far off from yours, I think." The waitress set their plates on the table. "You have to keep going," she said. "We all do. And I owe you so much…" She'd leaned on Louise, she'd barely expressed any thanks, and she'd made things worse for her. She had to find a way to help.

Louise was cutting into her burger, and she shook her head, eyes on her plate. "Let's talk about something else," she said. "Do you think I should get a new hairstyle too?"

★ ★ ★

The next morning, Virginia called Mimi Higgins, President Weissman's secretary. She didn't know how she'd explain wanting to meet with him, but Mimi only asked how much time Virginia would need. If she could come in at the tail end of the day, Mimi would squeeze her in.

She sat to write out her concerns and questions, tore the paper up. She wouldn't need to wait for Rebecca to come home from school, since Rebecca had to stay late for the ninth-grade orientation meeting, picking classes and clubs for next fall.

In the afternoon, she changed into a dress and checked her appearance, fluffing her short hair and running her new frosty lipstick over her lips. She did look like a stewardess—Louise was right. Louise's problem had never been that she talked too much and pushed ahead of others, as Oliver used to say. It was that she told the truth. Louise had tried to include Virginia, asked her to help out with something political, right after Oliver died, and Virginia had said no, and probably in a rude and hurtful way. The Gang of Four all welcomed her, and all she'd done was question that welcome, and then lure Louise into Oliver's old frat.

In the president's outer office Mimi Higgins gestured at a row of chairs. "He's on the phone, but he shouldn't be too long. I blocked off fifteen minutes for you. Will that be enough?"

"Yes, thanks, Mimi." Outside the office's windows, the trees lining the college green were almost fully leafed out. Spring in New Hampshire came on late, and every year the transition from buds and pale baby leaves to deep summery green took her by surprise.

"You can go in now." Mimi gave Virginia a quick smile, then bent to her typing.

"Thanks." She stood up and smoothed her skirt, as if she were heading in to a job interview.

President Weissman stood inside his door, and he took both her hands, kissing her on the cheek as though they were at a cocktail party. He leaned back and smiled, eyes crinkling at the edges. "You're looking wonderfully well, my dear," he said. "Very nice."

Virginia smiled back, wondering about the compliment as she followed him to his sitting area. Was he flirting? He was the president of a college, too remote for anything like flirting. On the chair across from him, she crossed her legs at the ankle rather than the knee.

"And how can I help?" he asked.

"Well, the thing is, I learned—that is, I wanted to ask—" She stopped. She began again more firmly. "I'm here because of Louise. Louise Walsh."

"Ah." His expression shifted at the mention of Louise's name, a closing off—he'd had enough of this tired subject. "Professor Walsh. Yes." He waited, tapping the ball of his foot.

"They're making a big mistake," she said. "Something needs to be done."

"A mistake," he repeated.

"Yes." Her mouth was dry, she needed a glass of water, but she knew what to say, and the words came tumbling out. "Did anyone on the committee, anyone at all, check to find out more about the women's meeting? Did any committee member take the time to talk to anyone who'd attended the meeting? Or did they see the headline in the

Clarendon paper and that was all they needed, one little push?"

He lit his pipe, looking at the glowing tobacco rather than at her. "As you may know, I'm not on the discipline committee. But it must be said that she hasn't always made things easy for others. She isn't much of a team player."

She thought of Randolph and Garland and the others in Oliver's department. "Oliver was a team player, and I don't see how it served him all that well," she said. "And I can think of a lot of his colleagues who aren't team players. It sounds like Louise is being held to a standard that no one else is being held to."

He leaned forward, pipe in one hand. "Here is the thing, my dear. It is a delicate time, and while it may not look like we're moving forward, we are. We simply can't have our faculty acting like radicals when we're trying to change. It hurts our case, subverts our argument. When there appears to be chaos, it annoys the alums and spooks the trustees, which makes it harder to get them on board."

She got it. Appearance, that was all that mattered. She let out a sigh.

"Mrs. Desmarais, I am trying." He looked weary, his whole face a frown, with his eyes turned down at their outer edges and the lines around his mouth deeper now. The job had aged him, worn him down. "Surely you know that I have been trying. I can see what Clarendon needs, it simply cannot go on as it has in the past, it must find a new way forward, and I have done what I can. And the young women have made their point. I don't blame Professor Walsh for the women's rights meeting—"

"I was there too," she said. "It wasn't just Louise."

He nodded. "The other day we received some information that certain groups are trying to make trouble on East Coast campuses," he said. "Outside groups, agitators. Clarendon isn't immune."

She thought again of the security officer sitting on her couch. Perhaps all these men had turned paranoid. But she'd been a fool to think that she could make a difference, an outsider like her. A housewife. Also a woman who started things but didn't finish, who made one bad choice after another. "But do you think it's right?"

He frowned at her, parsing her meaning.

"To just take away Louise's tenure like that."

"I don't think you've heard what I've been saying, my dear. And of course in the end, it depends on the committee, what they decide."

"No, I want to know if *you* think it's right." She heard herself sounding like someone else, someone who could ask hard questions.

He smiled. "I'm sorry, but I have another meeting I must get to in a minute. I'm so glad we had time to chat." He stood, waiting for her to stand up too, then walked her out, shaking her hand and kissing her again on the cheek.

He'd sent her away, just like that. With his usual courtesy, and without remorse. *Oliver, I hope you're still with me,* she thought. *I know a little of what you were up against.*

Chapter Eighteen

TO GET TO THE CHAPEL, Sam cut behind Lawrence dorm, avoiding the sidewalk and the Clarendon green, not that anyone would care what he was doing. The darkness felt thick tonight, heavy low clouds blocking the moon and stars. It would probably start pouring in a minute. In the gloom behind the chapel, he slowed down, but he didn't see anything. Good, because he didn't have the balls to do this—he wasn't brave enough or crazy enough.

He heard a harsh whisper, and then he caught the outlines of two people sitting with their arms around their knees, their backs against the far side of the chapel wall.

"What's happened to you, Hank?" Elodie was saying. "Where did your rage go? How can you not be enraged every single moment?"

Sam moved closer, cleared his throat. "Hey."

"Thank God you're here." Elodie reached up to press

something into Sam's hand. A flask. He took a drink, passed it back.

Hank spoke up. "I *am* enraged, Elodie. I'm just tired, that's all."

"We're all tired. But this project is your baby as much as anyone else's. You went and got the materials, remember? You scouted the locations—"

"Yeah, well, where's Jerry, huh?" Hank passed the flask back to Elodie. Hank was drunk, Sam saw.

"What is *wrong* with you? Jerry was never going to be part of this." Elodie gestured up at him. "Sit down, Sam. It's the simplest little timer and a very small amount of combustible material. You probably made this kind of thing in grammar school."

"Um, no. No one makes that kind of thing in grammar school." The things Sam had made as a kid—a potato clock, plastic models of WWII bombers and sleek jets—and the times he'd helped Zayde Waxman tinker with his shortwave radio—sure, he'd made a lot of things, but nothing meant to cause harm.

"Ohh-kay," Hank said, hoisting himself up to standing. "I'll drive."

"Maybe we don't need you," Elodie said.

"Yes, we do," Sam said. Ugh, he'd just said *we*. He'd been sucked into this project.

Elodie was still talking. "...just a handful of the frats. Hank scoped out the ones with the easiest entry. It's only symbolic, Sam. It's a Thursday night. No one's going to get hurt."

"How do you know?" Sam asked.

"Because we're being strategic, not stupid." A quarter moon slipped out from behind a cloud, and Sam and Hank followed her to the parking lot below the chapel, Hank whispering the frats he'd chosen like a chant: KA, Phi Rho, Delta Mu, Beta. Sam had to figure out how to take part in their crazy plan, but also stop them, all at the same time. It was like those dreams where he was both the main character and the audience, silently watching the action unfold.

In the lot, Elodie opened the trunk to Dougie's car.

"Huh. So you guys—" Sam decided not to state the obvious, that they'd taken Dougie's car. Elodie could have used any of the cars from Topos, but instead had stolen Dougie's, which she only knew about because of him.

"Less noticeable," Hank said. "He'll get it back, don't worry, man." Hank's flashlight illuminated a box. "All you need—wires, clocks, batteries, the material—is in there," Hank said, as Elodie pulled papers from her pocket and began to unfold them. Sam stared at the box, frozen with confusion.

"Okay, we'll each do two," Elodie said, then clicked the trunk shut. "Fair?"

"Elodie," Sam said. "We can't just walk right in and—"

"So it's an excellent thing you're here, Sam. You just tell me the best way in. I'll handle the rest." She was close enough to him that he could see that her eyes were big and pleading. She believed in this project, this action, and right now, at least, she believed in him. He reached for her free hand; she squeezed back.

As half his brain shouted to get out of here and away from Elodie, the other half went to work on this plan as if it were a perfectly logical thing to do late on a Thursday night at Clarendon. He could slip into the frats in a way that Elodie couldn't—he could come up with a story, someone he needed to talk to. But they couldn't drive Dougie's car down Frat Row, that would be insane. Sam heard himself agreeing that he and Elodie would put together the first kit—better not to dwell on what they were making—while Hank parked and waited over by the hospital, then regroup.

KA was the third house on Frat Row, first on Hank's list geographically. Sam thought of Teddy Burnham, Charlie Biddle, and all the other KA assholes who'd been giving him threatening looks since Spring Sing, and he felt a surge of nerves and energy. If anyone deserved a scare, they did. Where was a place where no guys would hang out on a Thursday night? KA had a library that was a dumping ground, a place to throw coats during parties, and to stash KA's trademark collection of old exams and papers—KA guys did all their studying and copying from them, sometimes selling them to guys in other frats. At least Sam had never paid for an old exam; at least he did his own work.

He went in through the back door, just like he would have if he were there legitimately, and he planned to say he was here to ask Charlie Biddle about Dougie's lost car, if he ran into anyone. But no one was around. Two guys were passed out in the flickering blue-gray light of the TV room, and from the basement came the banging of paddles on the pong table as someone scored a point. The main living room was deserted. He veered right, into the little paneled library, where he pushed open a side window and waved his hand to summon Elodie. From outside, Elodie handed up the components, and he crouched under a table to sort them out. His flashlight illuminated the directions, a simple drawing. He took a little comfort from the fact that no one had used his cipher for these instructions. One thing had to lead to the other. He attached the packet of

gunpowder to the paper-covered block of TNT, wrapping
the block and the batteries with wire. The chemical for-
mula for TNT floated through his head—he'd learned it
in chemistry class when they'd used it for charge transfer
experiments, and now he was just doing another experi-
ment. He twisted the wires around the clock, and then
wound the clock, setting the alarm for an hour from now.
He was like Max from *Get Smart*. "Good thinking, 99,"
he whispered. He was an utter fool.

Once Sam was outside again, Elodie took his face in her
hands and kissed him, a real kiss at last, and he kissed her
back, wanting to linger there. "One down," she said. She
took his hand and they ran for the parking lot to find Hank
and the supplies for the next house.

Sam waited with Elodie in the empty hospital parking lot, trying to stay out of the glow of the streetlights,
crouching behind the bushes that lined the lot. Still no
Hank. "He's probably just circling, trying to lie low," Sam
said. But maybe Hank had bailed on them; Sam hoped that
was what had happened. One crime per night was enough.
There was no way to convince Elodie of anything, though,
since she was pacing from one corner of the lot to the other,
as if she could make Dougie's car appear by perambulation.

Sam's brain veered back and forth too, telling him to bail
out now, go tell someone. At last Elodie said she'd find a
pay phone in the hospital, and that Sam should keep watch.
She sprinted off in the direction of the hospital.

This action wasn't going to work. The success of it de-
pended on a bunch of things happening at the same time,
and Hank's disappearance had screwed up the timing.
Sam had put an hour on the timer, but that wasn't going

to be anywhere near enough time to get all four devices set. He'd made a giant mistake, he'd fucked up badly, and he couldn't unravel the logic of how he'd arrived at this point. He still wanted Elodie—wanted her to see him the way he saw her—but this action's violence was too much. Jerry had been right all along. He couldn't set any more of those things. He turned and sprinted back toward Frat Row, legs pumping, his body moving faster than his mind could think.

After last week, Molly's mom had probably told her to be nice to Rebecca, *Just hang around with her more*, which gave Rebecca plenty of time to talk to Molly about her plan. Molly had been doubtful at first, a surprise, since Molly was the brave one, the one who used to talk Rebecca into doing crazy things like climbing onto the roof or skipping lunch at school.

But until now, as they approached Frat Row, Rebecca hadn't considered how scary this would feel. The frat houses loomed up, stolid brick and white-columned things, like a neighborhood for demented rich people. She'd already sussed out the location of KA, a brick house with green shutters and a columned porch, three houses down. In the Koslow-skis' station wagon that bad night, Kath had said she and her friends usually went around back, headed right down to KA's basement, and no one noticed or said boo to them.

Rebecca led the way, slipping through the side yard, staying close to some scraggly overgrown bushes, look-ing for the frat's back door. But once they got to the door, how would they keep going? They needed Kath, some-one older to tell them what to do, or to talk them out of it. She pictured Heloise and Dear Abby watching her and

Molly, Abby saying to Heloise what a foolish girl Rebecca had turned out to be.

They'd reached the back door of the frat, which stood half-open—practically an invitation. Even with the mascara and lip gloss they'd put on in her mudroom before they left, they didn't look anything like college girls. Technically they weren't even high school girls yet. She couldn't do this, and she spun around, bumping into Molly.

"Oh, come on, loser," Molly said, taking her hand. "This was your idea. We're going in." Molly pulled her through the door, and then they were inside the frat, at the start of a long hallway that led to a big front parlor kind of room. They took a couple of steps down the hall, still holding hands.

"Heeyy, girls," a guy said in a comfortable drawl, as if he knew them already. There was a room to their right that they hadn't noticed, where couches lined the walls and a TV up front played some old black-and-white movie. Empty bottles and plastic cups covered a table, and empty chip bags and newspapers littered the floor.

"Hey yourself," Molly said back.

Rebecca said nothing. She felt sick to her stomach.

The guy who'd just called to them got up, and two others had turned from the TV to see who was there. "So hey there," the guy said, in the hall with them now. He had wavy light hair, and even in the low light she could see his dimples when he smiled. He wore a button-down shirt, untucked over his bell-bottoms. "Join us for a beer?"

"Sparky, man," one of the other guys called from the couch. "Now's not the time."

"One beer isn't going to hurt anything," he said. "Follow me." He turned and went a little farther down the hallway, motioning them through a door and down a flight of stairs to a basement. He introduced himself—Teddy, his name was—and asked if they'd gone to the party that had taken over all of Frat Row last weekend. He kept talking without waiting for their answer, about how KA was on probation so they'd had to keep their party pretty quiet, which had only made it more exclusive, you know? Exclusive was good, but they'd have a bigger party, a complete blowout, in the fall, he said.

Rebecca took Molly's hand again as they followed him through the basement, which smelled sour and gross, to a long bar. Teddy went behind the bar and filled two cups from the beer taps, pushing them across the bar to them. "You're from Gilman Junior College, I take it?" he asked.

"Yep," Molly said, before Rebecca could figure out whether he was making fun of them, or what. "I'm Jenny, and this is Jessica."

Teddy came around the bar and clinked cups with them. "Nice to meet you, Jenny and Jessica."

Rebecca tried to sip at her beer as if she did this kind of thing every day. Teddy led them back upstairs and into the big parlor room, where she and Molly sat close to one another on a couch, and he turned a folding chair backward and perched on it. Two other guys came downstairs laughing about something and stopped near the couch. The guy with the louder laugh sank down onto another couch. His friend's sideburns reminded Rebecca of one of the Monkees.

Noisy-Laugh Guy asked who these chicks were.

"My new friends," Teddy said. "Jenny and—and—"

"Jessica," Rebecca said.

"From Gilman Junior College," Molly said.

The two other guys cracked up. "Gilman Junior College,

we love goddamn Gilman Junior College girls," Noisy-Laugh Guy said.

She didn't know what was so funny, and she pinched Molly to get her to stop saying they went to Gilman Junior College.

"So give us a reason you should hang out with us," Sideburns Guy said.

"We know every word to 'Joy to the World,'" Rebecca said. "The Three Dog Night version, not the Christmas carol." She didn't know where that had come from, or why she'd said it; it had just popped out. Molly looked at her, her eyes big with surprise.

"Okay, sing it," Teddy said.

Still looking at Molly, Rebecca started to sing. After that first line, Molly joined in, and they were singing together, badly, right through the chorus. But they did know every word. Now Sideburns Guy and Noisy-Laugh Guy sang with them, and Teddy went downstairs for more beers.

After a while, music blared from a stereo. Marvin Gaye and Tammi Terrell, and she and Molly sang that too. Then she drank another beer, listened to another Marvin Gaye song. She watched as Molly got up to dance with one of the guys, Bill, he'd said his name was.

Rebecca couldn't pinpoint the moment, but she realized that she'd been having fun for a while now. This was okay! She accepted another beer. A Ringo Starr song that she liked had started, so she got up and danced by herself, drinking her beer. Then someone was dancing with her, oh, it was Teddy, she knew him, and he was so cute and sweet. She liked his button-down shirt. He was a little more dressed up, maybe a little more proper, than the other guys in their ratty T-shirts. He took her hand and twirled her and they sang along with Ringo. He kept giving her sips of the drink in his other hand, which wasn't beer; she didn't know what it was, but it tasted pretty good.

She felt floaty and happy, dancing and drinking and singing, she floated around the big room holding Teddy's hand. And then, as if she were the lead in a movie, he told her how much he liked her, and she told him how much she liked him. He was going to show her the house, if that was okay with her, and of course it was okay because she was having a good time, she just had to go back and tell Molly that she was going upstairs for a minute, but Teddy pulled on her hand, tugging her toward the stairs.

"My room," he said—somehow they'd arrived at the doorway to a big room, with one bed in the corner and another on top of a high wooden platform. "What do you think?" He maneuvered her into the room, his arm draped heavily over her shoulder, and he kicked the door behind him so that it clicked shut.

Sam slipped back inside KA, where he could hear a couple of guys heading upstairs, the usual late-night banging around, and the thwacks and shouts of pong coming from the basement. Once again no one noticed.

A moment later, when he opened the frat's library door, a thin veil of smoke rolled over him, and a sharp smell of something burning, of singed fabric or carpet. The device must have caught on fire. But that couldn't be right— the alarm wasn't due to go off yet. He'd done something wrong, and he'd fucked up the fuse too.

Rebecca was still feeling wonderful and floaty, but a distant corner of her brain gave a little ping of alarm.

"Hey, I like you, you know that?" Teddy pulled her close, putting a hand on her back and then her bottom, pressing her to him. She liked him too, even though she shouldn't—he was way too old for her.

He kissed her, and even in her floaty state the kiss wasn't what she'd expected. It was sloppy and spitty and gross, his tongue pushing into her mouth. He smelled like chemicals, like alcohol was coming out of his skin. She pulled away.

"Oh, no," he said. "I thought you liked me. I mean, I really like you. I think I love you."

"I—uh—" But no more words would come. She found that she was sitting next to him on the bed in the corner. He tugged on her shirt, pulling her down, and she felt her T-shirt rip around the armhole. She was horizontal on the bed now, staring up at the ceiling, his body too close, his hand under her shirt, and with another tug he pulled on her bra until it ripped in the back. He turned away, and she felt him fumbling with his jeans. Something cut through her dreamy fog—her own brain, maybe—and she came to, awake and scared now. She rolled away from him and onto the floor, landing on her hands and knees. She caught her breath and started to scrabble away from the bed, but he rolled onto the grubby carpet as she'd just done, and she felt his too-big hands grab her ankle and tug. Her chin banged on the floor, burning as it rubbed against the carpet.

With his hand on her hip now, he flipped her over, and she looked up to see him smiling down at her, a sleepy, horrible grin, as if this were a game. She was going to die here.

She heard a thunderous sound, the sound of someone running through the hallway, banging on doors. The door swung open. "Get out!" a guy yelled into the room. "There's a fire! Fire department's on the way!" Teddy had let go, distracted by the sound, and she shoved him away with both knees, pushing up to standing, and then lurched toward the guy at the door. It was Sam the college guy, Mom's friend.

"Fuck, what are *you* doing here, asshole?" Teddy said from the floor.

She saw Sam's gaze taking in both her and Teddy, and she heard Teddy behind her, getting to his feet. She darted under Sam's arm and through the open door.

"Are you okay?" Sam asked. She tried to nod an answer. "I gotta check the third floor, but you need to get out." He slammed the door to Teddy's room and covered the hall in two big steps and ran upstairs to the third floor. She ran too, taking the hall in two steps like he'd done, and then down the curving stairs in a jumble.

A few seconds later she was in the frat's front yard, shaking, and college boys were going in all directions around her, yelling and calling to one another. She had to get away from this hideous place, and Molly had left her behind. Molly must have gone home. Molly hadn't even bothered to check if she was alive or dead. She started to cry.

"Bec!" she heard. "Rebecca!" It was Molly, on the lowest level of the frat's fire escape. Molly hadn't left, thank God. "What should I do?"

Rebecca darted over to the fire escape. It would be a long jump down. "Swing down and hold on, pretend it's a jungle gym. I'll catch you."

"I'll get her," a college guy said. Ugh, God, no, it was Teddy again, and she shuddered and started to move away from him. "Just drop through," he called up to Molly. "I'll catch you."

Before Rebecca could tell her not to, Molly dropped

into horrible Teddy's arms, and he staggered and fell under her weight. Rebecca whacked him on the head as best she could and grabbed for Molly, pulling her up and away. They started to run again, but Rebecca was off-balance and her legs went wobbly as Molly moved too fast. They'd barely reached the sidewalk when a police car pulled up in front of them, its headlights blinding. "New Hampshire State Police," the policeman called. "Don't move."

Chapter Nineteen

IN HER RUSH TO get out of the house, Virginia had forgotten her bra, and now she kept her coat buttoned, arms crossed over her chest. And she was cold after waking in the middle of the night. The girls were fine, the girls were fine, the girls were fine, she repeated, just as the policeman had said on the phone. But that knowledge didn't stop her shivering, didn't stop her teeth from chattering, as if it were a January night, ten below zero, instead of late May. Paul, Eileen's husband, leaned against the wall, tapping his foot. The Westfield police station at the back of town hall was so small that the waiting area held only two chairs. She sat next to Eileen, the two of them silent.

"Back here," a young policeman said, gesturing, and they followed him to a small conference room behind the desk, where the police chief, Gary Barton, stood waiting by the door.

He greeted them and started to talk as if he knew them all, but she couldn't listen to whatever he was saying; she could only take in Rebecca seated at the table next to Molly. Rebecca let out a sob and Virginia rushed around the table, leaning down to clutch at her daughter, who flopped onto her like a baby. After a minute, Virginia pulled back to get a better look. Rebecca's eyes were swollen from crying, her hair was disheveled, as if she'd been sleeping on it, and her shirt was missing a button. Molly looked about the same: runny nose, red-rimmed eyes, generally disheveled. Molly laid her head on her arms, either to sleep or to block them all out.

"What happened?" Virginia asked, holding on to Rebecca.

"Let's have a seat," Gary Barton said, gesturing at the chairs around the table. "They're a little intoxicated, so I'm going to run through what we know real quick, and then we'll have them come back later." The girls were found by the state police outside a Clarendon frat, drunk enough to be off-balance and slurring their words. They didn't seem to be with anyone else, although that couldn't be ascertained for sure as the circumstances of this evening were most unusual. "We were able to intervene and stop what seems to have been some sort of—an attempt at a bombing on campus. I can't give you details but a fraternity house got hit, leading to a small house fire. Everyone's safe. We'd have called you all in sooner but this was an extraordinary situation that's kind of taken over things here, having to sweep the entire campus and all."

Virginia felt struck dumb, and she heard Eileen's gasp.

"Just minor explosives, more in the realm of a prank, not that we'd call this a prank," Gary Barton said. "The kids were all out before the fire was contained. The fire department had to call on Bradford, Thetford and Royalton for aid because they didn't know what they might be dealing with, and the state police are combing the campus. Meanwhile, we got a confession from one perpetrator, and we know who the others are."

"Jesus Christ," Paul said.

Eileen turned to face Virginia. "I'm sorry, but I have to blame you, Virginia. You've radicalized our daughters. I knew something like this was coming."

Virginia was too addled to disagree or defend herself. "Wait—you think—that our girls were—what did you know was coming?"

"*Mom.*" Molly lifted her head from the table. "KA is where Lacey goes with her friends to buy pot. And Kath has hung out there. I'm not a radical, and neither is Bec."

"Lacey? Kath?" Eileen said, as if she'd just this moment remembered she had two older daughters.

"We just wanted to know what it was like in there," Rebecca said softly.

"Well, now you know," Paul said. "You girls could have gotten yourselves killed, or worse."

What could be worse than getting themselves killed? Virginia wondered. She stifled a laugh, which turned into a sob. She should have run out of tears by now, but she couldn't stop crying. She needed Oliver here, he'd know what to say; he wouldn't sound as harsh as Paul, or as crazy as Eileen. She put a fist to her mouth, trying to push the crying back inside.

"It's okay, Mom," Rebecca said. "Look, it's okay. We're okay. Right, Molly?"

Molly nodded. "We're fine."

The policeman gave Virginia a form to sign, noting that Rebecca was due back here at two o'clock tomorrow for further questioning. They all shuffled out of the police office, parting on the sidewalk. "We'll talk later," Eileen said. "I'm sure we'll get to the bottom of this."

Virginia could only nod. The girls were fine, that was the thing. The girls were fine.

At home, Virginia gave Rebecca two aspirin and a glass of water, then bundled Rebecca, still in her dirty clothes, into her own big bed, sliding in beside her. Outside, the night had lightened to gray, with a pale shimmer behind the gray. Rebecca drifted off after a minute, murmuring something unintelligible.

Virginia let herself cry again, sat up to blow her nose. *Nothing happened*, she reminded herself. Nothing happened, other than the fact that Rebecca had turned into a teenager without her noticing. She couldn't imagine why the girls would have gone into a frat, and then she was struck by the memory of her shameful episode with Louise, going into the frat to dance, sealing Louise's fate. And then her useless meeting with President Weissman yesterday. Weissman's words about the outside agitators came back to her now. What if Rebecca had still been inside the frat, trapped by the fire? She would never be able to stop thinking about that.

Sam was asleep, fully clothed as if he'd passed out after a night of partying, when he heard the banging on his door. *"Sam Waxman,"* someone called. *"Open up!"* He rolled out of bed and opened the door to a policeman. "They need to talk to you downtown."

The police car rolled through the early-morning fog as cheerful birdsong floated through the half-open driver's window. The cop said something into his two-way radio. All those surges of adrenaline last night had left Sam almost too tired to care that he was getting arrested. A minute later, a voice crackled through the radio. "President's office, not downtown."

At the threshold of the office, Sam stumbled from fatigue and confusion, and President Weissman, in a pullover and windbreaker, motioned for him to sit on the couch. A secretary handed him a cup of coffee, and he took a sip; she'd put milk and sugar in it for him. He took in the high ceilings and grand windows, and their view of the fog-obscured green.

A tall, narrow-framed man in a dark suit leaned against President Weissman's desk, writing in a notepad. He crossed the room to loom over Sam.

"Mr. Waxman," the tall guy said. "I'm Agent Stevenson. FBI. Few questions for you." He smiled: straightforward but not unpleasant. "Your friends gave us some useful information. Now it's your turn." He pulled some photos out of a manila folder. "Tell me who you recognize." He fanned out the photos like cards in a deck. Sam recognized an enlarged version of Hank's yearbook photo from freshman year, then Elodie—Elodie in New York, maybe Washington Square Park, walking with some guy—and he said so, feeling like a complete putz. A snitch.

"None of the others?" Agent Stevenson said. "You sure?" Sam could only shake his head no.

"As I said, your friends gave us some useful information. Mr. Atkins—" Hank "—tried to persuade us that he'd been tricked by a girl. That didn't sound so good since he was drunk and belligerent, in a stolen car with busted tail-lights and explosives in the trunk. And him with his rap sheet. I'm sure you won't waste our time with nonsense, Mr. Waxman."

Tricked by a girl.

"But as I said, Mr. Atkins and Miss Sewall—" Elodie "—have been quite helpful. Tell me what you see here." Agent Stevenson held up another photo.

It was a photo of something on fire, smoke billowing into the sky. He stretched to get a better view: a row of New York brownstones, downtown it looked like, with one in the middle mostly gone, dark smoke stretching up and out of a shell, the brownstones on either side untouched.

"We need to know how many were in there," Agent Stevenson said.

Sam's heart galloped and skittered so much that the pulses had to be visible through his sweatshirt. People had been killed. *Miss Sewall has been very helpful.* Not dead. He looked up at Agent Stevenson. "I—I don't know—I've never been there, I don't know what you're asking me."

"You sure you never—"

President Weissman spoke at the same time. "Just tell the man how much you were involved with these people." In his chair, President Weissman clasped his hands between his knees; he looked old and tired and sad. So Sam began the story, not the story he'd been telling himself, but the lame story of a guy who wanted to impress a girl. He heard himself going into the details of his relationship, such as it was, with Elodie. Of the cipher, the meeting and of last night. Of Hank disappearing, and of racing back to KA to undo what he'd done, and the fire. Of calling the fire department and trying to get all the guys out, and how most of the guys had just laughed at him. He heard himself talking; he sounded like a lunatic. After a while he noticed Agent Stevenson nod at President Weissman, and the two left the office to talk in private.

Sam leaned back against the couch. Outside, the fog had burned off and he took in the Frisbee players on the green, a woman walking a dog past the chapel, the stately old trees at the edge of the green that had probably seen two hundred years' worth of moronic Clarendon guys.

President Weissman had returned without Agent Stevenson, and now he stood over Sam. "They don't know what to do with you at the moment, and neither do I," President Weissman said. "I don't think this is going to end well, Sam."

Sam considered whether to tell President Weissman that he loved Clarendon, and he loved his classes, at least math and art history, and jazz band and Granitetones. He'd risked it all for a girl, so he could feel normal for a while. *Tricked by a girl.* But instead he said that he had screwed up badly, and he couldn't make it right, and he was sorry.

"I'm sorry too, Sam," President Weissman said.

Chapter Twenty

VIRGINIA WOKE REBECCA AT SEVEN. "Think you can get up and go to school, hon?" Rebecca only shook her head, and rolled over.

The weekend had passed, but Virginia couldn't stop replaying all the terrible things that might have happened, outcomes that Rebecca had missed by a tiny sliver of time and space. And Rebecca wasn't well. No fever, but she was pale and clammy; she hadn't eaten much of anything these past few days. "Okay," she said. "I'll come check on you in a while."

In the kitchen, she started another cup of coffee, filled a pan with water to poach an egg. Someone knocked at the side door: Eileen. She turned off the stove.

They hugged, and Virginia pulled out a chair for Eileen and got out another coffee mug. Eileen asked about Rebecca, and Virginia told her about letting Rebecca stay home from school, that Rebecca was a little worse today, not better.

"Molly cried all weekend, and now she's furious," Eileen said. "Furious at me, of all things. Even though she knows perfectly well that a severe consequence is in order."

Severe consequence, good God. "Didn't they already go through enough?" Virginia asked.

"We can't have fourteen-year-olds going into fraternities. Look what happened! Think of what might have happened!"

"That's what I mean. The whole thing was so awfully frightening that they won't do it again."

"They're all hippies these days, Virginia. All of them," Eileen said. "Kathleen and Lacey are getting their hands on drugs, and who knows what else they're doing. Molly may end up even worse, starting earlier." Eileen's lips quivered and she took a sip of coffee. "The world isn't supposed to be like this."

"What's it supposed to be like?"

"Like it used to be. Like it always was. When we knew what to do and how to do it. When we knew how to live a good life."

Eileen's words sounded so familiar, Virginia had probably said them herself. *I was like you, Eileen*, she thought. *I understand.* This knowledge filled her with a kind of empathy. "I'm not sure I ever knew what to do or how to do it," Virginia said. "But I think it's a good sign that Molly is angry." Anger had to be better than lying in bed, unable to get up.

When she leaned close to hug Eileen goodbye a few minutes later, Eileen remained stiff, as Virginia had been the other night in Eileen's kitchen, when Eileen had said

Virginia was off-balance and then folded her into a motherly hug. Virginia had lived lifetimes this year; she'd wandered through the dark and the rough, and there might or might not be light ahead to guide her. And no one needed to crack down on Rebecca. She wanted Rebecca to talk to her, she wanted Rebecca to live. She wanted Rebecca to grow up and find out who she was going to be.

She thought of the way things had gone last week, before all of this, when she'd taken Rebecca out for Mexican night at Mo's, when Rebecca was working hard to keep up her silent act.

"How about summer camp? You could go with your cousin Margaret to camp in West Virginia. Margaret's a CIT this year," she'd said, and Rebecca had scowled at her. "You need something to do this summer."

Rebecca said nothing.

"I'm sorry, Bec. No one will ever replace Daddy. No one. He will always be my husband and your dad. But I may not always be alone." She hadn't meant to say it, not yet.

Rebecca nodded, crying now.

"But you know, I need to work, and I'd like to finish my dissertation. I have to work to support us, you get that, right?"

"I get it, I know, I know," Rebecca said, finally breaking her silence. "The money tree in the backyard, right?"

Virginia laughed, and Rebecca smiled at last, and neither of them had to say any more. Oliver used to joke with Rebecca about the money tree, saying that Rebecca should go out to the money tree in the backyard to get some cash for the new record player she wanted or the new ice skates.

After Eileen left, Virginia went to the front door to grab the newspaper. The headline at the top of the front page was twice its usual size: Clarendon College to Admit Females. Underneath, the subhead: "Series of meetings this spring led to trustees' decision. Announcement made before night of campus chaos."

Mrs. Desmarais, I am trying, President Weissman had said. *The young women have made their point.* Maybe in some small way she'd helped to make a difference. But Louise—what about Louise? "We take this moment as an opportunity to bring new energy and a new approach to the college," the head of the trustees said in the article. "The first class of Clarendon women will graduate in 1976."

Imagine that.

1973

REBECCA

Westfield

IT'S BEEN MORE THAN two years since Dad died, and lately Rebecca pictures herself on a timeline, moving forward through the months and years, as Dad slips away into the past. She wonders if Dad would recognize her these days, and what he'd think about her running, about the tricks she learned from the doctor.

Last August, Rebecca and Mom made a summer trip to Virginia because Aunt June had bought a house at the beach, with an apartment in back for Grandmomma to live in. Rebecca's cousin Margaret, who hadn't given Rebecca the time of day for the last few years because Margaret was two years older, suddenly decided that Rebecca was cool and funny. Margaret was petite, with glossy dark hair and vivid blue eyes, and she tanned effortlessly—she didn't have to put on a T-shirt to keep from burning the way Rebecca did.

Rebecca and Margaret took long walks on the beach from the north end to the south and back again, the beach houses slowly giving way to hotels, restaurants, packs of tourists. Margaret showed her how to slip into hotel pools and swim for a few minutes, then resume their beach walk, as if the whole world belonged to them alone. Splashing through wavelets, she and Margaret talked about school and boys and college; Rebecca turned her terrible night in KA into a jokey story about two adventurous girls, leaving out everything but Molly and the beers, and the fact that Molly got in such big trouble that she got sent to a Catholic boarding school in Rhode Island. Even though she couldn't tell the truth about that night in KA, or about how much she missed Molly, Rebecca started to feel like a new person down here, an actual high school girl.

One night Margaret asked Rebecca if she wanted to go to a party. "You can meet some of my friends."

"Sure, I guess," Rebecca said. After dinner, they left Aunt June's house—Margaret told Mom and the aunts that they were going for a walk, which Mom and the aunts seemed to believe, even though she and Margaret had gone to their bedroom to change into halter tops, and they'd put on tons of mascara, their eyes dark, their lashes spiky in the bedroom mirror. Outside, Rebecca and Margaret crossed Atlantic Avenue, the August air thick with humid breezes, the cicadas whining and buzzing around them. Once you got a block away from the beach, the temperature went up about ten degrees. After a few minutes of walking, Margaret led her around the side of a little Cape-style house to a backyard where seemingly hundreds of people had gathered, talking and yelling.

"It's kind of a college party, but there's a lot of people here I know from school," Margaret said, leading her into the crush of people. One of Margaret's friends brought them beers from the keg, and they stood in a little circle drinking, Rebecca mostly listening to the way everyone said "Y'all" instead of "You guys." After a while someone turned up the stereo, an Allman Brothers song that she didn't care about but that people here seemed to love, since almost everyone had started singing along or slow dancing to it. Margaret had gone to the bathroom, and Rebecca was alone when a drunk guy in a tank top materialized next to her.

The drunk guy threw an arm around her shoulder. "Dance with me," he said, his words slurred. The feeling of his arm, the weight of it, and the way he looked at her set her heart pounding, her chest constricting, and she knew that she was about to die. She had to get out of there, and she wiggled away from him, turned around and then pushed her way out of the crowded backyard. She ran, flip-flops smacking the sidewalk, down Atlantic Avenue. She ran past houses and spicy-blooming crape myrtle trees, then apartment buildings, motels and a fancy hotel. When her breath overtook her, she slowed to a walk. She didn't know how much time had passed—twenty minutes? two hours?—since she'd left the party, but sweat dripped from her temples and between her breasts.

Rebecca turned around to run back toward Aunt June's house. The panicky about-to-die feeling had faded, but she couldn't remember Aunt June's street number or phone number, only the area code 804, which was of no use. She traced each cross street, looking for the house and her aunts' cars, the streetlights illuminating her search. By now most of the houses were dark, the people inside them asleep in their air-conditioned bedrooms.

She saw the police car's lights before she realized she'd reached Aunt June's. The worst had happened, she thought, and she sprinted into the house, where a policeman sat at the kitchen table—Aunt June had called the police when Margaret came home without Rebecca. Mom started to cry, and Rebecca felt time collapsing: losing Dad all over again, and the night in the frat, and Mom coming to get her at the police station in Westfield.

Later, after everyone else had gone to bed, she told Mom what had happened in the frat.

Back at home, Rebecca went with Mom to see a doctor. A psychiatrist. This doctor turned out to be a woman who kept toys—stuffed animals, Legos, puzzles, hand puppets—on shelves in her office. She and Mom talked to the doctor, Rebecca telling the story of going to KA, and Teddy, and then the party in Virginia Beach and the guy's arm on her shoulder. Then the doctor asked Mom to come back in an hour.

"Eventually, you're going to rewrite your story," the doctor said, after Mom left. "You can tell it to me however you want. You can use these props—" she picked up a Fisher-Price farmer from the coffee table "—or you can draw it."

This whole endeavor seemed stupid and pointless, the toys childish and wrong. "That's not going to work," Rebecca said. "I can't rewrite it so that my dad is alive. I can't change what happened."

"You can't change what happened," the doctor said. "That's right." But then they spent the rest of the hour sitting on the floor cross-legged, eyes closed, just breathing.

This seemed stupid too, until Rebecca noticed that she'd started to feel the way she sometimes felt in the ocean, just floating, being buffeted here and there by the gentle waves, or the way she felt near the end of a ski trail, when she pulled her body into a tuck to glide the rest of the way down, all movement, no thought.

She's fine, she guesses, but she's still lonely. Molly wrote a ton of letters when she first started at her boarding school, asking about the kids at home and telling about the girls from New York who had so many dresses and skirts and boots you wouldn't believe it, and Rebecca always wrote back, filling her in on what Todd and Josh and Sydney and Beth Karpas were doing, what the teachers at the high school were like. This year, the letters don't come very often. "That means Molly's settled in," Mom said. "I hope she's doing okay there." Mom's expression, eyebrows lifted, mouth pulled to the side, said she thought it was a dumb idea that Molly got sent off to boarding school.

Last spring, Rebecca rode down to Cambridge with Mom, where they stayed in a hotel for a couple of nights, and Mom had to stand up in front of all these frowning men and answer their questions designed to trip Mom up instead of being actual questions that needed answers. But after all the questions, those serious men turned friendly, shaking Mom's hand and congratulating her, calling her Dr. Desmarais. Rebecca sat in the back of the classroom with Louise and Corinna and Helen and Lily and Jeannette, who'd come down for the day, and they went out for Indian food afterward.

Next to her at dinner, Corinna asked Rebecca about

high school, and Rebecca told her about track. One thing she'd learned that panicky night in Virginia Beach was that she could run a long distance without stopping; she could run and run and run. So now she has her track friends, and she's learned that she's a pretty good distance runner. She runs the longer relays and the 3k. She likes the long practice runs, the way once a week the distance-running group will leave the track to head uphill and out of town, where little farms spread out on one side of the road and woods cover the other, with the Green Mountains off in the west. She can see spring arriving on those mountains, a shy pale green frilled with pink; it's the maples' buds that glow pink in the spring, Dad once told her. She likes the moment her team turns around, looping back like one long organism, and then the easy downhill run to the high school. She likes the way she can think about nothing and everything during those runs.

Yesterday, Josh talked to her after track practice—at the high school, kids mill around after practices, hanging out or waiting for the late bus. She hasn't said more than "hey" to him in a year—she doesn't know what he knows about what happened in the frat, and she doesn't want to find out. She asked him about baseball, and he said it was okay. "I don't get much playing time, and I'm always outfield," he said.

"You could come run track, there's a whole bunch of things you could try. High jump, hurdles, javelin—" She told him about throwing the javelin, how she was terrible at it, but throwing the spear-like thing into the air and watching it land with a thud was fun. A lot of times practice was just funny, everybody laughing, since most people were pretty bad at it. "You have to stay out of the way, especially with the bad throwers."

"Yeah, you wouldn't want to get hit in the head by a javelin," he said. "It sounds like medieval warfare."

"Kind of," she said. "Mostly track is just running."

"Okay, maybe I'll try it next year," he said. "If I do, can you give me some pointers on running?"

"Sure," she said. Maybe next spring she'll be running and Josh will too, and they'll have one of those conversations you have with people when you run. You talk a little bit, first a joke, and then if something's bothering you it's okay to let it out. Or if you're thinking about your big plans for the future you can talk about that too. And then after a while you're just running, and the other person is still with you. Not talking, just running.

SAM

New York

WHENEVER SAM HAS TO get Dad to agree to spend a little money on computer stuff, he waits until the moment after Rich, Red Wagon's A and R guy, has lost an argument with Dad, which happens a couple times a week. This morning, Dad and Rich are back to their most frequent argument; Sam can hear them clearly from his own desk at the other end of Red Wagon's narrow Herald Square office.

"That's not us, Richie," Dad says. "Jazz fusion has no meaning, it isn't jazz. It's a big barrel of other crap trying to glom onto jazz." Sam knows this exchange well enough that he could carry on Dad's bluster for him—Dad's about to tell Rich what jazz is, what bebop was, who the *real* jazz guys are.

"Come on, Harry. Chick Corea, Carlos Santana, *those*

guys are where it's at," Rich says. "We've got to take a more modern approach, add some prog rock—"

"Prog rock, my ass," Dad says. "I don't want to know what that is. And no more telling me jazz is dead," Dad says. "We have a mission here, and we're going to fulfill that mission. That's all."

Sam jumps up from his desk to tell Dad about a new data module he wants to buy. "So good news, IBM says there's a new kind of disk drive for—"

"Sure Sam," Dad says, refreshed after his righteous declarations. "Just don't go too crazy."

Dad never used to talk about *having a mission*. Maybe it's Patty's influence. Patty's gone back to school at Hunter College, and she's always reading some fat book. When Sam goes to the West Side to take his little brother, Adam, to the Museum of Natural History or a coffee shop for ice cream, Patty stops him before he and Adam head out. She wants his opinion on Margaret Mead's book about adolescents in New Guinea, or some philosopher he's never heard of.

Most likely Patty is responsible for Sam having this job at Red Wagon. He was pretty sure neither of his parents would ever speak to him again after he got kicked out of Clarendon, much less the criminal mischief and attempted arson conviction. In exchange for his suspended sentence, Sam spent six months tutoring inmates in math at the New Hampshire state prison in Concord—only three hours a day, but he wasn't very good at it, and he was scared most of the time. He rented a room from the widow of a Clarendon alum who wanted to hear exciting stories about his radical activism. But he had no stories, other than the story of Elodie.

He knows that President Weissman had something to

do with his work at the prison, along with the suspended sentence and the fact that he was convicted of misdemeanors rather than felonies. He knows he's lucky. He figures he'll write to President Weissman after he finishes his degree. He's part-time at City College (NYU and Columbia wouldn't take him, not after the expulsion), where he neither stands out nor blends in, because there's every kind of person you can think of. Mom is beside herself about having to say the dreaded phrase "City College" to her friends instead of "Clarendon," but math is math, and the teachers are okay.

One of these days he'll be sorry he took the job working for Dad, but for now it's going okay. Most days, he has to explain so many things to Dad that Dad doesn't have time to yell, and Sam's the one everyone comes to with a question about the new computer. Now they can keep track of sales, ad buys, radio contacts and billing receipts a lot more easily. Sam is his own little department, and some days it's like being back in the math building at Clarendon, trying something weird that turns out to work. And the guys at IBM are helpful—they don't mind his phone calls about whatever jam he's gotten the computer into.

Tommy helped out last summer with Red Wagon's accounting before he started law school. The law school was for Tommy's girlfriend's sake; Tommy said he wanted to live up to Jane's expectations and now Tommy's at NYU Law. Jerry's in law school too, Brooklyn Law School. Sam hasn't seen Jerry since last summer, when they met up for the John Lennon benefit concert. Sam didn't mention Elodie that night, and neither did Jerry.

He wonders if he'll ever see Elodie again. She's gone— she disappeared after she was released on bail. The people she'd gotten involved with were planning to bomb police stations in New York and other cities, but they'd blown up Elodie's aunt's town house by mistake, badly injuring two men. Were they the men who'd picked up the phone when Sam had called Elodie? he wonders. It took him a long time to get up the courage to go downtown and look at the destroyed town house, and by the time he did, the remains had been walled off with plywood, just another sad graffiti- and poster-covered space that people walked past without seeing. Still, as he stood across the street on a clear June day, trying to see what was no longer there, he shivered. His own actions had touched this larger destructive force that might still be at work.

He's written a few letters to Elodie. He hasn't mailed them—he's not that stupid, Elodie's a fugitive and Sam doesn't need the hassle of being questioned—and knowing that his letters are going nowhere, he's said more than he would in person. He wrote that he still feels confused and different, that sometimes he doesn't know who he is. That he misses Clarendon a lot more than he would have guessed, and he wishes he could see what Clarendon's like with girls on campus all the time. If he were writing her today, he might say that there's a guy at City College, a graduate assistant in his American history class. Last Tuesday they met for beers at one of the student bars near Columbia, before some other grad guys and girls joined them. They're maybe going to get together this weekend. But he might not say any of that to her, not yet.

VIRGINIA

Clarendon College

ON THIS LATE-MARCH EVENING, as wet flakes of spring snow fling themselves against the classroom window, the students have all taken turns introducing themselves, and Virginia has just finished her own introductory words to the group. It's the beginning of spring term, and some of the young women sit cross-legged on the hard chairs, willing this overheated, echoing classroom into a more comfortable space. Two sit on the wide windowsill, smoking, one with her hand up, eager to speak. Connie, a sophomore transfer student.

Virginia calls on Connie, who unwraps her legs, sets both feet on the floor and leans forward, her long hair swinging forward like a punctuation mark. "So I signed up for a class with Professor Parker because I'd heard good things about him. I mean, he's pretty famous, right?"

Virginia and Helen exchange glances—Elgin Parker is old-school in the worst way. Long ago, he made a name for himself in the English department at Columbia, one of the celebrated brash young critics of the '30s. But he's been coasting ever since.

"And so last week Professor Parker said to the whole class, 'This is Restoration drama and poetry, and some of the texts may be a little too much for feminine sensibilities.'" Connie is an excellent mimic—she's captured Elgin Parker's wavery voice and plummy faux-English accent. "Then he read some dumb ancient sex jokes from this dumb play *The Country Wife*, as if we've never heard this kind of thing before." Connie stops for a breath, keeps going. "And then. And *then*! He just stared at me and Jenny for a whole minute, or maybe longer. Long enough that all the other guys turned around to look at us too, like it was their God-given right to do that. Jenny dropped out of the class and now I'm the only girl, I mean woman."

"Old sexist pig," another sophomore, Nora, says.

"Who seems to think he's God," Connie says. "But who mainly wanted to embarrass us right out of the room."

Virginia waits for Helen to speak up, since she knows that Helen has her own long-held professional opinions about this particular sexist pig. Helen reminds the girls— the young women—that Elgin Parker is about a thousand years old, and he'll be retiring in a year or two. The rest of the English department can hardly wait for him to go, she says. Nora snorts and says that's not enough.

"No, it's not enough," Helen says, "but I want to remind you that he's out of touch, he hasn't published anything in decades, and he gives the same tired lectures year after year. We all know that intimidation is a tactic that's as old as time because sometimes it works."

The girls—the young women—talk all at once, voices rising and falling over one another, about the unfairness of who gets tenure, and why tenure really should be taken away from people like Professor Parker. Virginia catches Helen's eye again and they both smile, remembering. Yes, girls, there's a lot of unfairness out there, she'll have to say. Sometimes tenure doesn't get granted, and sometimes it gets taken away. Unfairly.

Virginia and Helen meet with these young women on Wednesday nights. These meetings aren't part of her job, but something that she and Helen agreed was needed, and so here they are. Everyone who shows up has to agree that nothing expressed here is to be shared with anyone outside the group. Last year, Virginia voted against having women faculty assigned to advise the young women. There weren't enough women on faculty to accommodate them, for one thing, and it would have sent a signal that the young women were still second-class citizens at Clarendon. But the young women do need extra support because in most ways the college hasn't moved on. The college seems to want to make it as difficult as possible for these young women. "Are you keeping notes on the things Professor Parker says, the ways he tries to intimidate you?" Virginia asks.

"No, how could we forget something like that?" Connie says.

"Well, from now on keep close track of anything else like that you hear," she says. "Write it all down. We'll need ongoing evidence in order to take it up with the administration."

"As if his rudeness to them isn't enough by itself," Nora

says. "Seems like someone should prosecute him for general obnoxiousness."

"Shoot him and put him and everyone else out of their misery," says another girl. Annie, she thinks the girl's name is.

These young women are sharp and funny, and often Virginia feels like she's a few steps behind them. Still, they listen when she speaks. They cry in her office about professors like Elgin Parker, or about the asshole guys who hold up numbered cards to rate the coeds as they enter the dining hall. There are times when she wants to murder every single boy—every young man, be fair, call them men—on campus. She pictures Rebecca's eyes, so big and sad, as she tried to tell Virginia what was wrong after the terrible night two years ago. Virginia failed her daughter, failed to ask what happened. She doesn't know how Rebecca lived with the assault on her own. All she has to do is remember Rebecca's expression from that day and she feels like she could single-handedly kill every young man at Clarendon. And Elgin Parker.

Don't get mad, get even, Virginia's dad used to say when she or Marnie or June or Rolly had a complaint about someone being mean or someone's unfair treatment. Dad had learned that phrase from his Irish grandmother, and Momma would always shush him and say, *Stop it, Roland, that's not Christian talk*. Virginia hopes she's getting even. She was able to see that Teddy Burnham had to take a year off—no expulsion for him because his father (and grandfather, years before) was a trustee. She didn't have the heart to pursue a criminal case, the possibility of Rebecca having to take the witness stand and be questioned about that night and her own behavior. But the other getting even was rewriting her dissertation—what would she have done without Jeannette, and Louise, and Helen, and Lily, she couldn't have done it without them—and then running the gauntlet of her committee at Harvard, which gave her something back, a confidence that she hadn't expected. She brought something new into the world; she brought a little of Sarah Miriam Peale's work to the light of day. And she's a better teacher now than she was a few years ago. Oliver would be happy about that, she thinks. She hopes. She likes to imagine him standing beside her, supporting her, still with her.

And the truth about Elgin Parker's anti-female obnoxiousness is that if they do keep track of it and establish a pattern among the older professors, they might be able to make something happen. With this new Title IX law, a federal antidiscrimination law, they can cause Clarendon to lose federal funding if they can show that Clarendon is keeping young women from the same opportunities it gives young men. A few months ago, Virginia and Helen and Lily organized a Title IX seminar with the young lawyer from NOW, and she was surprised and pleased to see so many show up—two administrators, the entire admissions office and more male faculty than she would have guessed.

The most unexpected part of the decision to admit women to Clarendon was a mandate to hire more women faculty members. Louise was offered her old job back, and she turned Clarendon down; she's happy at Wellesley and being closer to Boston. Clarendon's hiring of new women faculty meant firing the most recently hired men in every department, including Henry Jernigan. Henry teaches at University of Vermont now, but he runs a multi-school computing conference and he comes back to Clarendon twice a year. Henry, who sees the world's details in his own peculiar and lovely way.

But even now, the burden is on those affected by Elgin Parker's kind of discrimination. (What irony, that the worst offenders, like Elgin Parker, remain firmly in place, while better men like Henry have been shunted off.) These young women have to stand up and shout about it, as Connie is doing now. Maybe it will serve them well. And Virginia hopes she's doing her part, for Louise, who was so badly treated by the college, and others like her. And for these young Clarendon women. But mostly for Rebecca.

"Let Helen finish, please," she says to Nora, who's interrupted again. These young women have so much to say that they can barely contain themselves. She's glad for them, and for herself, that she gets to be here with them. At this time, as they inch closer to the last bit of the twentieth century, in this awkward new world of a coed Clarendon.

"Oliver, so much has happened," she says out loud on the way home from the meeting, shivering as the car's heater blows cold air on her legs. "I wish you'd come visit me sometime." She knows he won't. He's only with her in that sense she gets sometimes. But *she's* still here. She lets herself go back to the beginning for a moment; she and Oliver had a lovely beginning, and after a while they made a family. Their marriage, unexpectedly broken right in the middle of life, will always be unfinished. There will always be blank spaces and unanswered questions. Oliver is gone, and she'll carry those blank spaces, those questions, her failings and his, his love for her and hers for him, into the future. But she's still here.

★ ★ ★ ★ ★

Acknowledgments

Writing is solo work, but publishing a novel is a group endeavor, and this book would not exist without the care, thought and good eyes of many people. To Sharon Pelletier, my intrepid and insightful agent, thank you for sticking with me. And thank you to the team at MIRA Books, especially April Osborn, who pushed me (gently) to make this a better book, and Laura Gianino, Roxanne Jones, Ashley MacDonald and Gina Macedo.

Thank you to Sarah Stone, Laura Gabel-Hartman, Debby Prum, Lisa Sands, Heather Newton, Julie Hubble, Emerson Bruns and Carol Rifka Brunt, who read my early drafts—their suggestions improved the novel in so many ways. Likewise, many thanks to my workshop-mates and teachers at Vermont College of Fine Arts, especially Abby Frucht, Brian Leung, Ellen Lesser, Clint McCown and David Jauss, who helped me grow as a writer.

To Anne Boedecker, who shared her memories of being a female exchange student at Dartmouth College, and to Ann Crow and Liz Russell, who shared their memories of New England women's colleges, all my thanks. Although Clarendon College bears some resemblance to Dartmouth College before coeducation, Clarendon is a more hapless, and of course fictional, place. Dartmouth gave me a wonderful education, an introduction to New England and lifelong friends, especially the Green Girls.

I'm lucky to have a host of bookish and creative friends; many thanks for our talks about books and other arts. And to my stalwart reader-writer friends—Laura Gabel-Hartman, Jessica Benjamin, Lisa Sands, Emilie Burack—thank you! I'm also lucky to have parents who shared their love of reading, making me a reader at a young age. To my own three readers, Jack, Bea and Alice, thank you for your confidence and love. And to Peter: none of this would have happened without you. Thank you.